unbound FIRSTS

Our Unbound Firsts titles are inspired by Unbound's mission to discover fresh voices, new talent and amazing stories. As part of our commitment to amplifying diverse voices, Unbound Firsts is an annual opportunity for writers of colour to have their debut book published by an award-winning, crowd-leading publishing house.

Solange Burrell grew up in Bristol and then moved to London to study Journalism at London Metropolitan University. *Yeseni and the Daughter of Peace* is her first novel.

T0346937

YESEMI
AND THE
DAUGHTER
OF PEACE

SOLANGE BURRELL

unbound

First published in 2023

Unbound
c/o TC Group, 6th Floor King's House,
9-10 Haymarket, London SW1Y 4BP
www.unbound.com
All rights reserved

This is a work of fiction. Names and characters and places are
the product of the author's imagination and any resemblance to
actual persons, living or dead, is entirely coincidental.

Text design by Jouve (UK), Milton Keynes

A CIP record for this book is available from the British Library

ISBN 978-1-80018-221-9 (paperback)
ISBN 978-1-80018-223-3 (ebook)

Printed in Great Britain by Clays Ltd, Elcograf S.p.A.

1 3 5 7 9 8 6 4 2

Never-ending gratitude to my mum, Grassarah Burrell, for always believing and encouraging me no matter what. Deep appreciation for my husband, Carl Gordon, for his unwavering support, unconditional love and patience, for reading the first draft.

To the following people for their generous
support of this book:

BOOKSHOP PATRONS

Grassarah Burrell
Carl Gordon
Dave Butko
Tom Dillon
Mark Gamble
Mrs Jay-Shelley Heathfield BaMA
Russell Mackintosh
Webster T. Mudge

Fr. Mulligan
Jervis Pereira
Melaney Pereira
Dino Sicoli
Mike Tomaino
Jaclyn Turner
Paul Turner
Tina Turner

PATRONS

Tony Aitman
Robert M Atwater
Debbie Elliott
Mike Griffiths
E Hall
Emilia Leese
Garry McQuinn

John Mitchinson
Tom Moody-Stuart
Jackie Morris
Matthew Newman
Christoph Sander
Matthew Scott
Toni Smerdon

From a very young age, the reasons for war were explained to me in depth, or as much detail as I could comprehend at the time. Papa said that I was implying questions with my tone as soon as I could make sounds. He said that I would point at things and raise the inflection in my voice, uttering obscure non-words, then await an explanation from them.

Papa would often joke with Mama that I even wanted to know why the breeze blew through the trees. He would do this when I asked the more difficult questions. The ones that did not really have an answer, or, at least, not one that could be articulated in a nice, neat package and finished with a bow. I think this is how Papa felt when I asked him why we had been at war with the Okena for so many years. We sat in our back yard on chairs Papa had hand-carved from an old tree stump and leftover logs from the debris of the last tropical hurricane. The sun was low in the sky, and it was nearly my bedtime, but Papa had promised me one last game of Choko before I went up. I used the game as a way to pry answers to the many questions I had, and I remember him smiling and shaking his head at me. I think I was around six or maybe seven years old at the time. After looking at me, he stood up, turned around to the faucet and loosened it to wash the blood off his hands.

'Pass me the cloth, Elewa.' He pointed over to the row of clean cloths that he used as makeshift bandages: they were hanging on the washing line. The rope used for the washing line was made of plant fibres that were delicately twined or braided to form the cord. Papa nailed each end of it to the exterior back wall of our house and whenever it was full of clothes, it made the house look all festive and spruced up, but the clothes would cover the back door, so we would have to crouch to get in and out until they dried.

Elewa was the nickname that Papa had given me; it literally meant 'pretty' in his native tongue. Papa always said I had a face that the world should see. Mama loved the name as well.

'It means more than just pretty you know!' she would say, but at that time I was content with 'just pretty'.

I strolled over to the washing line, purposely dragging my feet along the red dirt to make a pattern in the ground before a gorgeous agama lizard with a bright orange head scurried through my feet.

'Hey!' I yelled.

'If you want to play one last game before bedtime, you will have to hurry up!'

I jumped up underneath the washing line and grabbed a clean cloth for him.

'Now hold there and do not let go,' he said. It was the first layer of the bandage to be wrapped around his wounded hand; he needed me to hold it firmly, so that it would stay in place. I felt so important and proud that I could assist my papa in this way. The wound was quite deep and just off the centre of his palm. As Papa wrapped the cloth around his hand, my finger, which was holding the first layer of cloth started to feel trapped.

'So, your question was, why do we go to war?' he asked.

'Why we have been at war for so long. Yes, Papa,' I said, feeling my face heat up then twist with discomfort before a single cold salty tear rolled down my cheek and into my mouth. I wanted to ask him if I could release my finger – I was sure that the other layers were now secure enough to hold the bandage in place.

'Sometimes, Elewa, you think you are helping by holding something important in place for someone that you love . . .' He looked at my finger, now suffocating underneath the pressure of his fresh bandage. '. . . and so you do as you are told. You hold it in place until the pressure becomes uncomfortable and instead of simply holding something in place, you are being suffocated.

'You wonder to yourself, perhaps I should have given them the space to help themselves, then perhaps I would not be so . . .' He supported my hand and pulled my finger out. *Finally*, I thought. '. . . deep inside this nightmare now.' He sat back down.

I still remember the relief I felt as the tingling sensations came back to my finger and yet I had no idea what Papa was talking about at the time. It was not until years later that I figured out what he really meant. Papa was my finger, stuck and suffocating in this war, only there in the first place with the intention of doing good, and the bandage was either his beliefs or his comrades or maybe both.

While massaging my finger, he continued.

'Elewa, people will give you all kinds of excuses for war in your lifetime, I am sure. But really, there is no good reason for war.' He took a deep breath, stood up and walked towards the boundary wall wearing his typical house clothes: a faded indigo robe with a deep neckline and wide sleeves. He spoke the next sentence at a faster pace, as if he had practised it before.

'War is a result of bad choices, bad advice and, sometimes, well-meaning people trying to help, who ultimately just end up making things worse.'

~

In the years that followed, Papa would tell me how he had got that wound. It was from an Okena musket ball that tore through his hand as he prepared to launch his spear. He told me that he fell to his knees, mainly in shock, at the speed and force of the weapon. He said that he had to be carried out of battle by a man called Diallo, who died on his return to combat just a few hours later.

I know that Papa always felt awful about this, because while he was carried out for his hand wound, Diallo suffered a musket ball through the neck, and he lay there on the field in agony as people stepped on him and over him while the very life inside of him slipped away. It seemed there was no one around to close his eyelids or even say a short prayer for his soul.

Diallo was special; he did not have to help Papa that day. His death made Papa realise that there were hundreds of special people being thrown into mass graves every day, who either could not be identified or who had no living family left. Papa promised himself that he would do everything in his power to put an end to the war.

I thought about our entire discussion late into the night as I lay up listening to the sound of tree frogs filling up the darkness.

~

Mama said our house was built by farm hands that did a half-job before abandoning the project for their next enticing undertaking.

'It is not suitable for a man of your standing . . .' Grandma would complain to Papa every time she visited, but we were all content with our lot. The walls were thin and had tiny little holes in corners and joints where the rays from the sun would beam through at different times of day as the sun moved across the sky. Or the wind would push the sweet, loamy air in dusty surges and wanes throughout the house, creating a small indoor cyclone, which was fun for me and my brother Komi and my little sister Fumi, but the bane of Mama's life.

~

As I grew older, I began to understand the reasons, or excuses, for our war with the Okena. Admittedly, though, my perspective was greatly shaped by the hours I had spent inadvertently fraternising at Omolara's indoor market, which contained a treasure trove of goods beneath its palm roof.

When Omolara entered the room, the light softened somehow; her presence conjured up soothing, pacifying feelings, and she opened up the hearts of everyone in her presence. A lavish display of colourful beads hung on both sides of the walls, jingling every time someone entered or exited.

'Elaaaywaaah . . .' She always stretched out my name in that exaggerated way, as if my entrance was a momentous event. and I do not know how, but she knew all of her customers by name, and could sometimes even identify them by sound. This deeply baffled and frustrated me, until the day I found out exactly how she did it.

It was an exceptionally busy day at her indoor market, and Omolara had been organising merchandise, so her back was turned away from the entrance when Mr Sizwe, a local merchant and regular visitor, came through the door.

'Good morning, Mr Sizwe.' She stretched up to the top shelf

5

to place a glass vessel of what looked like a luxury oud perfume obtained from one of the many merchants she traded with.

Mr Sizwe turned to look at me in a *did-you-see-that?* sort of way. I shrugged my shoulders at him and gave him *of-course-I've-seen-it* eyes but just like him, I had no idea how she did it. I was hoping he would have some answers, but he just smiled and shook his head in disbelief.

'Morning, Lara!' he replied, before heading to inspect some fabric.

I had witnessed her greet numerous customers like that, when they were out of her field of vision, and every time it happened, it astonished me all over again. Customer visibility was challenging due to the monumental towers of earthenware pots and enormous piles of bark cloth, baskets and woven fabric at every corner.

Aside from the low visibility inside, I had seen her welcome customers by name when she was tidying, with her back turned away from the entrance or when she was helping another customer and facing the opposite direction. It was as if she recognised their vibration as they entered. I wondered if there was some kind of trick to it, like a reflective panel on the back wall of the store that helped her view the person entering, but when I checked, I found nothing of the sort.

My curiosity erupted that day. 'How do you do that? How do you know who is there without even turning around?' I blurted out. *Well, surely everyone else was thinking it too,* I thought.

Everyone in the store, including Omolara, looked at me. My cheeks heated up and my heart started to race. I wanted the ground to open and swallow me, so I tried to fill in the painful silence.

'Sorry, I just wondered how you do it, because . . . it is kind of . . . strange.' I had never shouted anything out; in fact, I do not think anyone else had either. Thankfully though, her face gradually melted into a soft smile, which seemed to signal to everyone gawking that everything was congenial, so they started to move around and browse the market again.

She set aside the stock she was organising and walked over to the basket of scarves I had been muddling through before my outburst.

As she approached, her curls bounced with the rhythm of her strides. She had thick, black, tightly coiled hair; there was enough hair on her head for at least three grown women. Most of the time she wore her hair in ringlets formed by the fashioning of intricately twisted knots the night before, a technique Mama used too, but only for very special occasions. For Omolara, though, where her appearance was concerned, it seemed like every day was a special occasion. That day she wore an amethyst-coloured wrap with a thin beaded belt to match.

She scanned the scarves then reached out and grabbed a vibrant pink one; it had a spiral pattern on it, like a chameleon's tail. She placed the scarf around my neck and gently turned me around, so I was facing a looking glass that was fixed to the wall behind me.

'Everyone is special . . .' She fussed with the scarf, looping the long end around my neck twice before letting it hang. Her glossy, thick black eyebrows were now all scrunched together. *She disapproves*, I thought. Still anxious, I looked nervously at the customers behind me in the glass, relieved to see everyone appeared to have completely lost interest in my outburst – they all seemed to be busy riffling through shelves or browsing displays packed with fabrics in every colour, shade, weave and texture you could imagine. She stepped out

in front of me and unlooped the scarf from around my neck.
'. . . and the sounds they make when they enter a space are
unique and specific to them and only them.' She draped it
evenly around my shoulders and looked away briefly to smile
at a few customers that walked by and made eye contact.

'When you really start to listen, child, you will not need to
use these as much.' She wagged her fingers at her eyes and
chuckled, presumably at the perplexed expression on my
face.

I took a deep breath in, 'Well, I will try!' I agreed ambigu-
ously while still working out what I was agreeing to.

'It fits you!' She stepped to the side, out of the way, so that
I could see myself in the looking glass and admire the full
view of her ensemble. I felt a little swaddled by this beautiful
silk display around my neck.

I smiled respectfully, though, and nodded in agreement. I
did like the scarf, but I was still confused by her trick; it
reminded me of what Papa had taught me about how certain
animals navigate the world by sound.

I had so many questions for her, and maybe for Papa as
well, but the indoor market was full, and I was still too embarrassed to stay any longer than I needed to. Though they had
stopped staring, probably out of respect, I knew when they got
home to their families, my outburst would be the only thing
they would tell them about; it would probably be the only out-
of-the-ordinary thing to have happened in the market that day.
Besides, the long discussions I had with Omolara usually happened in the evenings, after she had closed for the day; or on a
slow day when most people stayed at home.

'I will take it!' I rummaged through my purse, desperately
looking for the coins that Papa had given me for helping him
with chores a few days before.

'It is my gift to you!' She removed the scarf from my shoulders, folded and tucked it into my purse. I knew better than to argue with her once she had made her mind up about anything, so I humbly accepted.

'Come and see me tomorrow – we can talk more,' she called out as I rushed off, making a beeline for the door.

A cool breeze circled around my clammy body as I opened the shop door. I did not go back the next day like I had promised, or for at least what seemed like the next one hundred days.

I did heed Omolara's advice though; I went over it in my head so many times . . . *the sounds they make when they enter a space are unique and specific to them and only them.* After a while it stuck and I started to learn the distinct sounds that the people in my life would make, the differences in pressure they applied to the objects around them, how their feet interacted with the ground. There was heavy and surefooted, light and rolling, or springy and enthusiastic, just to name a few.

It was not magic, it was just attentiveness, but her level of attention to detail was magical to me and to all of her patrons, I think.

'Very good, child!' she encouraged me once I finally returned to the market to share my success; how I could now recognise the people in my life by sound most of the time now.

'I recognise all our guards,' I bragged. 'Also a few of the people who pass our house on their regular travels.'

'Wonderful,' she sang. 'See, there is no "trick" – you are just using your ears as much as you use your eyes. And do you know your eyes have a power that can be sensed? Once you turn your gaze on a person, they change . . . Try to see what you can find out about the person without looking at them: there is more truth that way,' she insisted.

Once I started practising, I realised that I had been unknowingly using this 'trick' with my family as far back as I could remember. I knew the difference between Mama and Papa without looking, but with acquaintances, it was much harder.

~

Over time I also learned that every person has their own texture, like how they feel when they are around you: some are coarse and sharp, while others are velvety and smooth. The more people I studied, the more I learned that people can be coarse *and* smooth or sharp *and* velvety, and a million other complex combinations.

Omolara was simple, though; her whole purpose seemed to revolve around comforting people, making them feel welcome and connecting with them on a deeper level. It was simple because there did not seem to be any ulterior motive: no façade or underhanded objectives – it was just about respect, compassion and connection.

Through observing Omolara, I learned the importance of how to treat people. How to put people at ease and how to bring out the best in them; and although I found all these lessons fascinating, and even a bit enchanting, the most enlightening lesson Omolara taught me was about the history of our tribe, the Oleba.

After these lessons, I felt empowered, like I really belonged and, most importantly, I felt hope for peace.

~

My name is Ruru or Elewa, although some people call me Titi. When Mama is angry, she calls me Aje, but of my many names, I love Elewa the most. I think I love Elewa the most because she is adored without judgement and accepted without prejudice. Or perhaps I love Elewa the most because it is the nickname that Papa gave to me. Whenever I meet anyone new, I always introduce myself as Elewa and most people go on to call me by that name.

Where and when I am from, people prefer to observe how you act, your personality and your deeds, and then create their own name for you. That is one of the reasons why I have so many names. A popular proverb within our tribe is 'your actions will determine the name you are called'.

~

The Oleba are the descendants of nomads who eventually evolved into farmers. When I was growing up, young Oleba men were schooled in our tribal history and in our farming traditions. They were taught to understand the significance of our ceremonies, how to act and take part in cultural events that bound us as a tribe.

During the war, most Oleba men became warriors or wrestlers. They were the best wrestlers in their land, and they frequently partook in the seasonal matches that helped to bring the tribe together. The regular Oleba wrestling events represented a declaration of the Oleba culture, just like the knowledge of agriculture and farming served as an honour and remembrance to the Oleba ancestors.

In the earlier days, way before the war, when the first Oleba nomads decided to stop travelling, the men wrestled in order to win the land that we now call home. Papa said that our ancestors travelled from the south all the way up to the coast of the northwest, where we eventually settled. Apparently, this journey took those pioneers six full moons to complete. I am not sure why the Oleba chose to move, or why we chose the land we did, but Papa told me a fascinating story about what happened when we first arrived on the land.

~

When we first arrived in the northwest, we met an Animist tribe called the Chaandari. The Chaandari were hunter-gatherer people who were thin and tall. Papa told me they had been described as having a beautiful yellow-brown colour with delicately sculpted noses, elegant, full, heart-shaped lips, and wide, kind brown eyes. He said their hair formed tight circular curls that hugged their scalp closely. They wore beaded crowns and the beads formed gorgeous colourful patterns.

They ran for the best part of the day, hunting and foraging sustenance. The women wore a simple wraparound cloth skirt and a heavily beaded necklace, and the men wore loincloths made from animal skins with a simple beaded headband.

The land they had once thrived on had become scarce. Even so, the Chaandari still put up a fight to remain on it. Proficient with spears, they executed many of our tribesmen in combat. If we had allowed them to keep this up, our tribe probably would not exist today.

Papa said that both tribal leaders agreed to meet and talk through ways in which this problem could be settled, once and for all. Our chief managed to persuade theirs to have a wrestling match to the death: bare hands and no weapons. It is told that our chief picked one of the more feeble-looking boys to attend the meeting and told their chief he was one of our best wrestlers. Their chief quickly agreed to the match without enquiring who exactly would be in the duel. Our chief, naturally, picked another skilled wrestler and the Chaandari tribe were defeated.

Being an honourable tribe, they moved on to find other lands, leaving some of their women and children behind in the promise that they would be taken care of. We agreed that as long as they took our tribal name, learned our ways and ceased to practise their old tribal ceremonies, they could stay and form a new life with us. Some did so, adopting our ways and becoming like authentic Oleba. They raised families with us and let their past go. Others pretended to follow our ways and were later caught practising Animism ceremonies in secret. In those far-off days, they were immediately punished by death, or if our chief was feeling sympathetic, they were indentured for a period of time. Others tried to stay but eventually ran away in search of their old tribe.

Most of the Chaandari that stayed were those who could not physically make the journey east: pregnant women, their children, and elders. Our tribe has a mixture of Oleba and Chaandari blood in it to this day, and that is how we came to have the land that our tribe calls home.

I found this story interesting but sad, and asked Papa why the Oleba had not allowed the Chaandari to continue revering the spirits of animals and plants and rocks if they wished. What harm did that do?

'Elewa,' Papa replied gravely, 'all this was very long ago. The world was harsher and more brutal then. We cannot change the past. We cannot change history.'

2

Omolara's was more than just a market; it was a sanctuary of sorts. A place where young and old Oleba were welcome; they would either be captivated and mesmerised by Omolara's bursting collection of goods or unconsciously enthralled into a deep discussion with her or other patrons about tribal politics, the natural rights of people and the like.

The store had been around for many years. Omolara's great-great-grandmother had started a fellowship group for local women on the land; it had been a room for weaving fabric and baskets, and during the war it was a refuge centre where wounded fighters were brought to be treated by the herbalist, the bonesetter, and the healing rituals of the priest. It was always a place the Oleba gravitated to – the heart of the community. Although people said that under Omolara's ownership it had become more of a place of trade, even so, they still saw it as a shared place – theirs, the Olebas'.

At the north end of the shop there was a gathering space with a sunken floor. Large enough to fit around fifteen people, the steps leading down to the rectangular room from the market floor were broad and rustic. There were four huge wooden benches that angled in towards each other slightly, to form a roughly circular shape; they were generously padded on both the seats and back rests, embellished with a soft, luxurious fabric. There was a large wooden table in the middle of the room that almost always had cool water for guests, patrons and any villagers that dropped by. The room was intentionally designed for people to feel comfortable enough to sit and talk for hours, and Omolara encouraged it. I think it was her way of paying homage to what her ancestors wanted the land to be used for: the fostering of fellowship.

A few months after my humiliating incident, I had the most enlightening conversation with Omolara. Looking back now, I know that conversation was when I felt the first stirring of what I would come to know as Yeseni.

~

Mama had asked me to collect some fabric for a dress that she had pre-ordered for Papa's ceremony of recognition, a gesture the Oleba High Chief would initiate for his most revered advisors. I remember it so well because Mama never sent me to Omolara's – she liked to go by herself. It was a social event for her; she knew she would bump into old friends, and they would always end up talking for hours on end about the old days, so the whole excursion would be a treat for her, a chance to get out of the house, an opportunity to connect and be inspired.

The night before, Mama and Papa had been acting strange, in a nervous way. They sent me up to bed early. I had been doing yard work for Papa that day, so I was tired anyway and did not put up much of a fight. I fell asleep as soon as my head hit the pillow, but then I woke up to Papa's raised voice.

'He should not have been there in the first place – he knows just as well as everyone that Oleba are not free.' I crept out of my room so I could hear more clearly.

'What is that supposed to mean? The Oleba do not fall under any other tribe, and even if we did, that would not be an excuse for that kind of violence.' Mama's voice was breathy and quavering. They hardly ever argued or raised their voices, so whatever was stirring the still waters of our home had to be something serious, maybe even dangerous.

'There is more to freedom than that. There are paths we cannot walk, places we are not welcome.' Papa lowered his voice slightly, but I could hear his steps as he paced around the living room.

'Look, I just need him here. Whether he should have known better or not, after what happened to him, he needs to be with family.' Mama must have been standing up because I heard the squeak of the chair when she collapsed into it.

'And now we will need to explain to the children why Uncle Kwame is bruised and battered.'

I gasped, then covered my mouth with my hand, hoping the sound did not escape. A numb, tingling sensation in the leg that I had been leaning on started to spread, and as I carefully changed position, the floor timbers betrayed me with a loud creak.

I got up and ran back into my chamber. I jumped on my bed and hoped neither of them had heard, and if they had, that they did not plan on coming back to reprimand me. The mat on my low wooden bed was made from reeds interwoven with softer fibres for extra comfort. I settled on it as quietly as I could.

Now lying down, all I could hear were murmurs and my little brother and sister snoring. Sometimes it felt like they could sleep through an earthquake and other times a pin drop would wake them up. *What peculiar creatures they are*, I thought.

My mind conjured up a dozen variations of what could have happened to Uncle Kwame. I knew it was something terrible and that it was due to the Okena, but where was he now and why would he scare us? What did they do to him? I tossed and turned and contemplated going downstairs to ask them about it. I tried to think about something else and finally fell asleep.

~

The next day Mama woke me up at what felt like the crack of dawn.

'Elewa, I am sorry to wake you up, sweetheart, but I need you to collect the fabric from Omolara's and bring it to Kemi for me.' She gently patted my shoulder. Her voice was still tight and tremulous just like it had been the night before.

'Kemi is going to visit her sister; she will be leaving at nine and she needs to work on the dress while she is there, so it will be done in time for the ceremony.' My half-opened eyes revealed a blurry, unconvincing version of Mama standing over me. Although some might have found her story credible, I did not believe it. Mama had a network of seamstresses and tailors that she commissioned throughout the region, for this very reason; whenever one was away she would call on another one. Not just that, but she had never interrupted our sleep over an item as frivolous as a dress. I was tempted to play along, but I could not help but wonder about Uncle Kwame.

'What is happening with Uncle Kwame?' I lay on my back and closed my eyes. 'I heard you and Papa talking about him last night!' I felt her weight at the end of my bed where she sat down next to me.

'Elewa, what have I told you about eavesdropping on your

father and me?' I sat up and faced her. She looked distracted, like she was talking to me, but she was not really in the conversation; she was elsewhere somehow. Her eyes were red and puffy, and her hands started trembling. When she noticed she walked over to the bedroom window.

'What is wrong, Mama? It is all right, you can tell me.' She started fussing with the curtains.

'Please do this for me, daughter. I promise I will answer all of your questions when you return.' She sat back down next to me and put her arm around my shoulder and squeezed me into her chest. She reached inside her pocket and handed me the coins for the fabric, then wrapped her hands around mine and nodded in agreement on my behalf.

'Very well, Mama,' I conceded reluctantly then started getting ready to go.

I did not even say goodbye, I just left; I slammed the door and stormed all the way to Omolara's. I was pleased that Mama had sent me there; deep down I knew that there were answers in that place. I did not know if it had something to do with the land that it stood on; maybe the ancestors still watched over it – why else would all Oleba gravitate to a market? There had to be something else there, something cleansing, a force greater than Omolara's kindness. All I knew was that most of the time when I went there, I left with a clearer head than when I went in.

$\sim$

When I arrived at the store Omolara gave me my customary, momentous greeting.

'Ha!' she exclaimed. 'You back! What can I do for you today, my dear?' Her hair was still in tight knots covered with a blue silk scarf. The market had not officially opened yet, but if she was around, she would never turn a potential patron away. I flashed her a half-hearted smile and dove into a basket of discounted fabrics. I do not know why; I was only there to collect a specific order for Mama. It was as if I thought the answers to my questions could be somewhere in that basket.

I continued to vigorously rummage through the pieces of fabric.

'What did these cloths do to you, young lady?' she said as she stepped in front of me.

'Nothing, sorry I . . .' I dropped the bundle I had clutched in my hand; I was startled by how quickly she had manoeuvred between me and the basket. She reached down and grabbed them before they hit the floor.

'Come, child.' She beckoned me to the meeting room down on the sunken floor at the back. It was early in the morning and there was no one else around. I made my way down the steps while Omolara went to lock the front door.

'If they want me, they will have to knock!' she shouted as she marched down the steps to join me.

She sat down next to me with her hands lodged between her knees. We sat there in silence for a few seconds, but it felt like minutes. I started trying to think of reasons to excuse myself and then she bumped me with her shoulder.

'What do you know about the Okena and the Oleba?' She clapped her hands together in a *let's-get-this-cleared-up* kind of way.

'I know they want more power and control . . . and I know that we do not want to give it to them.'

She nodded and leaned back in the chair.

'That is what I thought,' she confirmed. 'Not much then.'

'Well what else is there to know?'

19

She raised her eyebrows and cautiously tilted her head from side to side as if she neither agreed nor disagreed with my point. Reaching over to the pitcher on the table, she poured a cup of water which she placed in front of me. I was not thirsty; I was just upset and confused. I shook my head and pushed it back towards her.

'Did you know that the Okena originated from a dense tropical forest where they are said to have lived comfortably and peacefully for thousands of years? This was until a young, ambitious chief took over after his father's reign. He managed to persuade his kinsmen that the tribe's destiny would be outside of the forest, where they would grow, flourish and prosper.'

I shuffled sideways and lay down on the bench. I was still tired, probably because I had been up eavesdropping on Mama and Papa for a good portion of the night.

'But how do you know that this is their true history and not just a story?' Lying on my back I could see the soft pink light from morning's sunrise emerging through the store and right down into the mezzanine. It made everything in its pathway look so mystical.

'It is more than just a folk tale, child; it is the word of the ancestors. The elders of the Okena say that the first Okenas were born of the earth, the very soil in a sacred spot, deep within their impenetrable jungle.' Omolara was animated now. I was not facing her, but I could see from the corner of my eye her limbs bouncing through the air as she sat on the edge of the bench.

The room was now drenched in the beautiful dreamy pink light, and I suddenly remembered Papa warning me about pink sunrises. He said they bring on erratic weather systems. I wondered if I would make it back home before that happened.

'Our own elders' accounts corroborate with those of the Okena; there are no lies to be found in what I am about to tell you. Are you ready to take this in or not?' She stood up and towered over me, raising one palm to the ceiling while the other rested on her hip. She seemed to have had her fill of my insolent remarks.

I apologised to Omolara and asked her to continue. She took a deep breath and sat back down.

'This situation with your uncle is distressing you, is it not?'

'How did you—'

'All will be well, Elewa. Your mother and father have it all in hand, your uncle is recovering, and they will explain everything to you when you get back home.' Gosh, it was like she had rehearsed what Mama had asked her to say verbatim. I rolled my eyes when I thought she was not looking. I did not understand why I had to wait for an explanation about my own uncle; it did not seem fair.

'You need to know your history to know who you are, child. So that you can make sense of happenings, like the one your family is going through now, with your uncle.'

Omolara removed her headscarf and started to unravel the Oleba knots in her hair in front of a looking glass that was fixed to the wall next to one of the tapestries. 'After the Okena migrated from the forest to the coast they met other tribes, like ours, who were of course already living on the land that they wanted to control. This created tension and ultimately war. The Okena vanquished many other tribes over time, but not the Oleba. That is why we have such uneasy truce now.'

Hearing her recite our history with the Okena felt so familiar. It brought up memories of the conversations I had either had with Papa or overheard him having with other people.

'Why are there so many members of the Okena Resistance then?' I asked.

'A lot of those Okena Resistance groups do not feel loyalty to the tribe, probably because their forefathers were from other tribes.'

I started wandering around the room. As I dawdled, I noticed that the space seemed much bigger than usual, perhaps because it was normally packed full of people consorting and mingling. I started to wonder what they would have to say about this subject. Whenever it was packed there were always multiple people putting the world to rights and debating tribal matters. Sometimes they acted as if Omolara's meeting room was the official Chief's House of Oleba.

One of the tapestries on the wall caught my attention. It was an embroidered picture of a blue man and woman embracing. I had never seen anything like it; although it was just thread and material, the detail was impeccable, and the image was so intense it made me feel like I was witnessing an intimate moment. They seemed so real that I felt like one of them would tell me to mind my own business or that it was rude to stare.

'There are so many grey areas – it is a complicated history, child.' Omolara had nearly finished with her hair, and she was transforming into the 'Omolara Odessa' that everyone recognised and loved.

I started to feel uncomfortable staring at that tapestry, so I walked away in search of something else. Underneath the rustic steps I noticed there was a nook covered by a thick woven curtain that matched the embellishment on the benches. I pulled the curtain back and saw an intriguing little grey box.

'It is hard to imagine.' I replied '. . . because it has always been like this . . . but I would love for there to be peace within our land. I would sacrifice anything for peace between our people, to know my family do not have to live in fear.' I closed the curtain before Omolara noticed my interest in it; something told me she would not want me looking in there. It was the only space in the whole building that seemed personal.

'Be careful what you wish for!'

As those words left her mouth an edgy feeling ran through my body. It was startling – it stopped me right in my tracks: I froze and started to feel lightheaded.

There was a sudden pounding of rain that started thudding against the windows, but Omolara did not seem to notice. She looked at me strangely.

'Are you feeling well, child?'

'I do not know, something strange just happened to me when you said that. A tingly, panicky feeling ran through my whole body. What happened to those who resisted if they refused to accept the Okena rule?' Omolara now only had two knots to unravel, then she would be done. I wondered what she would keep herself busy with next.

'For some tribes, peace was the most important thing in life. Living in peace was the same as living with the creator and so they would surrender more readily. Other tribes fundamentally believed that the land belonged to them and only them, and they would rather die than submit to the Okena or anyone else's rule, so their fate was written.'

There, she had finally finished. I imagined having to do that to my hair every day. And although her hair was done, she still needed to paint her face.

She walked over to that nook under the steps, pulled out a little black bag and returned to the looking glass. The bag contained small pots of clay paste and coloured paints. As she carefully applied the traditional Oleba marks to her face, she grew more beautiful.

'Papa said that if you were defeated during the war and did not concede, the Okena could take your entire family as slaves or prisoners of war.' I grew tired of watching Omolara carefully applying different coloured marks to her face, so I started to wander around the room again.

'Yes, but that fate was a lesser evil than the alternative.'

'What was the alternative?'

'Being sold into the white man.'

I stopped and looked at her: the white man? Those exotic men from across the ocean? *Interesting*, I thought. I had seen them from time to time, but I did not know much about them. I only knew I should be fearful of them because they were the only people that Papa seemed to be afraid of.

'Papa fears the white man but not the Okena,' I said.

Omolara nodded. 'Your father knows what the Okena also know: that our two tribes must learn to trust and to make peace. There is a much greater enemy in the white men who steal our people, whether they be Okena or Oleba.'

Suddenly there was a loud banging at the shop door.

'It is probably a customer. I will go and see what they want; I must open the market soon anyway.' When she was out of sight, my mind immediately drifted to the box in that nook. I thought about what was inside. Then I heard Omolara's footsteps coming towards the stairs.

'It is Kemi – she is leaving for her sister's house in fifteen minutes. I have given her the fabric your mother ordered but she also wants payment for half of the work now.'

I handed her the coins and this time, as soon as she was out of sight, I crept over to the nook, pulled the box out and opened it. It contained a small painted picture that looked

24

like Omolara hugging an Okena man: I could tell he was because of the tribal marking he had on his face. I wanted to look more closely, but I quickly put the picture back, returned the box and closed the curtain.

When she came back down, I could not help but look at her in a different light. I was even more intrigued by her – maybe she was not the perfect Omolara everyone thought she was after all.

Somehow, too nervous to sit down, I worked my way back to the tapestry with the embracing blue couple again. Omolara came to stand beside me.

'I have never seen anything like this before, it is . . .' I tried to think of a word to describe it. '. . . curious!'

'A very kind and talented friend of mine made it.' I wondered if that very kind friend was the man from the little painted picture.

'Omolara, I want to thank you for today.' I went to grab my bag and headed towards the stairs.

'Child, you know you are welcome to come and speak with me any time you want to.' She smiled and hugged me goodbye.

After that conversation the anger I felt towards the Okena was alleviated somewhat, because I had learned there was a strong desire for peace from both sides. I also saw that there was more to Omolara than just the 'simple' welcoming heart of the community. I imagined she had a rebellious side now. I thought about that man and wondered who he might be and how he was related to Omolara. *Maybe one day I will ask her.*

3

I intentionally prolonged the fifteen minutes it usually took me to walk home from Omolara's to an hour and a half. I deviated from the main route, worried about what I would find once I got home. I wondered if Uncle Kwame would be there, and if he was, would he really scare me like Papa suspected? Papa was not normally wrong, so I was preparing myself for a great fright. In my mind I practised what I could say that would be appropriate, and how I would control my facial expressions to hide the fear in my eyes.

'He should not have to feel bad for me,' I mumbled under my breath while kicking a small shingle pebble along as I walked. 'He is the one that is suffering, not me!' I looked around to see if anyone had noticed me talking to myself. I felt relief when I saw no one had.

I did not want Uncle Kwame worrying about me when he had his own troubles.

Selfishly, I hoped that he would not be there when I got back. I knew it would be much easier to cope with any horrifying news if I did not have to look it right in the face. If Uncle Kwame refused Mama's invitation and decided to stay home instead, then I could see him once he was fully healed. I could send messages and gifts to him with Mama. Then, once he finally recovered, he could come and visit and tell me all about the incident, like a bedtime story; he might even show off his scars as if they were badges of honour.

Something deep down inside of me knew that it was all just wishful thinking though. I knew Mama would never take no for an answer and if Uncle Kwame was not there when I got home, it would not be long until I had to face him.

Normally once I left Omolara's I would turn right and walk straight down the red Panapana Road past the Jamarah Memorial Gardens, then right again past the myriad of mangled footwear outside Mensah the shoemaker's. I would then make a left after Famara's fish stall, then head straight through the Makutano market, which was only about five minutes away from home, depending on how quickly I dodged the market traders and their regulars.

This time, though, I decided to turn left instead. I did not know how to get home that way, but I knew I could always just retrace my steps if I got lost. All I knew is that I needed more than fifteen minutes to prepare myself for whatever was waiting for me back at home.

Omolara's was in the middle of two derelict buildings that used to form part of a lively bazaar. Apparently, both adjoining buildings closed down during the war, but since I had been going to Omolara's they had always been empty. Mama said there was a baker to the right and a blacksmith to the left; she said the whole area was vibrant and bustling before the war.

But, looking around the place, you would never imagine a lively marketplace existed there. *It is funny how time can almost obliterate evidence of the past, leaving just a memory as proof of what once was*, I thought.

I had heard something about Omolara taking over the buildings and expanding her business, but she had never mentioned anything like that directly to me.

I had been wandering in the opposite direction for around thirty minutes when I started to feel a little lost. The plan was that I would just walk in a straight line so that if anything happened, I could simply trace my steps back, but while I was in deep thought I may have turned left or maybe right a few times by accident. I saw women gathering in the distance and decided I would go and ask for directions. When I got about two metres away, I heard the women talking loudly in a language I did not recognise, and I saw a face with Okena tribal markings. I started to panic and hid in some bushes on my right. Normally in daylight there was nothing to fear but after what had happened to Uncle Kwame my imagination started to run wild, conjuring up all the things that could happen to an Oleba if they met with an Okena on the street.

I stopped for a moment in the bushes to catch my breath.

I hastily paced back in the direction that I thought I had come from and sure enough, after thirty minutes or so I heard the sales cries from the Makutano market and knew I was not far from home.

~

As soon as I opened the front door, my worst fears came true: a warped version of Uncle Kwame sat on one of the living-room chairs, directly across from the entrance door. He looked weary and tortured, with puffy, bruised eyes that were dark purple with blood-red streaks through the whites of his eyeballs.

'Elewa, niece, do not be afraid!' He held his swollen hand out towards me but had no strength keep it raised for more than a few seconds, and it abruptly fell back down to his knee. I was rooted to the ground in the doorway. I could not believe that he was so badly hurt. It was even worse than I had imagined. He seemed like an imposter somehow. It was deeply distressing to witness what the Okena had done to my uncle.

'Is that Elewa?' Mama shouted from the kitchen.

'Yes, she just got back,' Uncle Kwame said.

I moved to sit down beside him. 'What happened to you, Uncle?' I placed my hand over his.

'You should see the other men . . .' He tried to laugh but it just caused him more pain and seemed to incite a vicious cough. 'I got on the wrong side of an Okena mob and was outnumbered.'

'He is lucky to be alive!' Papa burst through the kitchen door. 'They found him in Dokanta province late at night . . . in that state,' Papa turned to face Uncle Kwame, flashing him accusing eyes.

'I never would go that far across the disputed land; I have told you a million times! I was walking home, and a group of men rushed me, beat me, and left me for dead there, in Dokanta!'

'Hmmm . . .' Papa stood over Uncle Kwame, still unconvinced. 'What were you doing out at night alone? You live far too close to the border to be acting so carefree . . .'

Uncle Kwame kissed his teeth and brushed the air towards Papa, then he turned to me and squeezed my hand.

'The Okena are a wicked, wicked people, niece, always remember my battered face whenever you encounter one!' I nodded in agreement to please my poor and unfortunate uncle.

'Do not plant fear inside my daughter's mind, Kwame!' Papa walked over to me and patted the top of my head. 'People do wicked things for many different reasons; the Okena are no more wicked than the Oleba. Your uncle acted

29

carelessly and that is why he is in that shape!' I nodded again at Papa's explanation. Then Uncle Kwame looked back at me with a furrowed brow. I shrugged my shoulders, and he shook his head as if I had betrayed him.

Uncle Kwame again sliced the air upwards with his hand, in a quick sharp move, towards Papa, using as much effort as he could muster. 'Why do you fill your child's head with all that diplomatic gobbledegook?'

Papa took a breath in to respond when Mama came through the kitchen door.

'Enough! What good is bickering about this going to do now?' She turned to face me and dumped a stack of clean dish towels on my lap. Folding the dish towels was one of my chores, so I got on with it and was glad for the distraction.

'Elewa, we will be looking after your uncle until he is fully healed and ready to go back home.' I looked up from my task and nodded. 'We are just grateful that all his wounds are superficial.' She walked over and gently squeezed Uncle Kwame's wrist.

'Yes, and his thick skull may have finally come to some use!' Papa mocked.

Uncle Kwame's mouth sluggishly started curling upwards until he started hissing a restricted laugh. When we could be sure he found it funny, we all started laughing.

'The man is in pain – stop playing around!' Mama chuckled as she grabbed a towel from my lap and wrapped the end of it around her hand, then whipped Papa on the buttocks with it. This set Uncle Kwame off into what looked like an even more intensely painful hissing and coughing fit, and we all laughed until our stomachs hurt.

I was glad that we could still find some humour in the horrific incident. Seeing them joyful made me understand that we were laughing because we were fortunate enough to laugh. We were pleased because we did not have to mourn. We were glad because Uncle Kwame was still alive, and even if he was a tad sore, he was safe and with family and that was all that mattered.

4

It rained for five whole days during Uncle Kwame's first week with us.

'The heavens are grieving your plight, little brother!' Mama assured Uncle Kwame when she caught him drearily gazing through the window. 'After the rain, there'll be good fortune for you, my dear,' she added.

I was no longer worried about Uncle Kwame; he was healing quicker than I had imagined and he had promised Mama and Papa that he would not go out after dark until both tribes had reached a peace treaty.

Besides, I had found a new endeavour to worry about: I had started a small flower garden in the back yard a few weeks before the heavy rains. I was anxious that the rain would wash away all the plants before they had a chance to settle in. I did not want to have to start all over again. I had planted Tulbagh Satin Flowers, Yellow Bush Lilies, Emberglows and Sabi Stars.

'You will be surprised how resilient plants can be. They were here long before us and they will be here long after; do not worry about them, Elewa,' Mama declared, when I asked her if she thought the rains would wash away my new garden. I just could not imagine those delicate seedlings surviving through that type of rain.

Only time will tell, I told myself.

~

When Kemi returned from her sister's she dropped off Mama's outfit. Mama was not home at the time, so I waited until she got back so that we could open the package together. It was ritual; something Mama and I always did together with any kind of packaged purchase, whether it was a luxury or general necessity. I think it was probably an excuse to be together and indulge in the pleasure of one another's company.

'What do you think?' she asked, beaming from cheek to cheek as she unfolded the clothing and laid it out onto her bed. It was a stunning two-piece ensemble with a smart fitted V-neck blouse and a full overlay skirt. The material had been carefully hand embroidered to achieve a gorgeous floral pattern.

'It is beautiful, but any seamstress could have made this. Why did it have to be Kemi? You have a whole network of seamstresses.' For some reason I just could not let that go.

'Oh, Elewa! Kemi came recommended, if you must know.' Looking at the detail, I could see why.

'So, are you excited about Papa's ceremony?' I asked, changing the subject.

'I am, but I am wondering what the chief wants from us this time,' she replied as she carefully inspected the needlework on the outfit, making sure there were no flaws that ill-mannered guests could use as an excuse to shame her. 'Whenever he makes these grand gestures, there is always something that he asks for in return.'

I helped her check the left-hand side; if we found a small blunder Sessie could probably fix it, she was like my older sister and far more skilled with a needle than anyone I was related to by blood. But if it had a serious mistake, it would have to go back to Kemi.

'The last time he threw one of these "ceremonies in honour" for your father, he asked us to move our whole family to Idan-bule, so that we were closer to him and his wife.' Mama turned the outfit over and we started to inspect the back.

'Oh, so that is why we live here then?' I chuckled. Satisfied that there were no holes, rogue threads or missing sections of embroidery, Mama hung the dress up in her wardrobe. She had the same wardrobe from as far back as I could remember. It was a gift from the chief's wife, from their travels. It was a rich brown solid wood with double panelled doors and iron hinges.

'Yes,' she sighed.

'They have no children do they, the chief and his wife?' I had visited their house on a few occasions, and I could not remember seeing any children there. I did recall how immaculate it was. It surprised me to think anyone actually lived there. There were no rumpled beds, the floor was always swept, the elegant carved statues and wooden furniture shone, and wall-hangings hung just so; every single element of their home was in the most pristine condition.

'No. I think they did want children at one point, but they did not have any in the end.'

'So will you find out at the ceremony if the chief is close to making real peace with the Okena?' I walked over to the window to see if there were any signs of life in my garden.

'All we can do is hope, Elewa; we can only do what we can do. The Okena have to meet us halfway!' Mama joined me, and we sat opposite each other in the window nook staring out at the rain.

5

We lived in Idanbule, a small village where the Wiri River met the ocean on the coast of B'eri. It sits on the eastern half of the bank, close to the border with Taolulwe. Idanbule was just one of a number of small villages along the mouth of the river. Our house was not too far from the shoreline, close enough to hear the hustle and bustle of the seafolk when the ships docked, but far enough not to be caught in the middle.

The sanctity of fresh air filled my lungs as I strolled along the shoreline near our house. Papa's ceremony was that evening, and the chief would be announcing 'the new plan for peace' either after or during the event. I had a strange sense of unease, though I could not say why. It was the first beautiful day without rain in over a week and I yearned for that feeling of freedom that only the ocean could offer.

Fishermen were burning dead palm leaves on the beach and the smoke from the fire created a haze of sooty fumes that contrasted with the gorgeous clear blue water. The soothing crackling of flames felt sedatory when combined with the salty sea air. I took a deep breath in.

'I never get bored with being near the ocean!' I exhaled.

'You what?' shouted my little sister Fumi as she darted past me.

'Nothing! Stay close by!' I yelled back, while she raced to

catch up with Komi, my younger brother. As I watched the two of them playing in the distance all I could hear was Papa's reprimanding voice in my head: 'Not only did you disobey me by going to the beach, you brought your little brother and sister with you as well?' I pushed the voice to the back of my mind and rushed ahead to catch up with them.

When I caught up, they were playing Tak Tak, a jumping game we played on the boulders in the shallow ocean water. Fumi was losing, of course – she was far too small to jump the wider boulders, and too proud to allow me to choose narrower ones. She never really paid attention, even though she insisted on tagging along, and she always ended up soaking wet.

'Pay attention, Fumi. Remember, you wanted to come along. If you end up in the water again, I am not explaining it to Mama . . .' I prayed my firm tone would encourage her to try harder. 'Now, bend your knees, step back, swing your arms backwards and jump.' She hesitatingly followed my guidance, placing her right foot backwards, shortly followed by the left. *Her feet are too close together*, I thought.

'Spread your feet further apart!' I called. She quickly adjusted them, bent her knees, and closed her eyes.

'Come on, Little Tretra, we do not have all day,' Komi yelled, 'and if you want to make the jump you must open your eyes, *Little Tretra*.'

Little Tretra was Fumi's nickname. It was the locals' name for a little bird that had the brightest yellow feathers and the loudest, most obnoxious, never-ending song. When she was born, she never stopped crying and it sounded strangely like the tretra bird's song. Uncle Kwame came to visit the day after her birth and called her Tretra; the whole family laughed the first time he said it and the name had stuck ever since.

Fumi opened her eyes and gave Komi a look of contempt.

She did not like being rushed, but this time, she had a point to prove.

She took a deep breath and leaped into the air in a forward motion.

'*Fifty Okena worth half an Oleba . . .*' A group of boisterous children bolted past us.

'*The tribe without glory! The tribe without grace! Befriending the white man to save face, yeah! Fifty Okena . . .*' they chanted at the top of their lungs. One of them even ran backwards – he was motioning circles with his hands towards his torso, trying to encourage us to join in.

'Shush!' Komi screamed at them. 'You are distracting my sister.'

Fumi looked over to the children, already distracted, and inevitably fell short of the other side of the rock. My eyes rolled back up to the sky and my head sunk into my hands. Komi and I ran over to check to see if Fumi was unhurt and, thank the guardian spirits, she was.

'Enough for today – we are going home,' I ordered.

'Oh, but we just got here, and I have not had my turn yet,' Komi whined.

'I do not care! We should not even be here.' Fumi's eyes welled up and her lip started quivering in a downward motion. *Oh no, please do not start sobbing*, I thought. 'Fumi, you did well, Tre.' The left-hand side of her mouth started turning in the opposite direction, upwards towards her eyes. *Phew*, I sighed.

'If those children had not come by you would have made that jump!' Komi reassured her while ruffling her hair. I looked over to see if I could recognise any of them, but they were now just little dots beneath the sun.

~

There was a time when we were able to go to the beach and play whenever we felt like it – that was until Papa changed his mind. He told us stories of white men coming to the shores and capturing children then taking them to faraway lands. To me this sounded like a thrilling adventure, and I was secretly jealous of those children who got to go to those exotic lands, far far away. Although he meant to scare us, his stories just encouraged my curiosity.

There was nothing Komi loved more than being at the shore; Mama said he knew how to swim way before he could walk. It was hard for me to avoid the beach because I had grown up around the water and loved it there, but as hard as it was for me, it must have been much harder for Komi. He had a deeper connection to the ocean that was inexplicable. He just seemed to understand it like no one else – all his joy and bliss were there, part of his substance, the essence of him was there too – and sometimes it felt like he left it there, when we would leave to go back home. Which is why I apprehensively defied Papa's rules and let him come with me to the shore every once in a while. We took Fumi, because if we did not, she would probably tell.

'Can I go in for another swim, please?' Komi begged.

'Not today, Komi, we have to head back. You have been playing in the water with Fumi for long enough; sorry but it is time to go home now!' I prepared myself for a long debate with Komi on how much time he got to spend in the water and how unfair it was. Every time we had this argument, I swore I would never bring him back but then time would pass, and I would cave in once again.

'You are so mean,' he stormed off in front of me.

'Komi, please, as soon as it is safe again, and as soon as

Papa allows it, I promise you, we will be able to come back here every day, like we used to.'

'And go fishing too?' he haggled. It did not surprise me that at the age of eleven years, Komi was one of the best fishermen in the family. Papa said he had something he called *bolasina*. The gift of eternal sustenance or a bountiful palm. I did not agree; I thought that his talent was linked to his connection to the ocean. I felt his fortune was there and whatever he chose to do in the water would work in his favour.

The fact that he had not been allowed to do what he loved the most, for so long, was hard for him and it showed. Since Papa banned us from going to the coastline, Komi had not seemed himself at all. He was not as upbeat or as bright as he normally was, and at times he actually looked hopeless. The spark in his eyes had dimmed and his energy levels seemed altogether sapped. I worried about him a lot during those times, and I would take him to the coast, to bring back his buoyancy and sense of self.

'Bolasina!' A local fisherman had recognised Komi and shouted out to him, 'Come and bless my boat.' Komi's face lit up, but I grabbed his arm and pulled him back.

'He is not allowed to do that anymore . . . sorry!' I shouted. Would one of these fishermen tell Mama or Papa that they saw us? There was so much risk involved in the escapade that I decided in that moment that I would not do it again.

The fisherman looked confused. Whenever they had asked before, Komi would just run over and shake their hands or wish them well on their trip out to sea. They swore it brought them good luck every time and I think it made him feel special. I wondered if me stopping Komi now would trigger people to talk more. *Maybe I should have just let him do it,* I thought.

'Is that where the white men take children?' Komi pointed to the horizon, where the sky met the sea.

'I guess so?' We all stared at the horizon and I wondered what lay beyond. I started to feel envious again of those who were captured and were now exploring foreign lands. *Oh, why can you not capture me*, I wished secretly to myself.

'Why does Papa say that it is dangerous here? It just looks normal to me,' Fumi remarked, and she did have a point. The coastline looked as benign as usual – what dangers could possibly be there?

'Papa knows better than us, Fumi, we should not question his judgement.' I felt like a hypocrite because not only did I bring my little brother and sister to the seashore against orders, but I was also secretly hoping to see one of the 'villainous' white men do something vicious like in Papa's tales. I scanned the whole coastline but there were just local fishermen working, women washing their clothes and a few children playing. Further up the coast, I could see huge forts in the distance and those criminals chained up to board that gigantic boat but nothing threatening or out of the ordinary; it was all just a typical day in Idanbule.

'And . . . why do their parents let them play in the water?' Fumi persisted. I questioned the same.

'That is enough, Fumi. Come on, you two, we must go.' I said the words, but we stared into the distance for a little longer. The loud squawks of the seagulls shocked me out of my daydream. 'We had better get back home before we get caught.' We linked arms and headed home.

~

Luckily by the time we got home Mama and Papa had already left for the appreciation ceremony. We seemed to have gotten away with our insubordinate day out.

But when they returned, they appeared irked.

'So . . . how did it go?' I was so eager to find out all the details of the ceremony that I could not sleep; I had decided I would just wait up for them. I sat on the edge of the chair in the living room and prayed for good news.

'Elewa, there is something we need to talk to you about.' They looked hurt, almost as if someone had ripped their hearts right out of their chests at the party.

'What is wrong?' I asked. 'Why do you look so worried?' Had one of the fishermen told them we had been at the shore? Were they about to lecture me on the dangers of the white man? But no, they did not look angry or frustrated; instead their faces were full of pain.

'Why not wait until the morning? We do not have to do this now.' Papa's eyebrows tilted up towards each other to form a mountain-like shape, and instead of standing up straight and proud with his chest protruded, he cowered over as if he were ashamed of something. I had never seen him stand like that before.

'You are starting to scare me now. What happened?'

Mama looked shocked, then her hands started trembling. When Papa saw that, he put his arm around her. Her eyes welled up and looked as shiny as glass.

'Is this about the peace treaty?' They sat down either side of me and held each of my hands.

'The Okena and Oleba chiefs have decided that the only way peace can be established between both tribes is if the firstborn of both tribes' chiefs are betrothed,' she said.

'Oh, well that is good news, is it not?' I paused, trying to figure out what I was missing. 'But the Oleba High Chief has no children.' Mama looked at me intensely, and Papa would not meet my eye.

'Wait, me?' I blurted out, sure that it would make them laugh, but as I said it, tears started to flow down Mama's face.

'Yes. You, Elewa, you will be the Daughter of Peace.'

'But I am not the chief's daughter.' None of this made any sense to me.

'The chief will be stepping aside; your father will be the new Oleba chief.'

'Papa?' I ripped my hand out of my mother's grip and looked over at Papa for confirmation, clarification or at least some form of eye contact.

He stood up, his shoulders now back and his stance proud. He glanced at me then looked right over me. This was not my papa, my kind-hearted companion. This was a stranger; this was the new Oleba chief.

'As soon as you are of age you will be marrying Ojuro Okena. It is your duty, for the peace of our people.' And with that he walked away, through the kitchen and to the back yard. I turned to Mama, but she just nodded in agreement.

'Get some rest, child; once the dust settles, we will explain everything to you,' she urged. I felt like Papa had abandoned me; he had not even looked me in the eye. Papa was my ally and, in that moment, I had never felt so alone, confused and afraid. Mama was as brave and reassuring as she could possibly be, but I needed Papa to tell me that this was a good thing, that all would be well, and instead he had walked away.

6

In my world, a woman's greatest gift in life is her fertility, her ability to conceive a child. As far back as I can remember I had Leba, a carved wooden fertility doll given to me at birth. Leba was not just given to me though; every Oleba girl had one. She was an artefact of virtue, a birthright, and above all, she helped young women gain the blessings needed for a joyful marriage, and many healthy children if, and only if, she was properly cared for.

As an Oleba woman, one of the first life lessons you are taught is to look after your Leba, at least until you are married. *Look after Leba and she will provide*, they would say.

When I was little, I adored her more than anything in the world and I treated her even better than I had been taught to; I carried her with me everywhere I went, handled her with care, adorned her with beads and jewellery and even washed and clothed her every day. I was truly captivated by her. I played with her for hours on end, creating imaginary worlds together, and I even built a bed for her, right underneath mine. We went on exciting adventures all over Idanbule, and I managed to persuade Mama to sew us matching nightclothes. But, as the years went by, Leba's mystery began to fade. If I saw her in a room I would put her in a cupboard, kick her under a chair or hide her so she was out of sight. Somehow even seeing her lying around embarrassed me. Eventually all I saw in Leba was a drab piece of old wood.

'Where is Leba?' Mama would ask, once she noticed I had started leaving her behind on our days out. 'Remember, Elewa, if you look after Leba, Leba will look after your destiny.' She would look down at me with stern, berating eyes.

'She is boring!' I protested one day.

'Well, she is not supposed to be interesting; she is not supposed to entertain you, Elewa. Do you not want to get married and have children one day?' I shrugged my shoulders. 'If you look after Leba—'

'Yes, I know she will look after me,' I interjected while thinking, *Why do I have to get married anyway?*

One day I just came right out and asked Mama that question. She was hanging clothes on the line in the yard, with a basket full of pegs sitting on her hip held in place by her elbow; suddenly she lost grip of the basket and the pegs fell all over the ground.

'Well, Elewa, it is what every Oleba woman does. It is the natural way, child.'

'What if I do not want to get married?' I asked while grabbing the hem of my skirt for a pouch so that I could collect the pegs and put them back in the basket.

'Do you not want what Papa and I have? Or would you prefer to live alone for the rest of your life?' She was standing directly in front of the sun, which made her into a striking silhouette. She was dark and bold; the background was soft, warm and enchanting, like a watercolour painting.

'Marriage is a great union; it is a lifetime of friendship; it means you will not be alone in this world. Papa and I will not be around forever you know and we need to make sure

44

that when we are gone you will be safe and happy and not be alone.'

'But why is it so bad to be alone?' I had found all the pegs now and decided to hold the basket for Mama this time, so it did not happen again.

'People need to feel connected to one another; we need closeness and affection so that we can feel fulfilled in life.'

'So why can I not just have friends then?' I shuffled beside her so she could take the pegs when she needed them.

'You cannot have children with your friends, Elewa. And, when you have children, you can teach them all the lessons that you have learned from us, and by then you and your husband will have lessons of your own to teach them too.'

'Why can you not have children with your friends?' She paused and flashed me an irritated glare.

'Stop being argumentative, Elewa. My point is, your husband will be your friend; he will be your best friend. But you need not worry about this now. For now, all you need to do is enjoy your youth and look after Leba, because . . .'

'Leba holds my promise, I know.' My arms started hurting, I had been holding the basket up for too long. I noticed I could probably hold the remaining pegs in my palms if I used both hands.

Mama took the pegs from my hand and threw them back in the basket. I was relieved for the respite, as our garden was west facing, so the heat from the afternoon sun started making me feel stifled and dizzy.

~

It was after that day that I decided to intentionally neglect Leba – not because I did not want to get married and have children, but just to see what would happen if I did not follow the rules. I imagined the worst that could happen is that I would be unmarried with no children, and that did not seem like such a diabolical fate to me.

Mama started taking care of her on my behalf, presumably in the hope that as long as someone was looking after my Leba, she would still gift me with all the virtues of my destiny.

One day, when Mama was out shopping, I went into her room, stole my Leba back and took her to the river. I found a heavy rock and tied it around her waist then flung her as far as I could into the water.

As she sank to the bottom of the river, I felt truly exhilarated, as if I was going to be starting a journey that no other Oleba girl had been on.

There was a slight sense of sadness that did come over me though, when I watched the ripples from the water spread through the bank. Deep down, if I am honest, I knew that I did want what Mama and Papa had someday. I did want to have children so that I could teach them all the lessons they had taught me. But if I were to be married one day, I knew I did not want it to be because of a chunk of wood that I had been bound to since birth. I wanted it to be because of true destiny or I did not want it to *be* at all.

The night that they told me I was betrothed to Ojuro, I could not sleep; I tossed and turned all night. I felt so guilty; I knew it was my fault: *This has to be because of what I did to Leba.* I had thought the worst thing that could happen was not being married and having no children; I never thought Leba could curse me, by condemning me to a marriage with a blood-sworn enemy, someone from a tribe of people that had been killing my tribe for generations.

I pictured Uncle Kwame's bruised and battered face and

I wondered what type of hell I could expect from this marriage. If only I had listened, I might not be in this situation now.

I thought about going back to the river to find Leba. Maybe if I found her, she would forgive me, and make this all right again. Too many years had gone by though; she was probably rotten, damaged, or flushed downstream into the sea. It was hopeless, I thought; I would just have to learn to live with my new destiny somehow.

'Is this happening because of what I did to Leba?' Mama and Papa were already downstairs speaking quietly amongst themselves when I came down, the morning after they told me about the betrothal.

'What did you do?' Papa asked.

'I stole her from your room then drowned her in the bottom of the river.'

Papa's food fell from his fingers; he slapped his hand on the table, shaking his bowed head slowly, and finally looked up at me. 'Why on earth would you do that?'

Mama fixed her critical gaze on me. 'I thought you had lost her, Elewa. I bought you a new one years ago. I have been looking after her for you until you were ready to start courting.' *She is always one step ahead*, I thought.

'This is not a curse, it is a blessing. You are the Daughter of Peace. This marriage will bring about the peace between our tribes once and for all,' said Papa.

He stood up and walked over to me; he looked me in the eyes, just like normal.

'I am so proud of you, daughter. When I become chief, I will . . .' he corrected himself, 'We will have to let go of the life we have now. Everything will be different, daughter. Mama and I want everything to be clear before we prepare for what

47

lies ahead of you. If I had it my way you would live with us forever. I would not give you away to anyone; you are my precious Elewa. But peace is more important than my feelings. It is more important than any of our feelings. You understand, Elewa?'

'I am scared, Papa!'

'I know, Elewa, but you have to trust me. Have I ever put you in any danger?' His eyes were piercingly convincing, then a sense of calm washed over me, and I started to believe all would be well after all. The loneliness I had felt the night before faded: if Papa was on my side, I knew I could do anything. He got up and beckoned me to the table and put a bowl at an empty space for me, between him and Mama, then sat back down.

I sat down to join them. It was a beautiful breakfast, the type we would eat for a celebration. In the middle of the table there was a dish full of oto, a boiled, mashed yam infused with onions and garlic, a bowl of boiled eggs, and a platter full of sweet fried plantain. These were all my favourite foods and normally I would dive right in but with all the excitement, I had lost my appetite.

'This is the best thing that has happened to our tribe in decades. I always knew you would do something great, Elewa, I just did not know it would be this soon.'

'This soon? How soon will it be?' When Mama saw I had not dished any food out for myself she stopped eating and started piling food in my bowl.

'Your seventeenth birthday is in six months, so we will start making arrangements very soon, my dear.'

I started moving the food around my bowl with my hands. I would force myself to eat if I had to. Anything to avoid a conversation about needing 'to keep my strength up'.

Mama reached under the table and squeezed my hand.

I took a handful of oto and looked over at her gleaming smile. 'Be careful what you wish for,' a familiar voice, as clear as day, warned.

'What? What did you say?'

'I did not say anything, Elewa.' He and Mama exchanged perplexed glances.

'There was a voice, did you hear that?'

'Be careful what you wish for.' There it was again; it was Omolara's voice, but it sounded warped somehow. My mind flashed back to that day when I told her I would do anything for the peace of our kingdom. I started to feel that awful stifling feeling I had felt after she had said those words, the feeling that stopped me in my tracks.

'It was Omolara's voice . . .' They both gave me a worried look.

'You should go and lay down, Elewa; the excitement of the morning has just got you a bit flustered, that is all, sweet child. We have a big day today; the chief is coming here to go through the transition with Papa and he wants to meet with you for a few minutes as well.'

'I will bring the rest of your food up to you, okay?' Papa added.

I politely smiled and left. *Was I losing my mind?*

I had not slept properly and that must have been why I was hearing things.

But as I sat there on my bed, I started to connect the dots. I had declared on Omolara's sacred land that I would do anything for peace, and there was that eerie feeling I felt after she warned me to be careful what I wished for. Then I had felt that sense of unease at the shore. A day after being told that I was to be the Daughter of Peace, I had heard Omolara's warning again.

How could I hear things that other people could not? Could these be coincidences? It was all too much, so I decided to take their advice and lay down. As soon as my head hit the pillow, I fell fast asleep; then woke up a few hours later to a cold bowl of oto on the stool next to my bed. And strange voices downstairs.

~

Fumi and Komi were yelling at the top of their lungs, and everyone was talking at once. I could not understand what was being said, and then thankfully, Fumi and Komi went out into the back garden to play. Once they had left the room, I could tell exactly who was downstairs. Papa was talking to Babatunde, the Oleba chief, and Mama was talking to Olivia, his wife.

'She is upstairs resting, I will wake her up soon,' Mama answered, presumably to a question regarding my whereabouts.

'Oh yes, no problem, let her rest,' Olivia replied, before finishing her previous thought. 'As I was saying, every tribe is well known for one specific quality.' She sounded worked up, the way people get when they are talking about something they are passionate about. 'Like their industriousness, intelligence or their flair for politics . . .'

'Uh-huh, uh-huh,' Mama encouraged her, but she sounded slightly disinterested or maybe just distracted.

'If I am honest, pride in tribal qualities can cause divisiveness; the war, for instance,' Mama said nervously.

'Well, now that we have this new peace treaty, hopefully it will be the end of the war and the start of unity!' Olivia seemed to raise her voice when she said the words 'peace treaty', as if she and the chief had agreed on code words for the purpose of keeping to the matter in hand.

'Did somebody mention peace? Where is the Daughter of Peace?' Chief Babatunde bellowed, making my code-word theory more convincing.

'Oh right, yes – I will go and get her now!' With that, Mama came to find me.

~

'Eleeeewaa!' Mama called in her high-pitched singsong voice. It was the voice she used whenever we had company. When she marched into my room, she gasped when she saw me already awake, sitting on the edge of the bed.

'Oh, you are already up. How are you feeling? Did the rest help?'

Before I had heard Omolara's voice at breakfast, I had been coming around to the idea of the betrothal, but now I was starting to feel very apprehensive about the whole thing again. Perhaps this was just a process my mind had to go through to make peace with my fate.

'I guess so.'

Mama looked at me in a dubious way. She knew I was nervous. In that moment, though, it did not seem to matter how I felt.

'Well, the chief is ready for you now!' I still had so many questions. I wanted to talk to Mama and Papa before I spoke with anyone else, never mind the Oleba chief. It was all starting to feel too rushed.

'How do we know that this whole arrangement will work – the betrothal of a chief's daughter to an enemy tribe? How do we know it will result in peace?' The hinges on the door let out a whining creepy wail as Mama carefully closed it. She seemed to be concerned that either Olivia or the chief would hear. *Surely they would expect me to have questions and be apprehensive?*

51

'Not only am I sure it will work, Elewa, I believe it is the only thing that will work. A female, especially a first-born female child, is the most precious thing in the world for Oleba parents. In our tribe females are highly revered. We are a matrilineal tribe; we trace our ancestry through the female line. You know this! The Oleba believe that females are closer to our creator than males will ever be.' She spoke only a fraction louder than a whisper.

'Do the Okena not value women, then?'

She pressed her index finger into her lips and scrunched her face at me. 'Of course they do, but to them, while a girl is a wonderful gift, a son is a divine favour, the most venerated offering from the creator, just like you are to us, so it is the opposite for the Okena. You see, child, we are both bestowing our most cherished family member for peace in our land.'

Mama went on to explain that a similar peace treaty had been proposed by the Okena many years ago, during the war and before Babatunde was chief. The Oleba chief at the time refused to allow his first-born daughter to marry and suggested another solution. But the Okena believed that engaging in peace talks had to begin with a betrothal for the negotiation process to be sincere. And so, the fighting had continued.

'How do you know they are not pretending to go ahead with this so they can gain some advantage over us? Maybe they think you will not consider it; maybe they really want something else from us . . . maybe—'

'I think you are thinking too much, Elewa,' she interrupted me. 'Everyone, both Okena and Oleba, are desperate for peace now, and this is the only way to prove it to ourselves and to the kingdom.' Then she came and sat down next to me.

'Well, what about our differences?'

'Which ones?' she chuckled, flinging both her hands in the air.

'Our principles – like how the Okena sell men from our land to the white man in exchange for weapons? We do not believe in that! Will those differences not cause an uprising amongst our people?'

'That is the whole point of the peace treaty, Elewa. It is an opportunity to resolve our differences. The marriage is just a part of the treaty; the rest will determine what will and will not be law, based on what your father and the Council of Elders are able to negotiate.'

I wondered what people would say. I imagined them all in Omolara's community room, on the streets and in the social halls in heated debates about the new Daughter and Son of Peace.

'All we can do is have faith, Elewa. Come downstairs now; if you have any more questions, the chief will answer them.' She took my hand, and I reluctantly followed her.

∽

'The Daughter of Peace, I knew from the moment I first laid eyes on you that you were a rare, exceptional gift from the ancestors.' Chief Babatunde's voice was so deep and raspy it shook me to my core.

'Eh heh, the first-born child,' Papa chimed in.

'Hello, Elewa.' Olivia wrapped me in a heartfelt embrace. The truth was, although I had known Chief Babatunde and Olivia my whole life, this was the first time I had felt truly noticed or seen by them and it felt encouraging. It was a powerful feeling, to feel genuinely valued by people, important people, other than my parents. As I stood there at the bottom of the stairs with everyone looking back at me, I allowed myself to revel in that feeling for a moment. *Maybe this was what I was born to do.* I pictured our land without borders and our people without anxiety and fear, and then I realised that this was what I wanted, probably more than anything in the world. Perhaps Mama and Papa were right, maybe there was nothing to worry about. And then a more sinister feeling crept into my mind. It dawned on me that the look in their eyes was hope and all their hope rested in me. If I let them down would that hope in their eyes turn to regret?

A heavy force suddenly overpowered my body and almost knocked me off my feet. I held onto the banister to stop myself from falling to the floor.

'Are you feeling well, my dear? Sit down,' Olivia suggested.

'Yes, just a little dizzy,' I replied.

'I can imagine you must be feeling overwhelmed, child,' she added as she placed her hand on the small of my back and guided me to a seat next to her.

We all sat down and Chief Babatunde outlined the plan for the acceptance of the Okena's betrothal offer. He explained that we had thirty-one days to respond and that the process could take up to two years to complete and they would want to commence proceedings within the next year. He warned that negotiations could not take place until the wedding ceremony had occurred, and explained the main points of contention from both sides. Of course, one of ours was selling our people in exchange for guns or anything else, and one of theirs was disputed land and back payments owed to them from the Oleba residing on that land. He added that both tribes would vote on the matters, and whichever gained the most votes would become law.

'But why does the marriage have to take place before all those matters are resolved?' I asked.

'Good question – it gives the chiefs of both tribes an incentive to see the peace treaty through to the end. If you do not get married, either chief could pull out at any stage. But if they have already given up their most precious gift in this life – their precious son and daughter – they are much more likely to follow through.'

'I see!' *So, we trap them first and work out the details later.*

'He is called Ojuro? Their first-born son?' I faintly remembered him; he was always on the beach practising wrestling with older men. He often seemed distracted and absent somehow.

'Ahh, he is indeed – a fine young man, a wonderful match for you, Elewa!'

I told myself that, for all I knew, that aloof behaviour was just shyness, or a stage Ojuro was going through.

'Will I get to meet with him beforehand, to see if we get along?'

Mama and Papa gave the chief and his wife apologetic eyes. Chief Babatunde chuckled.

'My dear, this marriage is bigger than the two of you. We hope with all our hearts you get along, but whether you do or not is neither here nor there. You are doing this for the peace of our kingdom, and if you get along that is an extra bounty.'

I was annoyed by their responses but then I remembered the promise I had made to myself at Omolara's. I said I would do anything for the peace of our kingdom. I really did mean it, but I just never imagined that this would be what I would have to do. I told myself I would have at least twelve months to get used to the idea and that there was a possibility that I would love Ojuro and maybe he would love me as well.

'Do you have any other questions, my dear . . . ?' the chief asked.

'I do have one: why do the Okena have the same name as the tribe?' That had always puzzled me, but I had never gotten around to asking anyone, I'd just accepted it. But now that I was about to join them, I felt that I really needed to know.

'Ahhh, that is because the Okena chief has always been an inherited position. It has gone down from father to son for, possibly, hundreds of years, whereas for the Oleba, it is passed on to the most deserving man for the job, like your father now.' He chuckled.

'Very well, and what role does each of their family members have within the tribe?'

The chief explained the roles that each family member held; he said their chief was called Chukwuemeka-Okena, and that he had many duties. Promoting peace, resolving disputes, governing the tribe, allocating land, and much more. Chukwuemeka-Okena's wife was called Afua. She was also involved in countless activities, from adjudicating on women's matters to encouraging better relations between all the tribes that fell under the Okena's rule, which sounded fascinating.

He said that the Okena family lived further inland and closer to the forest, and that three of their four daughters were married to men from both Tawa and Mandemi tribes. I had been promised to their first son, Ojuro, and that left two sons who had not been promised and one daughter, who was called Iyùn.

Ojuro's brothers were called Folo and Akin and they were both on the Council of Elders, helping to govern. Iyùn, on the other hand, seemed to be an advocate for women and a family counsellor.

The way that Chief Babatunde spoke about the Okena

made them sound like reasonable, intelligent people. But I had always thought our tribe was more sophisticated and that they were the more crude and unrefined people.

'Why do you look so shocked?' Chief Babatunde asked me.

'I do not know; I just did not expect them to be so inclined to good order.'

'You must remember, Elewa, the Okena have inherited much of what we are dealing with now. The fact that they have initiated the peace treaty on the last two occasions says a great deal about the Okena who are in power now. I think we must give them a chance.'

'Yes, Chief Babatunde is right, but we will always sleep with one eye open. That is to say, I am not sure they could ever be blindly trusted, but I do believe we can live in peace one day,' Papa added.

'They just seem contradictory,' I said. 'They want peace, yet they sell our people to the white man for guns and other goods. They have a sophisticated tribal system, yet they have many tribes under their reign whom they would have killed if they had not surrendered to them.'

Papa looked over at me, in a proud way, as if to say, *That is my daughter.* Papa and I had had many discussions like this over the years. He had always encouraged me to think and question what had been laid out in front of me, especially when something did not seem right.

'As I said, Elewa, the Okena in power now are not the ones who made those terrible decisions in the past, and maybe initiating the peace treaty is their way of trying to right some of those wrongs.'

I thought back to my conversation with Omolara and the painting with her and the Okena man – there had to be more to these people than their bad decisions.

'Things are not always black and white, Elewa. In time you will find out just how many intricate layers and shades of grey exist within both the Okena family and tribe.'

After that Chief Babatunde and Olivia went home. Although I was still apprehensive, I had a better understanding of what was expected of me. I decided to take this new journey one moment at a time and trust Papa because, as he said, he had never let me down before.

7

Out of the four Okena daughters, Iyùn was the only one unmarried. Not only was she not married, but she had not even been promised to the son of any noble family yet. Iyùn was deaf and many tribes believed she was cursed or would bring difficulty onto their family, so they would not accept her.

Iyùn was bright, charismatic, and used sign-language to communicate her needs, thoughts, feeling and desires to her family. In turn her family learned the language and used it to communicate back to her and to one another, when Iyùn was around.

This visual language started off very simple but grew to become quite comprehensive. The language developed with Iyùn and by the time she was eleven, she was able to communicate abstract ideas.

The fact that their tribe could communicate without words gave them an edge against other tribes. Chief Chukwuemeka-Okena, Iyùn's father, knew this and appreciated that their success, as a tribe, at least partially, came down to Iyùn. Although this was not true for Afua, Iyùn's mother, who fretted for her deaf daughter. No matter what Iyùn did, her mother still looked upon her as a worry, even though she could sense so much more than her hearing brothers and sisters, and on countless occasions she had got them all out of trouble – the kind of trouble only hearing people could get into, when, for example, they missed the subtleties of communication that they had come to take for granted. They would often go away from an encounter thinking they had understood what the person wanted because they only listened to their voice and nothing else. Iyùn would often tell her family what she understood from the meeting and more often than not she would be correct. When her father saw this, he started to insist that Iyùn attend all his important business meetings, and then he would consult her when the attendees had gone. Her siblings would do the same, but in a more informal way, like with friends and potential partners. The family deeply valued Iyùn and believed that she was very gifted. Iyùn's gift saved the family a great deal of hassle and affliction during the course of their lives.

~

When we lived with Grandpa and Grandma, before Fumi and Komi were born, Grandpa always told us stories of the Okena's grandmother, Mama Iyeniye. He claimed that Mama Iyeniye was the one that had the Yeseni, the gift of sight. At first, I could not really understand what he meant, but his eyes would change as he described the miraculous acts he witnessed as a young boy, like Mama Iyeniye's ability to suddenly appear in different places, to foretell the future and to know what could not be known by other people. His pupils would dilate, and his skin would turn flushed, and burnished with sweat. Grandpa would stand and get really animated and excitable during parts of the stories. He could never really stand up much in those days, so I could tell something really left a strong impression on him. I cannot say I disbelieved

Grandpa but I could not know then that one day, I would come to truly appreciate and understand the meaning of his fantastical tales.

~

As the weeks went by, Papa and Chief Babatunde started to make regular trips to the Okena for joint tribal meetings and discussions about the betrothal. Everyone was keen to start peace treaty dialogues, but they knew that that could not happen until after the wedding. There were details regarding the marriage that needed to be ironed out and due to our tribe being matrilineal Mama needed to be at many of those meetings.

Although we had not been in open battle with the Okena for years, we were still in wartime, and with no agreement in place between our tribes, people were on edge; constantly anxious, afraid and restrained. I knew that people felt that they could not live their lives freely. We all knew that if we did not broker peace soon, any kind of frivolous incident could cause us to break into a vicious battle. That would mean losing more innocent lives and costing more than either of our tribes could afford.

Papa knew deep down that if we did engage in another battle, the Okena would probably win. They had been trading with the white men at the coast for years now and so they had many guns and other exotic warfare tools that our tribe did not possess. Instead, we used traditional combat tools, which, at times, gave our tribe the advantage, because sometimes, the Okena's guns would fail them. They could not really fight unless they had gunpowder and gunpowder was not unlimited.

Papa said that catching the Okena off guard or unexpectedly was our only hope of winning battles. During the war, when we had caught them unprepared, we were mostly victorious, but ultimately, at that time neither side could sustain another bloody battle. Both sides were desperate for a solution.

~

Fumi and Komi were at Uncle Kwame's house and our beloved Sessie came along with us to one of the betrothal meetings. It had not yet been officially announced, but somehow word about it had gotten out, and since then, there had been a few Okena raids in our area, and consequently, Oleba outrage started to intensify. It felt like there could be some kind of retaliation at any moment, so Mama and Papa did not want to leave us at home alone.

During the meeting, the men from both tribes were shouting and debating over land, gold and agriculture, even though those discussions were not supposed to take place until after the wedding. People could not seem to wait to get those subjects of contention off their chests.

In the heat of the commotion, I felt a sudden urge to be outside, away from the hubbub of the raised voices and heightened tempers. I slipped out of the meeting room and into the fresh air. As I breathed deeply and tried to calm the jangling in my head, I became aware of a small hut ahead of me. Something pulled me irresistibly towards it, even though I knew I should not be trespassing in Okena houses without permission. I crept towards the doorway, fearful that I would be spotted but drawn so powerfully that my fear could not stop me.

'Come in, my child,' said a voice from inside. I peered in at the figure of an old women dressed in an indigo head-dress, wrap and a tunic covered in traditional ivory prints. She had her back to me and was looking out through her southern-facing window, onto the fields. It seemed impossible, but I knew with certainty who she was. She was Mama Iyeniye.

'Come in, my child,' she repeated. I held my breath. I think I was worried that if I let it go, she would curse me. *How did she know I was there?*

'Breathe,' she said, in a calm, drawn-out tone, almost like a mantra or the bass tone of a melody. She finally turned around and I stood there in the opening of the doorway, as still as a statue. She had so many wrinkles on her face; they appeared likes lines on an enigmatic map. They were deep-set and folded in around her eyes, from her nose to the corners of her mouth, and her lips had vertical lines leading down towards her shrivelled chin, and on the top lip they led up, towards her Cupid's bow. Her eyes were brown and wide, almond in shape, and her nose was small and round. It looked like it belonged to another face.

I finally let my breath go.

'There you go,' she said as she smiled at me. 'How can I help you?'

Just as I knew her, I felt she also knew who I was, knew me deeply, and had done all my life.

'Grandpa said you have Yeseni . . .'

'Did he now? You would think by his age he would have learned that gossip serves neither the creator or the spirits and is for the idle of mind and heart.' She placed her hand on her hip and walked back towards the window. 'Come, child,' she ordered, 'sit.'

I walked into her room and sat on the wooden chair that she had gestured me towards. I sat back and my feet did not touch the ground, so I shuffled forward until they did. She sat opposite me and rested her hands on the table in front of us; I kept mine on my lap.

'You are Mama Iyeniye?'

'Tiiandas, Mama Tiiandas,' she corrected me as if she had been used to people mixing their names up. 'My younger sister is Iyeniye,' she clarified.

'Sorry, Mama Tiiandas,' I repeated back to her for approval. *So much for my intuition.* She smiled and nodded in one firm motion.

The room smelt of frankincense, soil and delicate flowers, the kind you find in the Mambi Valley, just before you reach the Suwhetu Lake.

There was a single bed to the east side, dressed in exotic cotton sheets; I had never seen anything like them before. She must have acquired them during one of their trades with the white man. They were immaculately arranged on the bed in such a painstakingly flawless fashion that I could not imagine anyone curling up and sleeping on such a thing.

On the north-facing wall she had a reflective glass panel, like Omolara's looking glass but larger, and I could see the opposite side of the room through it. *It is true*, I instinctively knew, *this woman really does have Yeseni.* Underneath that panel was a wooden cabinet with three drawers that were framed with metal ironmongery. Four fancy little legs held the structure together and they were carved in what appeared to be the likeness of lion paws.

On top of the cabinet there were four candles sitting on two small, shiny, foreign-looking plates. I looked back at Mama Tiiandas, who was studying me as thoroughly as I was studying her quarters.

'When someone comes to me with a spirit like yours, they are usually looking for something. Tell me now why you are here.'

'Mama and Papa had to meet with Mama Iyeniye's son to arrange peace—'

'Why have you been drawn here to me?' It clearly was not the answer she wanted. Either that or I had not understood her question properly. *Why* had *I come all the way out here to seek out this strange elderly lady? In fact, Mama is probably looking for me.* I hastily got up from the chair.

'Give me your hands,' she instructed me and immediately I placed my hands in her palms. The room disappeared; my whole body jolted. It felt like I was in a different world. Only I was not there either, in that other world. I could just see that world and I was viewing real people in motion.

I saw a man surrounded by gold, plenty of exotic foods, slaves and servants. He had dark brown skin with a reddish undertone, the same colour as Papa's. He wore bright clothes with colours I had never seen before.

'Excellency, are you certain you will be travelling with all of this?' A second man gestured towards the packed luggage filled with luxury items.

'Do you question my judgement, Ola? I have travelled to many lands, as you very well know . . .' The first man casually strolled around the room and wherever he went, it seemed, the light followed him, reflecting off the precious metals he was wearing. He wore a thick gold bracelet that had a serpent's head on one end and the tail on the other. The serpent's mouth was open, and the cleft tongue became the lock that fixed the bracelet securely to his wrist; I had never seen such craftsmanship, such detail. *How beautiful.*

Around his neck he had numerous woven gold chains; the one that he wore on the outermost layer held a pendant of a large gold mask. I had seen this type of pendant before, but mostly made from wood, bark, or tusks; they were normally worn by folk for protection from evil spirits in my tribe. The first man continued, 'This is the way you gain respect from those you meet when you travel on a pilgrimage.' Various people came in to check on every aspect of his person. They treated him like he was the most precious thing in the world. Even more precious than time, which is why they dedicated all of theirs to him.

They checked his temperature, his clothes, fixing them with impeccable accuracy to his shoulders and pinning them around his body in a deliberate way, but to look effortless.

While listening and nodding agreeably to the golden man, Ola directed the other servants around the room, almost like a conductor in an orchestra, and they moved hastily with his direction. The golden man continued.

'People are capricious, Ola; they are not divine like Allah or wise like his prophet. They judge your worth based on what they see with their eyes and nothing more.' The golden man walked over to Ola, placing his hand on his shoulder and staring directly into his eyes. 'If we are generous with gifts, they will respect us, so we will give them what they want, do you understand?'

'Yes, master,' Ola timidly replied.

I started to feel a tingling sensation in the tips of my fingers and then another person's hands touching mine. Mama Tiiandas's hands. My heart started pounding and I could not catch my breath. *Was I holding my breath that whole time?* I moved my hands out of hers and rested them on my knees, planting my head deep in between my shoulders. With my chin to my chest, I was now gasping for air.

'You will be fine, child, just breathe,' she reassured me in a calm, deep voice, rubbing her hand between my shoulders.

'What just happened to me?' I asked in between violent intakes of breath. She gently lifted my head up and held my chin in place with the tips of her fingers, my breathing calmed down.

'What did you see, child?' she asked eagerly.

'I need to go,' I shouted, as I scurried out the door.

'Mama, Mama!' I called out. I do not know how she heard my cries over the loud deliberating in the Okena debating chamber, but I saw her come running around the corner.

'Good grief, child, where have you been?' she exhaled as she grabbed me and pulled me to her chest.

My heart was still pounding, and I could not bring myself to speak.

'We are leaving now,' she ordered, as we walked over towards Sessie and the carriage. I stopped to look back at the house and saw Mama Tiiandas peering through the window.

'Who are you staring at?' Mama quizzed me. I did not respond; my stomach felt like it had repositioned itself to the back of my spine and my mouth was numb, fixed shut. *Yeseni, did that really happen to me? What did the vision mean, and who were those people?* I had so many questions.

I must have fallen fast asleep during our journey home, as the next thing I knew I was waking up to the sunlight through my bedroom window. The birds were singing a strange song, one that I had not heard before. Had they migrated from another part of our land?

In the weeks that followed, I found it impossible not to think about that day. I had thought that the feeling I got after Omolara told me to be careful what I wish for was the strangest thing I had ever felt, but that day with Mama Tiiandas was of a different order. She had shown me another world and it haunted my thoughts day and night. I found myself thinking about Ola and the wealthy man's journey; I wondered if they ever got to where they had planned to go and if the wealthy man ever achieved the respect he sought.

I remember noting that even though they were wealthy,

certain aspects of their lives seemed in comparison with my own. The clothes they wore were elaborate, but old-fashioned. The way they spoke, although comprehensible, felt archaic. That is why I concluded that the world I had seen was probably from the past.

After that night, I tried living my life as normal, putting the experience to the back of my mind as much as I could and trying my best not to dwell on it too much. I did not try to seek out Mama Tiiandas again. I was afraid it might happen again and for once, my fear got the better of my curiosity.

8

After Mama Tiiandas shared her vision with me, I felt like a different person somehow. Before, I lived in the moment and reacted to everything that was happening in my life as if the world revolved around me. But after the vision, I began observing the happenings of my life in a detached way.

'Step outside of yourself for a while, child, the view is much clearer from the other side' was something Omolara used to say to me whenever I came to her wound up about some trivial situation. I never truly understood what she meant by that until after Mama Tiiandas shared her vision with me.

Now that I had seen another land – had smelled the air, heard the voices and felt the tension, the courage and optimism in the atmosphere – it felt like almost anything was possible, and I began to get excited about my future.

'It was not just a vision,' I mumbled to myself as I lay on my bed, 'it was stronger than that. I was there.' Sometimes I found that saying things out loud was more powerful than just thinking them. Physically putting the words into the world made them more solid, more real; they existed.

And if that world existed, the world with Ola and the

golden man, and my world existed, then did any other worlds exist as well?

～

When I heard the news of Mama Tiiandas's death, it deeply troubled me. I regretted my own cowardice and bitterly wished I had visited to talk with her again, to ask her questions and try to make sense of the vision she had shared. Yet now there was no chance of that.

I had left it too late and I worried that I would be stuck in this mundane world with no visions or thrilling experiences, just the memory. I would be just like Grandpa: telling my grandchildren tales of a mystical time that they could not possibly understand.

～

The death ceremony was a sombre affair and because of the betrothal, we were all expected to attend. Everybody wore white, which was odd to me. White was normally worn in remembrance ceremonies, not funerals, but perhaps that was just the Okena way. After all, every tribe had different customs and practices.

At the house of the deceased, all decorations were taken down and put safely away out of respect. As we arrived, I saw Mama Tiiandas's immaculate bed, being taken out by three sturdy-looking men. An older woman stood behind the men, giving instructions on where to put the bed, so that Mama Tiiandas would not come back and haunt the living and would instead move on to the afterlife and ultimately, rest in peace. This was a tradition that I was familiar with because the Oleba had a very similar way.

The women could be heard crying for miles. The ceremony

was held so that all you could think about was the deceased. It brought structure to your mourning and left no space for your mind to wander to other selfish thoughts. Through their cries my heart sank, and a deep sorrow came over me. After the women's mourning cries, it was the men's turn. Mama asked me to go to the kitchen and help the family prepare food for the mourners.

Several carcasses lay bloody on the kitchen table. I wondered how many goats had been slaughtered for the guests. Suddenly, I felt a hand on my waist. I looked up and saw a younger version of Mama Tiiandas. I gasped in shock.

'Tiiandas told me about you,' she said. I composed myself.

'She was a—' I was about to try and think up something clever and respectful to say about Mama Tiiandas, but she interrupted me.

'About the day that you came to her quarters.' I just nodded; I was unsure what she wanted from me.

After an awkward silence I replied, 'You look just like her – what is your name?' She really did. We had been speaking in a low tone, not quite a whisper but low enough so the women around us could not make out what we were saying.

'Iyeniye, Mama Iyeniye to you.'

I raised my eyebrows, smiled, and nodded agreeably at her, then repeated her name back to her.

This is the Mama Iyeniye of Grandpa's tales, I thought, the one I had initially mistaken Mama Tiiandas for.

'It is nice to meet you. My name is—'

'I know your name, child. You are promised to my grandson. I know I am old, but I have not lost all my faculties . . .' she chuckled, ending the sentence with a wink. She went on, in a more serious tone this time, 'All she asked is that you shared with her what you saw that night.' I broke eye contact with her and lowered my head. She was right, I knew she was right. I should have gotten in touch with Mama Tiiandas sooner. She welcomed me into her quarters and shared her gift with me and the least I could have done was told her what I saw.

Mama Iyeniye lifted my head and smiled back at me. 'I have not met anyone that could receive a vision in that way for many years. To get a vision, like the one you received, you would have to have Yeseni.'

'I should have come to see Mama Tiiandas before. I wanted to, but I was still afraid. I thought I would see her soon enough,' I confessed.

'It matters little; she is always around. In a few days come and see me and I can answer any questions you have, since I was the one you were first seeking, was I not?' She said this in such a blasé manner: *she is always around.* The woman had passed away, moved on to the afterlife, how could she always be around? I had so many questions, but I did not want to make a scene.

'Yes, you were the one that Grandpa told me about. I thought Mama Tiiandas was you.'

'She told me,' she said with a smile. 'When we were younger, people used to get us muddled up all the time. I shall see you soon.' She gently rubbed my arm then walked away.

'Mama Iyeniye!' I called, and everyone in the kitchen looked at me. She turned back around, her eyebrows inched up towards her hairline and she raised her shoulder to the ceiling.

'I am sorry for your loss,' I said, and with that everyone continued with their tasks.

'Yes, we are all sorry, child, you never recover from losing a sibling,' she replied, as she walked away and into the living room. I thought that was a strange response from someone who had *just* lost her sibling; it seemed as if she had been grieving her death longer than a few days.

'Come on, child,' an older lady scolded me, 'you have been standing in front of that meat for ages, it will not chop itself – we have hundreds of people to feed!' I put my head down and focused on the task at hand. I cut the meat into small cubes like I had been shown to do and then I seasoned it and took it outside to another lady cooking on an open fire.

By the time we were finished I was soaked in sweat and my hands were sore from the relentless chopping. I was so exhausted that I just wanted to lay down in a dark room and think of nothing.

Hours after the food had been served, people were starting to leave, and Mama asked Papa if we could go home as well. He agreed and we left, while he stayed on for the rest of the ceremony. I planned on taking Mama Iyeniye up on her offer and visiting her as soon as she had had enough time to mourn. I was not going to make the same mistake that I had with Mama Tiiandas. Now, I was more curious and determined than ever to learn more about the gift they called Yeseni.

9

The weeks after Mama Tiiandas's funeral were some of the strangest weeks of my life. The most peculiar things kept happening and Papa's anxiety seemed to be worsening.

The Oleba were used to the presence of the white man in our village every now and then, but during that time it felt as though their appearances increased tenfold within just a few weeks. We were not surprised to find out that they had been visiting other members of the Oleba tribe because Chief Babatunde warned Papa about that. But we were shocked when they visited Papa, the soon-to-be Oleba chief, in the weeks leading up to the betrothal.

Any extra freedom I had hoped for before my marriage was completely out of the question because Papa doubled down on all his restrictions and rules for us children and I started to wish they would just disappear so that we could live our lives without these extra constraints.

～

One day, we heard a loud knock at the door, and we all went running down the steps to open it. Sessie was already making her way there; she had a basket full of clean cloths balancing on her hip. We ran so fast past her that we knocked them onto the floor. You must understand that knocks at the door like this could mean any number of thrilling things for us all. Often, they meant a surprise parcel that Mama and I could unpack together – or even better, Uncle Kwame. He would bring the tastiest treats: coconut and honey drops or citrus candies, the gooey kind that stuck to your teeth. Occasionally he would bring a new toy and Fumi and Komi would spend the day fighting over it, only to abandon it once the novelty had worn off. We were all hoping it was Uncle Kwame when we heard that knock. Later that day Mama made us rewash every single cloth that we had made Sessie drop. Mama was very protective of Sessie and very particular about how we treated her. We were to call her Sister Sessie. She had been with us since she was a baby. Mama always said without Sessie we would fall apart.

When we arrived at the door, standing there were two white men, with the reddest coats I had ever seen. We did not have a name for the colour red in our language; names of colours were sort of grouped together, described by their tone rather than their hue. Their coats were very thick and made of what I now believe was a felt material. They had engraved brass buttons going down the breast. I remember them looking very shiny, uncomfortable, sweaty and hot. Their clothes were not suitable for our climate.

'Hello, little lady,' the older one with the nose that pointed slightly to the right said to me. 'Where is your father, Mr Olan . . . Olanie . . .' He desperately turned to his colleague for help, who quickly jumped in and saved him. 'Mr Olanre-waju!' When Mama heard their voices, she came rushing to the door and sent us to play out the back, but I told Fumi and Komi to go while I sat nearby to listen in. Mama closed the front door after she told them that she would see if Papa was available, so I ran to my bedroom window, which looked out

75

to the front yard, and there they were, waiting in the heat for Papa to come out.

Mama went to tell Papa that the white men from the sea were here again, hoping to speak with him. After a heated discussion between the two, Sessie was asked to let them in, offer them some refreshments and have them seated in the living room, which she did.

Papa took his time getting ready. We never knew exactly when they would appear, so when they did, it would always cause a sense of apprehension.

Other families in the area had been speaking of them showing up on their doorsteps, unannounced, with all sorts of exotic offerings, in return for which they would be expected to work for them as slave catchers, betraying their own people for trinkets, knives and guns. The entrance to my room was opposite the steps and Papa's was even closer, so I had to wait until he went downstairs before I could listen in. I sat by my door so that I could listen to as much as possible. I heard Sessie leave the room with the slight clinking of the jug against the serving plates. I heard her steps towards the kitchen, setting the tray and jugs down and heading to the back, presumably to ask Mama if there was anything else that she could do. Mama must have said no because Sessie left. I heard Papa leave his room, head down the stairs and into the living room. I followed and sat on the top step.

'Mr Olanrewaju, allow me to introduce Captain Williams. I am Captain Lewis.'

'How may I help you, Captain Lewis?'

'Well, first of all I would like to congratulate you – I hear you are to be the next Oleba chief?' I did not hear a response from Papa and there was silence for what felt like minutes but was probably only seconds.

'I see you are a man of few words; I respect that.' I heard the sound of footsteps walking around the living room. I knew they were not Papa's; I knew his stride off by heart. The footsteps followed the voice around, so I thought it must be Captain Lewis. He walked in a menacing, dull thudding pattern; there was no spring in his step whatsoever.

'Captain, I ask you again – what is it you want from me?' The pitch of Papa's voice seemed slightly higher than usual, almost like pleading.

'Of course. Williams, show Mr Olanrewaju the contract.' There was a rustling of papers.

I heard Papa pacing around while riffling through the document. He let out a loud, piercing cackle.

'You people are unbelievable – so if I sign this contract, you will stop supplying guns to the Okena and you will supply them to us instead, if we help you do your filthy work?' I imagined him shaking his head in disbelief. 'Have you learned nothing about the Oleba, in all your years of prying around us? We never have dealt with you, and we never will.' Papa marched over to the front door and stood next to it, presumably waiting for an opportunity to ask them to leave.

'Ah, Mr Olanrewaju, I like you . . . you are the only one, the only honest Oleba left.'

'What are you talking about?' Papa asked.

'We have been doing business with the Oleba for years – Chief Babatunde understands this. We have had a long-standing contract with him, and the Oleba chief before him. Why do you think your families are all protected and have never been captured? Because we have an agreement.'

Papa chuckled. I am not sure if they bought Papa's façade of confidence, but I did not – I could tell he was using everything in his power to hold his temper. These men were accusing Chief Babatunde of making an agreement with them behind Papa's back.

'The first mention of peace in our land and you cannot bear it – you are terrified that we will finally wake up and you will lose all your profit from our free labour. Well, your nightmare has come true. Maybe I am the only honest Oleba left, but you will have to put a musket ball through my head before I will sign any contract with you. If I find out who has been doing your dirty work, I will kill them with my bare hands, the Oleba way,' he panted; I had never heard him so enraged.

'So, you will kill your wife's only brother, as well as your oldest friend, Chief Babatunde?' Captain Williams' voice was as cool as the sea breeze before sunrise. 'Do not look so shocked, Mr Olanrewaju. As I said, it seems as though you are the only honest Oleba left.'

Captain Williams had now accused Uncle Kwame of dealing with them as well. I could not for the life of me understand how this could be true. I could just about understand how a poor or vulnerable Oleba might give in to the white man's tempting offerings, but a well-connected Oleba chief and the kind-hearted brother-in-law of a soon-to-be chief? *He has to be lying.*

'Maybe so, but while I am chief, there will be no dealings with you.' Papa paused and the tone in his voice dropped. 'I have been to your lands – I know what you do to our people once they get there. I would not wish that fate on my worst enemy. Like I said, if you want to stop me, you will have to kill me. Now get off my land and do not come back!'

I could not believe what I was hearing. Papa had been to the land of the white man of the sea, but he had never mentioned it to me before.

'I will leave this with you. You look tired, Mr Olanrewaju. Get some rest, sleep on it. I think that after some rest you will find you value your life more than your principles. We will be back!'

He sounded so confident and self-assured. Maybe he had had the same response from Chief Babatunde and Uncle Kwame when he first approached them, but he had somehow managed to coerce them into it.

Mama ran downstairs and wrapped her arms around Papa as soon as they had gone, and when I heard the front door close, I ran to the window and saw the men walk off, looking agitated and flushed in the face. After that day, Papa had a ten-foot-tall gate built all around the perimeter of our house and hired two security guards, one at the entrance and one at the rear door.

~

Our tribes were wealthy at that time, so I could not see why we needed trading relationships with the white man of the sea. What they needed from us was our labour in lands they had stolen to help establish and build their empire, but what we wanted from them helped to supplement our wars. If this peace treaty was successful, perhaps we would not need their tools of war any longer. Maybe then, I hoped, they would finally leave us alone. The Okena still had control of the trading and commerce of all the tribes they had defeated in battle, which brought in a great deal of wealth to their tribe. They also had an abundance of gold, which Chief Chukwuemeka-Okena ostentatiously exhibited, frequently commissioning great plaques, jewellery and ornaments to be made from it. No one really knew exactly where all the gold came from, but some believed it was found on their ancestral, sacred land, within the dense jungle.

Our tribe also had gold, which was mined in several locations inland. We mainly used the gold to trade with other tribes, for items like frankincense, other metals, materials to make weapons and certain foods and spices. We seldom wore it on our person as, culturally, within our tribe, bold displays of gold were viewed as slightly vulgar.

When I think back to the day of the unannounced visit from Captain Williams and Captain Lewis, I remembered how terrified Papa sounded, even though he was trying his hardest to hold his temper. There was an edginess that I had never seen in him before, and he stayed that way for days, maybe even weeks, after their visit. This went deeper than Papa simply following custom; he had been to their land, and I waited and waited for the best opportunity to ask him about his experience. I wanted to know what he had seen there and why just speaking of it that day made his voice so jittery and breathless. I wondered if the captains were telling the truth about Chief Babatunde and Uncle Kwame and, if so, I thought about why they might betray Papa in that way. I knew the truth would come out sooner or later. I told myself it was just a matter of time.

10

My concern for Papa kept him constantly in my thoughts. I remembered the love and kindness he had shown me when trying to teach me to throw a spear when I was younger. Most Oleba girls are not taught this, but Papa patiently persevered with my training, despite my constant complaints that I would never find myself on a battlefield.

'Papa, why are you are always thinking of bad things, like war, and battle and death?' I whined.

'You are my precious Elewa,' he replied. 'I would never forgive myself if anything happened to you and I had not prepared you for it.' His eyes welled up, and he looked right through me, like he was remembering someone he had lost for that very reason.

'Papa, you look like you are thinking about something sad?'

'You do not get to my age without a few sad stories.'

Now I knew that some of those sad stories must be from when he had travelled to the white man's lands.

~

My daydreams often took me to strange places but now I had learned that I had the power to see into another world, an odd but still recognisable world, I wanted to learn more.

I still did not quite know why or how the vision came to me that night with Mama Tiiandas. At first, I had thought that I was channelling her powers, until her sister told me it would not have been possible unless I possessed the gift of Yeseni myself.

The week before I went back to visit Mama Iyeniye, I must have thought of Ola and the wealthy man every day. I started to have dreams of the visions and each time I had those dreams they got stronger and more vivid. I would wake up in the middle of the night, panting and sweating, until I realised I must make it my business to go and see her without delay. I was terrified of what she would reveal to me, but I knew it was something that I had to do.

I started looking for clues of my power in my everyday life, but I could not find anything. Until then the only other strange thing that had happened to me was that morning when Omolara warned me to be careful what I wished for, just before that eerie paralysing feeling came over me. That was an inexplicable experience, but it was nothing like the vision of Ola and the wealthy man. When I could not find any clues of my powers, I started to doubt what Mama Iyeniye had told me on the day of the funeral; I even started to doubt myself. And I grew frustrated.

'If I have these special powers, where are they?' I mumbled to myself. If I did have them, perhaps I could use my powers to help Papa.

~

On the morning of the day that I finally made the decision to take a trip to the Okena, I told Mama I was going to Omolara's market to look for a present for Papa's birthday. She said that would be fine but asked Sessie to accompany me.

82

Sessie agreed and we set off. I told Sessie where we were going on the way.

'This is something I have to do, Sessie.' She gave me that look, the look she gets when she disagrees with a choice you have made.

'Please do not make your face like that,' I implored her. 'We will be going to the market afterwards.'

She replied as if I had not said anything, and she was just finishing her sentence.

'And what if your mother asks me where we have been? Do you expect me to lie?' She looked at me as if I had lost any sense that I had. Sessie had known me longer than I had known myself, so she knew how to make me feel like I had disappointed her. To be completely honest, I did not expect this to be easy, but I knew she would take my side; she always stood by my side in the end. Even if she gave me a hard time at first, she would always help me through whatever disaster I had gotten myself into. Sessie acted a little bit like my conscience at times. I knew her concern was always out of love, so I put up with her reproof. I rolled my eyes.

'No, Sessie, I just expect you to avoid the conversation, make up an excuse or change the subject – do whatever you need to do, but I must do this.' I was normally concerned with impressing Sessie, but right now I honestly did not care what she had to say. Mama had asked her to come along with me and that was what she had to do. Finding out about these powers and the meaning of that vision with Mama Tiiandas was more important than pleasing Sessie.

'Elewa, there has been time set aside for you to get to know Ojuro, you do not need to sneak around like this,' she droned on. Why did I not explain to her what had happened that day? *At least so that she would understand and get off my back*, a voice inside my head suggested. *Because I did not even understand what happened that night myself*, another voice responded.

'This is not about Ojuro, Sessie, I need to see Mama Iyeniye. Do you remember the day of the treaty when we accompanied Papa to the Okena?'

'When you sneaked away,' she replied in a tone that was more condescending than confirmatory.

'Yes. I went to see Mama Tiiandas. Something happened and I need to find out what it meant. Are you coming with me or not?' I started to lose patience with her. If she did not want to come, fine – she could go back home and tell Mama that she had left me to gallivant around alone. One of the voices in my head started again: *It is not a sin to visit a family that we are now in the process of forming a peace treaty with, a family that you have been betrothed into.* The other voice responded: *No, the sin would be lying to your mother about it in the first place.*

Ugh, these voices are mocking me, I thought.

'Very well, but please do not ask me to do anything like this again.'

I made my promises and Sessie came along with me. We did not talk much on the way there and she kept that uncomfortable look on her face for the whole journey. I did not care. If I had to put up with that face and this tension just to get the answers that would lead to clarity and peace of mind, I would do so. Sooner or later, I would tell everyone – Mama, Papa, Komi, Fumi and Sessie. Until then I was willing to put up with whatever I needed to.

I had to find out what these powers of Yeseni were and more importantly, how I could access them – if I could ever access them again.

When we arrived, the guards recognised me and one of them took us to the lobby to wait while he called the Okena chief's wife, Afua.

We sat on two large wooden chairs that were opposite each other. Sessie had her pretend pleasant face on now and I was just consumed by my surroundings. Soon this would be my new home. The walls were covered with a variety of art: some paintings, some plaques and what looked like silk rugs, probably gifted or traded with an Arab merchant. The plaques were bronze casts of the Okena family members' likenesses. The figures protruding from the plaques were so detailed they looked like they could step out of their display and shake your hand.

I heard footsteps towards the lobby, followed by Afua's voice.

'Elewa, my darling, how is my daughter?' Her eyebrows were raised, and she smiled enough to bring the sun out of the sky once again.

'Mama Afua, so nice to see you. I wish to apologise for turning up unannounced.'

'Dear, we are all excited about the joining of you and Ojuro, but your mother and I are planning the meeting ceremonies – you understand that these are fixed, and you cannot see each other before they happen?' She nodded while she said it, and I could see Sessie's *I told you so* face from the corner of my eye. I inwardly rolled my eyes at her and continued to try and explain to Afua.

'I know, Mama explained that to me, but I am here to see Mama Iyeniye. She invited me to come by the other day; she said that I had left something of mine with her.' I had to think quickly, make something up. I could not tell her the real reason I was there.

'Very well. I will get Ada to see if she is available.' She gestured to Ada, who was loitering around the hallway and perked up when she heard her name. Ada nodded back at Afua and hastily scurried away.

'Now, ladies I hope you are thirsty; Ada made some fresh clove tea and I was just about to have a glass.'

'Thank you, we would love some tea.'

She disappeared to the kitchen and returned with two cups of delicious clove tea for us both.

Sessie made me ask Ada for the recipe, and I thought it was the least I could do for dragging her into this. When Ada returned, she advised us that Mama Iyeniye had been resting but was happy to see me. I followed her to Mama Iyeniye's quarters, while Sessie waited for me in the entrance chamber.

～

Mama Iyeniye's quarters reminded me so much of Mama Tiiandas's. Strange wood carvings, perfectly made bed, the alluring scent of frankincense and that obscure reflective panel on the wall.

'You came . . .' A warm smile formed across her face, and she opened both her arms as she walked over to hug me. 'How are you, my dear?' She let go and held my cheeks in her palms. I wasted no time with small talk.

'I am well, but I need to know what that vision meant and what this power is that you say I possess.' I thought the best way to go about this was to be straightforward.

'Sit down, my dear. Tell me, what did you see?' She gestured me over to a wooden chair next to her immaculate bed. I reluctantly walked over and sat down. I honestly wanted to stay standing. Sessie was waiting for me, and she was not impressed with my antics so far that day as it was. If we took much longer, I was sure she would scorn me for life. Then Mama would start worrying about our whereabouts, which was the last thing I needed. Besides, did this really need to take an age? Nevertheless, I explained.

I told her how Mama Tiiandas had held my hand and how I felt the energy move from her into me and with that, the visions played out through my mind. I described the wealthy man who seemed to be preparing to go on a long trip. I explained how affluent he clearly was and how they seemed to live in a different time, although they were still the people of our land. I went into as much detail as I possibly could. I had been talking for what felt like an hour, non-stop, all the while Mama Iyeniye not appearing at all surprised by anything that I was saying.

'So, you said if I had any questions you would be happy to help. I want to know what this power is and what that vision meant.'

She rose from her seat.

'That was a powerful vision that you had, Elewa, but I am afraid I cannot tell you what it meant or who those people were. I can tell you that whatever or whoever comes to you in a vision means that Yeseni is calling you, giving you the chance to make a wrong right. It could be a message from the past, future or present.'

She moved to the other side of the window and inspected the frame. She was nonchalant and I wished she had stopped me earlier if she knew she could not tell me what the vision meant.

'So, you are saying that the vision was some kind of message and now I must decipher it, in order to right a wrong from the past?' I concluded.

'It would seem so, yes. We, that is, me and Mama Tiiandas, used to get them all the time growing up. We saved our father from financial ruin more than once. We also saved our village from being flooded and destroyed.' She turned her back towards the window and faced me.

'Very well. And the Yeseni – how do I access it on my own?'

'You already access it on your own, my dear.'

'With respect, Mama Iyeniye, no I do not. I have never had an experience like that again.'

'But you were by yourself that day.' This time she walked towards me and placed my hand in her palms.

'I was with Mama Tiiandas; I told you that and you confirmed it at her funeral, that day in the kitchen.' This was getting too strange now. *I will make my excuses and just leave.*

'Mama Tiiandas, my sister, has been dead for nearly ten years; my child; the woman you saw that day was her spirit.'

Gravity must have taken over because I fell backwards into that chair. This could not be true. I had seen her face, every line, the whites of her eyes. I had touched her hands.

'What about the funeral, how can you explain that?' I glared at her, desperately looking for a sign of dishonesty, but she was as stable as a rock. Not a quiver in her voice or her eyes.

'The remembrance ceremony, you mean? We hold them for all our ancestors on the eve of the anniversary of their death.' She shook her head in disbelief, as if she could not imagine how I did not know these things. 'You summoned my sister in your vision that day, all by yourself,' she proclaimed.

My heart felt like it was in my throat. I froze on the chair, I could not move. How could something that seemed so real be so fabricated, and by my own mind as well?

'Do you see now that you do not need anyone but yourself? The you that believes in your powers. That is all you need to conjure them. You can use a vessel – Mama Tiiandas, one of your own ancestors or anything that helps you – but really all you need is yourself and your belief. Think back through your life, all the things that you willed to happen that came true. All the fortune your family enjoys, the reason our tribes are now working towards a peace treaty. It is all because of you, Elewa.

'I cannot tell you exactly what your vision meant but I can promise you that it is important and could be the difference between life and death, feast or famine. You must discover its meaning so that you can honour the Yeseni.' She put her arm around me.

'How do I do that?' I was still frozen. I wondered if she was really there or if I had conjured her up too. I just could not believe what she was suggesting.

'Where do you feel most at peace?' She squeezed me tight.

'Near the water, I suppose.' That was truly the only place I ever felt at peace, in fact I wanted to be there in that very moment.

'Go to the river or the sea, find somewhere comfortable and sit in silence. Focus on your breaths as they travel in and out of your body. Affirm your power and ask Yeseni to bring you the vision. Ask when you know and believe in your power.

'I must tell you, Elewa, you do not always have a lifetime to make the change. There are many visions I received that I did not act upon, and they caused devastating consequences.

So, I encourage you to act with urgency. You must do this.' She smiled and released me from her embrace.

'I know this is a great deal to take in and it will probably take you some time to understand it all. But if you look back, you will see, you have always had Yeseni, my dear.' She picked up a piece of linen that was hanging on the back of the wooden chair and began folding it. As if life just went back to normal, after being told that I had the power to see visions in both the future and the past.

'I would like to meet with you again when I understand better. I might need your help.' My voice quivered a little bit; I no longer felt full of the brash impatience I had walked in with, instead I felt nervous and docile as I made my way to the door.

'I am always here for you, granddaughter, just call around like you did today. Tiiandas and I had each other. I think Komi, your little brother, is also gifted with a kind of Yeseni, though his will be different to yours. He is too young yet to trouble him with naming it or trying to understand it.' My mind went to Komi and what we had always thought was a simple talent or a lucky streak. I could not tell him for now; he would not understand. Besides, he was not allowed to the water any more anyway. I thanked Mama Iyeniye and left. I had to sleep on this and decide what to do next.

I made my way back to the entrance chamber and Sessie was sitting on the same wooden chair with a cushion resting on her shoulder. Her cheek was pressed down on it: she had fallen asleep.

'Sessie . . .' I tapped her shoulder, 'we have to go now.'

Afua insisted that her servants drop us at the market so we had no choice but to accept and we went to buy Papa a birthday present.

On our way home, Sessie finally broke her silence.

'So, did you get all the answers you needed?'

'I am more confused now than I was when we arrived.'

'Elewa, I do not mean to speak out of turn but everyone in the village knows that Mama Iyeniye is slightly peculiar – do not waste your time trying to understand her mumbo jumbo. You are young and about to be married into a very favourable family.'

'Is Mama Iyeniye the only one in that "favourable family" that you disagree with then?'

'I am just saying, indulging her might just lead you down that same road. You are the Daughter of Peace. Play your role, do not get distracted.'

I was not going to tell Sessie what had happened, so what was the point in arguing with her?

'You are right, Sessie, what a waste of time today was. Never again.' Sessie seemed satisfied.

'I think there is some stewed fish at home left over from yesterday. I will fix you a plate when we get home then we should both get some rest; it has been a long day.'

11

In the days that followed my conversation with Mama Iyeniye, I started seeing strange and beautiful, almost hypnotic patterns of colour whenever I closed my eyes and thought about Yeseni. When I focused on them long enough, they sent me into a deep, tranquil sleep. I thought that they were probably Yeseni's energy intensifying throughout my body. It just made it all seem so real; my world was opening up and the confidence I had in my Yeseni began to grow. Then, one morning, I woke up and decided to try and access it alone for the very first time. Mama Iyeniye claimed that I had accessed Yeseni by myself when I, apparently, conjured up the spirit of Mama Tiiandas, yet that morning felt like it was the first time I intentionally did it alone. I decided not to go to the sea. After Captain Lewis's visit, Papa was increasingly concerned about the possibility of one of us being captured by the slavers. I did not want to tempt fate either; after hearing their conversation that day I finally saw that Papa was not overly fearful after all. I recalled the cruel sincerity in Captain Lewis's voice, and the sinister thudding of his footsteps. Just thinking about those men sent a shudder through my body, and we speculated on when they would attempt to visit us again to try and seal the agreement. Papa had been avoiding both Chief Babatunde and Uncle Kwame since that day.

My childish fascination with being captured and taken to foreign, exotic lands had long since evaporated and I had realised the wisdom of fear and caution. So that morning I decided that instead of going to the sea I would walk to the Wiri River. It was a quiet river to the south of our land that hardly anyone visited because it meant that you had to walk through dense Okena forest. Oleba were still quite hesitant about walking through the Okena land alone, even though we were working towards a peace treaty.

~

Even though I was travelling through the forest in a more peaceful time, I was still afraid. My heart rate accelerated and then sank to the base of my stomach. *There it is,* I thought, *the fear of the unknown, eating me from the inside out.* Now, I just decided to embrace the feeling and let it in. It was there anyway, rearranging all of my organs, and if I fought it, surely that would just make it worse. Moments after I made that decision the feeling had gone. Vanished, just like that. *Maybe there is something in this,* I thought.

There were many Okena working throughout the forest, carving wood, digging, sawing down trees or making tools. As our tribes were now working towards a peace treaty, we greeted each other, and I continued on my journey with only the occasional acknowledgement from the few who recognised me.

'Ahh, the Daughter of Peace; bless you, my dear sister!' some would say.

When I arrived at the river it was as serene as I had expected it to be. I sat down on the banks and closed my eyes. I could hear the gentle movement of the water travelling downstream. Above me I could hear the calling of the birds and the air seemed to lighten, lose weight, and so too did my mind, as light as a piece of lint carried away with the breeze. I thought about Mama Iyeniye and what she had advised me to do.

Go somewhere that you feel at peace, close your eyes and command your Yeseni.

And so I asked out loud, 'Yeseni, if you are truly mine, I ask you now to come to me.' I saw a wave of colour, a kaleidoscope, like the pattern I had come to recognise. But this time the shapes in the pattern were in motion; they started moving faster and faster and circling all around me, then a tingling cold sensation covered my body and my muscles seemed to contract, making me feel stuck in my position. The hairs on my arms stuck out and the texture of my skin changed from smooth to bumpy. Then suddenly the kaleidoscope that surrounded me was replaced by another vivid scene. It was the wealthy man, the man I had seen with Mama Tiiandas and the man I would come to learn was Oba Yemisola, or King Yemi.

∼

King Yemi sat in a grand foyer with his servant, Ola, but this time he was amongst people who looked very different from him. They appeared to be wealthy: the building's interior looked like it was made of solid marble, with gold embellishments here and there, and there were two large pillars to the entrance just below the stairs. King Yemi looked a lot more anxious than before.

A man with light brown skin and jet-black hair came from another room into the waiting area. 'His Majesty will see you now.'

King Yemi and Ola followed him into this other room, in

which there was another man. He was wearing a loose turban, so the front strands of his hair were not covered.

'Yemi,' he said as he raised both of his hands in King Yemi's direction, 'I am glad you made it here safely.' King Yemi smiled and thanked the other man, Bilal, for inviting him.

'Bring in the refreshments please, Omar!' he commanded his servant. An assortment of fruits, juices, meats and sweets were brought into the room and spread across the table.

They sat and shared Bilal's hospitality, as King Yemi showed him the gifts of gold he had brought.

The vision changed. King Yemi, Ola and Bilal disappeared and now all I could see was static black and then another vision abruptly came to me. It was Bilal in the same room, although this time King Yemi and Ola were not there. He was sitting with ten men around the table. He was plotting against King Yemi, telling them all about how the king had so much gold on him and of his vast gold reserves. He was mocking him for his stupidity. He told the men his plan to befriend King Yemi, gain his trust and then raid the land of its riches.

Another startling flash in front of my eyes and I saw a different land: it was the white man's land, I think, because there were many of them. This time Bilal was telling them more about King Yemi, 'the richest man in the world'. The men seemed impressed, and they all started planning their voyage to King Yemi's land.

Then just like before, the vision ended and there I was again at the Wiri River, panting for breath. I felt a small hand on my back.

'Are you feeling well?' It was a young girl.

'Yes, I am well, I just need to catch my breath . . .' I said in between gasps of air. 'Thank you.' She smiled and walked away.

I calmed myself down and made my way back home. I went over in my head what I understood the vision to be. King Yemi thought he had impressed Bilal, but he planned on betraying him and raiding his land. Not only that, but it appeared that King Yemi's ostentatious displays of wealth had brought undesirable attention to his people. Bilal was not the only one who wanted to acquire some of their wealth and now they were all plotting.

Perhaps it had been King Yemi's gold that had first attracted the attention of the white man; perhaps that was when they were first drawn to our lands. I spent days and nights trying to work out whether, if that was true, I was meant to use Yeseni to prevent that happening – if I should, or even if I could. I did not know how, nor where the right answers lay.

12

I desperately wanted to talk things through with Mama Iyeniye. I needed her advice on how to stop Bilal from taking advantage of King Yemi. Instead of showing up at the house, I decided to send a messenger to her.

His name was Ade; he was an orphan and once a slave. He later managed to buy his freedom and acquire a responsible and respectable job. The only problem I had was payment for his services; I had no gold of my own but fortunately Ade did a lot of work for Papa. I decided that I would ask him to bill us in a few weeks while I found a way to make up the fee.

Ade had no qualms with this; in fact, he said he would have done it for free – I just did not believe in that type of favour. Papa always warned me.

'Be careful, Elewa, who you accept goodwill from. You never want to be indebted to an evil spirit.'

The truth was that I did not know Ade very well as an adult. But one thing I did know about him was his ambition, and ambitious people will do anything to achieve their goals. You could see from his past and in his eyes that he wanted, needed to be, more than a messenger and I believed that he would do whatever it took to get there.

'What does a young, beautiful, noble princess want with a crazy, senile old witch?' he said as he chuckled.

'Do you want the job, or should I do it myself?' I looked at him impatiently.

'Of course I do! I am at your service, Elewa, Daughter of Peace!' He made a rolling gesture with his hands, stepped back and sort of bowed forward.

'You need be discreet, Ade,' I warned him quietly.

'I would not have gotten this far without discretion; between you and me, the things I know could start the next civil war.' I was interested in all the things that Ade must know. Being a messenger for the High Chief, his household and his comrades, I could only imagine what information he was exposed to. But I had no time for idle chat.

'I would love to stay and talk, Ade, but I just need you to do this for me.' I told him to get Mama Iyeniye to meet me at the Wiri River on the fifth day of the week. 'You will be compensated by the next full moon.' I walked away. Slightly worried, but desperate enough to take the chance.

'Fine, Daughter of Peace, at your service,' he shouted back at me. I lifted my arm up in the air and waved my hand back and forth, without looking back. If I let him carry on, we could be there all afternoon.

≈

True to Ade's word, there she was, Mama Iyeniye at the Wiri River on the fifth day of the week at sunrise. We sat by the river, and I told her all about my first experience in accessing my Yeseni. I told her what I saw, as well as my emerging plan to get a message to King Yemi, to warn him of Bilal's real intentions. I was uncertain whether Yeseni would allow this – whether I had only the gift of visions, or if I could communicate with people across time.

'That is excellent, Elewa, an auspicious start, but do you know who King Yemi is?'

I shook my head.

'He was the richest man in the world, one of the most powerful kings in the history of our land. Who do you think you will be if you appear before him?'

'I will be who I am now, Elewa, an honourable girl from a noble family.'

She smiled at me, like you smile at a child when they are trying to form their first sentence.

'No, you will be a girl from an unknown family and you will probably be jailed for insanity.' I stood corrected. 'You need to find out your reason for warning him and you will need to have solid proof before you go to him with this information.' I could not argue with her; she was right. I had gotten so excited that I had managed to get another vision and discover more about both King Yemi's and Bilal's motives that I had not thought through my strategy. Although the new information was interesting, it was not enough to go to King Yemi with. I would need to go back, dig deeper and find the missing pieces in this mystery ...

I remembered Mama Iyeniye telling me I needed to act urgently. I started to worry that I might not be able to achieve any of this quickly enough.

'You said if I did not act on a vision promptly something bad could happen? What if it takes too much time to find out everything I need to?'

'That is true: something bad could happen, something bad could have already happened or something bad could be happening now. You just need to find out what that "something bad" is before you go to warn King Yemi. He will not just accept a stranger's warning. The next question he will ask, if you even get that far, is: what exactly will happen? And then what will you tell him? That you do not know?'

She was right. I still did not know what was so bad that I had to travel through time to warn King Yemi against it.

It was not the worst thing in history if the richest man in the world was robbed of money, but I knew there was more to this story.

I asked Mama Iyeniye if she thought I had the power to travel through time or if my powers were restricted to visions alone.

'Your powers are what you allow them to be. Your primary power does appear to be visions, but that does not mean that you would not be able to travel and do other things, with practice and patience. I cannot confirm that once you travel, you will be able to come back though.' She bit her bottom lip. It seemed talking about travelling back through time made her slightly uneasy.

'So you mean I could be stuck, in time, in another world?'

'How do you think we got here? Mama Tiiandas and I, we are not from this time, Elewa. We could not return, no matter how hard we tried. We might have been able to make it if we had tried individually but we did not want to risk leaving each other alone, in another time. So eventually we decided that if we could not return together, we would not go apart. That is why we stayed here in the past.'

My eyes widened and my mouth was glued shut – was what she was telling me true? Mama Iyeniye and Mama Tiiandas were from the future?

'When Mama Tiiandas died, why did you not return then?'

'Once you have a family and once you have created a life, it is not that simple; we lived most of our lives here in the past.'

'So, what is it like? The future, I mean.' I probably should have asked a more caring question, like how it felt to be stuck in the past, or about the people she remembered from the future. She leant towards me and flickered her eyebrows playfully.

'Elewa, you may not need me to tell you that.' I looked back at her blankly.

'You may need to go to the future yourself to find out how you can help King Yemi to make the right decision. I have a contact in the future, a four times great grand-niece. I can arrange for her to meet with you to help you find the answers that you need.'

'And what if I am not able to come back? What about my family – what about Ojuro, your grandson? We are betrothed; we are the only hope for peace.'

'Elewa, this is not just about helping to keep a rich man rich. This could affect many, many lives. Visions from Yeseni only come when they really matter. Yeseni would not have given you the vision if you were not worthy of the task. Ultimately, it is your own decision, but if you do decide to go, you will be risking your life, as you know it now.

'You must work out if this gift, this Yeseni, is yours or if it is just something that you have. The holder of Yeseni has a responsibility to the world, to honour its possession.

'Maybe it is something that you have, in which case you can go about your life and forget about this whole thing. But if this is something that you wish to own, you will need to honour it.

'You will have to find the answer to that question for your-self, but remember, you may be able to come back. I never tried without my sister so you may be more fortunate than we were.'

'Mama Iyeniye, this is not for me,' I panicked. I could feel my heart racing. 'I could never leave my parents, or my brother and sister, for a stranger that I barely know.' She gave me that same look that she did in her quarters, that day when I told her about my first vision: a placid and unconcerned look. What did she know that I did not? It seemed like she had been here before, seen this scene before somehow.

'You do not have to decide this moment, child. When you decide what you want to do, come and find me, but do not use Ade again. Come around the east of the estate. That will lead you to the side of my quarters. There is a gate there and I leave it open; just knock on my window.' I nodded and politely smiled.

'Do not worry. Whatever decision you make will be the right one – there are plenty of people with Yeseni that do not use it and they have their reasons. Look deep inside yourself and then we will talk again, my child.' She walked away through the dense forest, and I just sat there, gazing into the river, watching the rippling of the water.

13

Perhaps the most unsavoury outcome of war was, and always had been, opportunity. Unpleasant as it may be, the war had allowed the victorious spoils in the form of free labour from prisoners of war. It created despair, sorrow, loneliness and misery, not just in a few, but in thousands of human hearts. Imagine a world where everyone you know lives with some form of grief; that was our world for many years after the war. Countless lives were tragically lost: Okena lives, Oleba lives, all of them human lives.

One of the main ways in which a civilian could become a slave in our time was through the war with the Okena. For those who were captured rather than killed, an inevitable fate awaited: that of becoming a slave. It did not matter what their rank was, or who they were, or where they came from: if they were prisoners of war, they were taken into slavery. Many Okena had been taken this way, captured in battles long ago. Some escaped and returned to the Okena, others became like members of our extended Oleba families. Since the fighting had ended, there had been no more prisoners of war, for which I was glad.

Though I knew it was still used as a punishment for stealing, debt or violent acts, I agreed with Papa that it was a cruel fate to be a slave. Though our use of the word 'slave' was probably closer to the word 'servant', it was nothing like the slavery I would come to witness, and I still hoped the peace treaty would end the practice once and for all. Though it occurred to me that in some ways, our beloved Sessie would be categorized as a slave by any Oleba or Okena chief, even though we all knew better.

~

Whenever Mama told me about the day that she had found Sessie, her eyes would go all soft and weary. She and a group of friends had formed a group, helping to clean up after battle. One particular day she recalled an exceptionally disturbing scene, many more dead bodies and horrific wounds than usual.

'It felt like the field was painted in red,' she would say, 'empty bodies whose souls had abandoned them. Such a cruel thing, Elewa.' The spark in her eyes would fade, and when I stared into them, I could almost see the scene. The bloody bodies that lay on top of each other, the limbs dissevered and scattered. The multiple holes in heads, hearts, chests and groins. This harrowing scene would torment my poor mother for the rest of her life.

The bodies had to be cleared and most of the men that had survived were injured or exhausted, so it was left up to the women to remove the dead and sort out all useful items found on the corpses. These items would be divided out between the tribes and given to the chiefs to distribute, unless an official claim had been made on an item, like a family heirloom. The work took the best part of four weeks and once the men had recovered, they started digging the communal grave where the unclaimed bodies would be buried. Family members would be desperately searching the field in the hope of finding their loved ones to avoid them being buried in the communal grave.

If they found them, they would take them home and bury them on their own land, which was the proper thing to do.

It had been the second day of the clear-up and Mama said she heard what sounded like a cat next to a soldier who looked like he came from the Nuri tribe. When she lifted his arm there was the smallest, sweetest baby lying in the arms of a woman underneath him. The woman's fingers were still tightly gripping the baby.

'I never saw a corpse hold a grip on anything so tight before.' She had to prise each finger away until she could release the baby. Mama took the baby home and asked the other workers to bring the soldier and woman to our land where she planned on burying them.

'I had to assume they were the child's mother and father, but the truth is, they could have been anyone; all I knew is that they were all this child had left in the world.'

After settling the baby down for the night, Mama went to search the bodies for some clue of the child's name or identity, but she could find nothing. The father had a musket ball wound right through his heart and the mother had one just above her left ear.

Mama alone cleaned the two bodies and gathered all their belongings to set aside in a safe place for the child. She intended on raising the child as her own, but when she and Papa approached Chief Babatunde about it, he refused and said they had to stick to the laws of the kingdom. Any man, woman or child captured from the opposing side was to be taken into the capturer's family as a slave. And so, officially, Sessie became our slave, but to us, she was my older sister. Mama and Papa loved her like a daughter, and she had known no other family.

Sessie was a healthy baby for the most part. Mama said that she could be fussy if she did not get her meals on time, but this was the same for all babies. As Sessie grew she enjoyed learning and making friends. When she joined the village women to learn making clay pots, they said she had natural talent.

'Mama Olanrewaju, where did you get this daughter from? It is like she was born with a palm full of clay,' they would say, flattering Sessie. I mean, how good can a child really be at pot-making? I wondered if they knew and took pity on Sessie, overcompensating her with undeserved compliments.

One day Sessie came home from playing with the village children, very distressed and shocked.

'Why do I have to call you Aunty and Uncle? Why do not I call you Mama and Papa?' she sobbed. Mama asked what had brought this on. Some of the children had found out about her past, presumably through their parents. They confronted Sessie and it caused a massive argument. Obviously at this time Sessie knew nothing of her past.

'My friends said I am your slave and I have no parents. What is a slave?'

Mama explained how she found Sessie as a baby on the battlefield.

'Do you know who my parents are?' she asked anxiously.

'The woman I found holding you looked like she came from the Nuri tribe and there was also a man that laid intertwined with her, and his arm lay on top of you.'

'So, were they my parents?'

'Possibly; they definitely cared deeply about you. They protected you,' Mama replied. She went on, though perhaps she should have stopped there. 'I am not sure what would drive a mother to bring a baby to a battlefield; she must have been desperate.' Mama's hand motioned upwards towards her mouth, intending to physically stop the doubtful words pouring out. It was too late: a remorseful expression on her face appeared, her hand still in place.

'So, you are not sure if they were my parents?'

'They were the only people you had in the world at the time, and you looked like the woman,' she replied. She quickly removed her hand from her mouth and placed it on Sessie's shoulder. 'Papa and I are your parents.'

'I am your slave,' she said as she shrugged Mama's hand off her shoulder.

The rebellion had commenced.

I suppose all Mama could do from that point on was to ride the wave of discontent. She told herself that every parent goes through it at one point or other.

'We pretend you are a slave, so that we can keep you; you know we love you very much.'

'So are you saying my real mother and father could still be alive, still out there now? Why did you not try to find them?' Sessie grew frustrated.

'We thought you would be safer with us. The family that you were with put you in the dangerous situation that I found you in. And to be honest, it is very likely that the man and woman I found you with were your parents.'

Mama told me that Sessie was not happy with her response; she felt they could have tried harder to find out if she had any living family.

After that day Sessie distanced herself and would often sit out in the back yard, sometimes for hours on end. She would sit next to the grave of the man and woman that she was found with. They were the only people that connected her to what she felt was her true identity. Sessie started to resent the family and tribe that she was once so proud of. It was like she had lost something deep inside of her and she was desperate for answers.

As time passed, Mama gave Sessie all the possessions that she had found on the man and woman. A bronze brooch in the shape of a battle-axe, which was pinned to the man's cloak, and a silver pocket watch found in his carrying pouch. The watch was not native to our land, so Mama presumed that their tribe had successfully established wide trading relationships. The items found on the woman included a foreign gold coin and wooden pendant in the shape of a hand with an open palm. Sessie treasured these items and always kept them close.

When she had once spent her spare time playing with her friends, instead she now spent most of her time asking the elders all about the Nuri tribe.

Even though she tried her utmost to push Mama and Papa away they would always ask, 'Daughter, please share what you have learned. It is important for us too.'

Reluctantly Sessie would share with them all that she had learned about who she thought were her people.

From Sessie's research Mama found out that the Nuri were one of the aboriginal tribes in the west of the land and one of the largest ethnic groups, hundreds of years older than the Oleba. Their empire prospered before the Oleba arrived; they were already trading with Arabs and other inland tribes.

They made their own distinctive clothes and had their own drumming language, which meant that they could communicate with tribal members from many miles away. Their tribal proverb was 'When you kill a thousand, a thousand will come.'

After a few months of rebelling against our parents, one day Mama came home to find Sessie on the living-room floor in tears. Sessie explained that she felt she had been ungrateful and self-centred; she profusely apologised, her head and hands on the floor, crouching in her puddle of remorse.

'My daughter,' Mama commanded, 'never apologise for having feelings. We love you no matter what.' Sessie explained that she was confused, hurt, and felt alone. They sat and talked for hours that day.

Mama told Sessie of her fight to adopt her as a daughter and the chief's firm refusal; she told her about all the characteristics she had as a child and they laughed at the tales of her juvenile antics until their sides hurt. Mama said that since that day she and Sessie became closer than ever. The truth is, Sessie would always be closer with Mama than Fumi, Komi or I would ever be, and as I grew older, I understood their bond and respected it.

When I was younger, I thought Sessie was my blood, and I never quite understood the weird pretence in public. We all saw Sessie as no different to us, except the game we played in public, that game became second nature to our family, and we were not the only family who were playing the game to uphold Oleba laws.

Besides, my parents had always planned on granting Sessie her freedom, but they wanted to do it once the war was over and once Sessie had a valuable trade and a potential partner, so that she would not be alone.

By the age of eighteen, Sessie's curiosity about her own origins had widened into a fascination for learning about many other different tribes and cultures.

I heard Mama talking to Papa about the possibility of giving Sessie a job on the tribal council as a junior emissary. There were many misunderstandings between tribes in our land that required tribal representatives to meet and negotiate agreements upon, and Mama thought Sessie would be an asset in such a role. Papa agreed and said that he would speak to Chief Babatunde about it when the time was right.

Sessie never travelled anywhere without the brooch, pendant and coin. The empty lost girl had faded, and a happy confident one had reappeared. Sessie had many roles to play in her lifetime. She was Sessie the slave, Sessie the daughter, Sessie the sister, Sessie the orphan and now, quite possibly, Sessie the tribal emissary.

~

The little garden I planted, when Uncle Kwame was staying with us as part of his recovery, was doing so well. All those little weak-looking saplings had turned into fully formed gorgeous flowers. I could not believe they had survived all the volatile weather over the last few months.

'See, I told you that plants were more resilient than you expected.' Mama could never resist an 'I told you so' moment.

'You said they had been here before us and they will be here long after we have gone,' I replied. She had been right on that first day of torrential rain when I was sure they would be ruined.

'That is right, Elewa!' She smiled one of her wide, warm and encouraging smiles.

'What is going on with Papa, Babatunde and Uncle Kwame?' Uncle Kwame had moved back to his house a few days before Mama and Papa first told me about the betrothal. He had made a full recovery and could not wait to get home.

'I know you heard what those captains said when they came to the house; it was a lot to take in,' Mama replied. I noticed that they were not hiding things from me as much as they used to. I had noticed the change in them since the announcement of the betrothal.

'Why does Papa not just talk to them about it? Find out if there is any truth in it? He might be able to avoid Uncle Kwame, but he works with the chief every day – how can he negotiate a peace treaty while holding a grudge with his closest friend?'

'Everything in good time, Elewa; he will speak to them soon enough.'

'So, do you think Uncle Kwame did it then?' I could not help but ask Mama this. Uncle Kwame was her brother and Captain Lewis had accused him of treason.

'The only way your uncle would do a deal with the white men of the sea is if they threatened to harm us; there would be no other reason.'

'But it still does not make it right, does it? If they threatened him, why did not he come to us? We could have helped him!' Papa argued, coming into the yard from out of nowhere.

'That is something you will have to ask Kwame yourself,' Mama said. I could now see how desperate she was to get this resolved.

'Not yet, I still need to think.'

'Papa, how are you managing to work with Chief Babatunde on a daily basis without bringing up what those captains accused him of?' *If it were me,* I thought, *I would have met with Chief Babatunde the same day to ask him if what those men had said about him was true or not. I would have needed to know.*

'Elewa, if they are right, I cannot change what he did, and if they are wrong there is nothing to talk about. If I bring it up and he did do it, that could cause a huge problem between us, and it could potentially prevent me becoming Chief. That would affect your betrothal, which would affect the peace treaty, and then that would mean both tribes were back to square one and at risk of another war.'

'I did not think of it that way.'

'That is why I am the designated thinker for the family.' Papa chuckled and Mama flashed him a cautionary look.

I stood staring at my beautiful garden, hoping I could make sense of everything and use my Yeseni wisely to fulfil my destiny.

14

I needed the guidance of Mama Iyeniye, and so I began to meet her more frequently. She encouraged me to think about the future that she felt I must visit if I was to understand what my Yeseni had shown me. I expected her to enquire about my decision to go there, but she never did. She simply told me stories of her own time there in that future, applying a subtle, intelligent pressure on me.

'Is it not enough that I have Yeseni – why do I need to learn about all these elements of the future; can I not simply use my Yeseni to get by?' I looked at her, bemused.

'No, Elewa – if you get stuck there, all the "stories" I am telling you now will help you settle in and make a life for yourself. Your Yeseni has to remain a secret,' she warned me.

~

During one of our meetings, Mama Iyeniye pulled out a huge picture; the background was blue and there were seven odd squiggly shapes scattered all over the page.

'A picture of this world, is it not beautiful?' The strange shapes were landmasses, but I did not understand why there were so many different ones. Up until that moment, I thought that all humans lived on one joined-together piece of land surrounded by sea.

I started to wonder which bit of land we were on, and she pointed to one as if reading my mind. This was not the first time she had responded in such an intuitive way. What exactly were her powers – could she read minds as well? 'You ask a lot of questions,' she said. *Yes*, I thought, *she definitely could read minds.*

'Only when I have a connection to the person. I am not trying to read your mind, Elewa, but your thoughts are ...' she searched for the right word to use, '... speaking to me. You are opening up your thoughts to me. If you had a thought that you did not want me to hear, you could close communication with me. But a lot of people go around opening their every thought to the world, and it can be tiring for people like me. Tiring and very loud.' She rolled her eyes.

'So how would I do that, how would I close my thoughts to you?'

'Well, to begin with, do not ask questions that require *me* to answer them. The mind cannot differentiate between a rhetorical and a rudimentary question unless you train it to.' I was in awe of this woman.

Mama Iyeniye proceeded to point at one of the squiggly shapes on her map. This odd, top-heavy landmass was, supposedly, our land, the land we called home. Every large place had a name and Mama Iyeniye said ours was called Alkebulan, which, apparently, meant *Mother of Mankind*. Mother of Mankind – what a regal name, and if ours had such a name, I wondered what the others were called and what their names meant.

We were stood at her large old wooden table in her cluttered quarters, with the massive map laid neatly on the table. Mama Iyeniye had placed both her palms down against it, and her body, was diagonally positioned leaning over it.

Her voice had become the background to my daydreaming until I heard her mention a word I had never heard before: 'Africa,' she said. Some men from other lands were starting to refer to Alkebulan with another name. 'Africa' was easier for them to pronounce, and, as she was from the future, she knew it would soon catch on. She showed me where England was on the map. *How small*, I thought. *Surely it could fit into our kingdom at least a dozen times.*

'You may go there, Elewa – to England, I mean – if you decide to travel like we discussed at the Wiri River.' This was the first time that she had brought up that day at the river.

'Are there only white people in England?' The only white people I had met were Captain Lewis and Captain Williams, the slavers who had visited Papa.

'No, child,' Mama Iyeniye laughed. 'In the future, people from all over the world call England home. But people who look like you and me are the minority.'

'What do you mean, minority?'

'Like the white man in Alkebulan. He is the minority here, meaning there are few that look like him and more that look like us.' She lifted her hands from the table and turned to face me.

'So do they live in peace even though they are the minority?'

'A kind of strange peace, yes, some of the time.'

'Kind of strange peace? What do you mean, Mama Iyeniye? When is peace ever strange?' Peace was kind, but surely it was just peaceful and not strange at all. Now I was getting caught up in the web of words. I decided to let her try to explain.

'Do you see the slaves that are captured and held in the forts on the coast?'

'I did not know that slaves were held there – I always wondered what those forts were for,' I replied. What did they have to do with why the future was not entirely peaceful?

'I understand, but you must have seen the captives all chained up and boarding that enormous ship on the coast.'

'The criminals?' She chuckled in disbelief, tightly squinted her eyes whilst shaking her head at me. 'That is what we tell ourselves so that we do not have to deal with what is happening right in front of our eyes. Most of the people that look like you and me that live in England two hundred years from now are the descendants of those slaves being captured in the forts now.'

'So, they bought their freedom?' I smiled.

'No, child, it is complicated. It is happening now as I speak to you. If you choose to visit, it would have been abolished for around two hundred years by the time you arrive. So that is why the peace is kind of strange, because there is still tension and inequality in that world because of what is happening now with the captured slaves at the forts by the sea.'

'But surely I can visit whenever I like, can I not? I mean I can visit a week from now, a month from now, or one hundred years from now?'

'I am only in touch with one person from the future in that specific time, two hundred years after the abolition of the transatlantic slave trade. If you go when I suggest, I can ensure you have somewhere to stay, someone who understands your Yeseni and someone who can help you pick through your visions.'

I nodded, still taking it all in. I could travel any time that I wanted to, but she could only really help me in the timeframe that she suggested.

'Once you travel and meet my four-times great grandniece,

she will try to help you to return home, but as I mentioned before, sometimes it does not work, for whatever reason.'

'I might not be able to return, I know.'

'I cannot guarantee that, no . . . but you are thinking it over, are you not?' She gave me that look again, as if me *thinking this over* was just a pointless ritual, as if both of us already knew what my answer would be.

'Yes, I am waiting for the answer to come to me.' I do not know what she thought she knew, but I still had no clue what my decision was going to be. The only thing that would help me decide was to find out what catastrophic event I would be stopping.

Mama Iyeniye brought my attention back to the map and explained that all the other landmasses existed beyond the sea, so far, she said that they could not be seen by the naked eye.

Our land was gigantic, and our kingdom was minuscule within it. What were the other kingdoms like? The kingdom that I had once believed to be the entire world was just a speck on this map. The rest of Alkebulan had at least six additional empires, Mama Iyeniye told me, consisting of thousands of subjects each practising diverse beliefs with varied governing and tribal structures. Merely learning and understanding more about Alkebulan had an immense effect on me. While my perspective broadened, I started shrinking fast. It withered away at me, diminishing the view I had of my family, our tribe and myself. Now that I could see on this map how tiny our land was when compared to the rest of Alkebulan, I realised how small and insignificant we, the Oleba and Okena, really were.

Mama Iyeniye explained to me that hundreds of millions of years ago, there was only one landmass, which eventually broke apart and separated into seven segments; these were consequently called the continents. She told me that humans on all the other continents, no matter what they looked like, originated from Alkebulan: Africa. A handful of families from the west of our continent left their homes thousands of years ago and populated the rest of the world.

It all felt quite absurd and fantastical, but Mama Iyeniye had never lied to me before. If she had told me about my gift before I had physically experienced it myself, I would have disregarded her without a second thought, but I could not regard someone as a liar when all their outlandish claims, so far, had proven true.

I had to accept that Mama Iyeniye and I lived in the same bizarre world now and I would try my utmost to embrace her teachings. Although her claims were, at times, far-fetched, they had to have some truth. I mean, where did these strange white men sail in from? Was it England, or another one of those squiggly-shaped islands of land in the ocean?

15

I decided to visit Omolara. I had not seen her in what felt like forever, and I wanted her advice.

As soon as I walked through the door of her market, I felt tension in the air. People were whispering to each other, and it seemed as if they were muttering unpleasantries about me under their breath. A few people flashed me nervous smiles, but it all just felt awkward. I used to feel so at home there but now it felt hostile.

'Eleeeewa!' Omolara seemed to appear out of nowhere. 'Or should I call you the Daughter of Peace now? Welcome back! Where have you been?'

'Hi, Omolara, sorry I have not been to visit; I have been busy with all *this* going on.'

'Naturally, my dear. Everything is well though, I hope?' She ushered me by the small of my back to a quieter corner of the store.

'Well, I was wondering if I could talk to you for a few minutes; there is a conundrum that I need help with.' She had a heavy pile of fabric in her hands; she seemed to be in the middle of something. Maybe I would have to come back.

'Oh, sounds intriguing – can you give me a moment though? I just need to help a customer with an order. I will meet you in the back room. I do not think there is anyone down there.' Getting Omolara's view would really help to give me the clarity I needed; the only thing was, I could not tell her everything.

'Of course,' I replied. 'I might get some fresh air first and then I will meet you down there. Thank you, Omolara!' I stepped out of the door and heard an older woman, probably about Mama's age, standing outside the market talking with her friend.

'Daughter of Peace! Pft!' she scoffed. 'What makes her so special? I cannot believe they think a little Idanbule farm girl and a crazy wayward Okena boy could inspire peace between us!' Her friend laughed in agreement. I stepped back inside the door before she saw that I had heard.

'I thought you wanted some fresh air?' Omolara yelled from across the store.

'Changed my mind, I will just wait downstairs instead.' I made my way down the broad rustic staircase and there were people there. A few older men were deep in conversation. Curious, I sat on the step and listened.

'Well, I will believe it when I see it; there have been promises of peace treaties for years, and they never pull it off. Whenever it fails, it only makes tensions worse.' The peace treaty was on everyone's minds.

'Oh, why are you so negative? You never know, now they have the Daughter of Peace girl, it might just work. An Oleba and Okena marriage, come on! There could not be a better way to start a peace treaty. I think they will do it this time.' Hearing the people who believed in the treaty was almost harder than the non-believers. Letting a believer down somehow seemed more heart-breaking.

Then I heard Omolara behind me. I stood up.

'Oh, Elewa, people will talk – you cannot let them upset

you!' She marched past me down the stairs, and I followed behind her.

'Come on, out with you! We need some private woman time.' The men left, one tilting his hat towards me.

'So, is it just all the talk that is bothering you or is it something else?' We sat down on the wooden benches.

'No, it is more than that. I have barely been out socially since I found out about the betrothal, so this is the first time I have heard people talking about it.' What I meant is that I had not been out amongst Oleba, to hear their unfiltered opinions.

'Well, you know this is one of the only places in the village that Oleba feel free to express themselves.' It was probably the best place to find out what the Oleba really thought about, well, any political decision.

'It is not that. I am just scared. I do not want to let them down, the ones that do believe in this.'

'People are scared too, Elewa, but they will come around after the wedding.' I thought back to the ladies outside the store, how one called me an Idanbule farm girl. My grandparents were farmers, but so were most other Oleba.

'Well maybe they are right to be scared. Maybe there will not be a wedding after all.'

'What are you saying?'

I buried my head in the palms of my hands. 'If you had a choice to bring about peace between us and the Okena or, say, save our future generations from a true evil, what would you choose?'

'Well, what are you talking about?' This abstract, far-fetched situation was not working with Omolara. I would have to try something else.

'Very well, forget that. But imagine, if you had the choice of saving your daughter or your future great-great-granddaughter, who would you choose?' Omolara had no children, but we were speculating and maybe this concept was a bit easier to grasp.

'Probably my daughter. Because would not saving my daughter naturally save my great-great-granddaughter?'

'Not necessarily!'

'Well, I would still save my daughter!' That was what I needed to find out from her. The present, the here and now, was more important than the future.

'Hmmm, I know what you mean.'

'Do you? I am glad somebody knows what someone means because I have no clue what you mean!'

I wished that I could tell Omolara exactly what was going on, but I did not really understand it fully myself yet, and I did not want her thinking of me the way people thought of Mama Iyeniye.

'All is well, thank you, Omolara; you have really helped me.'

'Elewa, are you sure you are well?' she asked as I walked up the stairs.

'Yes, I am fine. I will see you soon! Thank you!'

I left Omolara looking more confused than I had ever seen her.

Omolara thought I should stay, but Mama Iyeniye thought I should go. If Mama and Papa knew, they would definitely want me to stay.

Staying seemed like both the right and most popular thing to do, but just because it was the most popular choice it did not mean that it was the most morally justified choice. I felt like I was being pulled in multiple directions while looking outward for an answer, but perhaps that was the problem – maybe the answer was inside of me. I needed to meet Ojuro before I could decide.

～

Ojuro was tall in stature with high cheekbones and a resting face that expressed distraction, anxiety, or perhaps it was ambition. He was subtly attractive, with kind light brown eyes and heart-shaped lips; his top lip appeared significantly smaller than the bottom one until he was completely relaxed. Then they would imitate a perfect heart shape.

Before he and I were betrothed, I knew little about him, only that he had two older sisters, two younger brothers, he was of the Okena tribe and that some people called him Jo for short.

During our betrothal I learned a great deal more about him, like his complicated feelings about having been unable to fight in the war. I knew he had a reputation as a fighter, but I would come to learn that he had cultivated this in the years that followed the war.

Wrestling was clearly not the Okena way, but the people around Jo, during that time, said he acted like he had a point to prove. They said he made it clear that he felt unworthy of the peace that he had come to enjoy, since he had not taken part in the war. They believed that he felt deeply bitter about this. Whether they truly believed this, or just considered it to be a pretence concocted by Ojuro to gain respect, was unclear.

His peers clearly viewed him as a troubled soul. They told me that Jo knew countless young men his age, fighting in the war, and that many of them had tragically died in battle. No matter how hard he begged his parents, they would not allow him to fight. Both his brothers fought, and even his sister Iyún took part in battle strategy, yet he was not allowed. All because the Okena viewed the first-born male child to be the most precious gift in the world, they treated him like the petals of a delicate rare flower, and this caused a terrible rift between Jo and his parents, and eventually his siblings too. Ultimately, this disagreement would create a distance so vast between them that they would forever struggle to find their way back to each other.

He began to deeply resent his parents for treating him that way, and I could imagine how frustrated he must have felt. I started to understand why he might have been seeking other ways to demonstrate his worth to the world and to himself.

Once the truce was called, Omolara told me that it was then that he first befriended some men from our tribe, old war veterans. Apparently, he convinced them to teach him their wrestling skills.

One day, I decided to venture down to the waterfront where Jo used to consort with the old warriors from our tribe. The closer it got to our wedding, the more eager I was to discover more about the man I was to marry. If I did decide to go to the future, I wondered if I could take Jo with me. I thought about whether I should even tell him of my Yeseni; I wondered if he already knew about it through his grandmother, Mama Iyeniye. I had so many questions and I was lucky to find an old man that knew Jo very well.

Oquie was one of the local fishermen that always asked me for Komi's whereabouts whenever he saw me. 'Your brother really has a special gift, you know,' he smiled as he brought the boat to shore. I asked him to tell me about Ojuro because most Idanbule fishermen were old war veterans, so he was bound to know something about him. 'Well, I can tell you more about him if you can channel some of your brother's luck my way today?' I needed to steer the conversation away from Komi and towards Jo, so I just asked him directly what Jo was like when he was younger.

'Skinny and stubborn,' he said, as if he was retaliating against my ignoring his request for Komi's help rather than answering my question. 'You are marrying a very determined man, Elewa.' He continued, but in a more reassuring tone, telling me how Jo would hang around with him and his friends from sunrise to sunset to perfect his fighting skills. So much time, he said, that Jo had started to understand our tribal tongue and mannerisms.

'Some of the men grew uneasy with his constant presence, which would have been expected, since not long before this we were slaughtering his kin on the very land that we were teaching him to wrestle on. They thought he was a spy, sent by the Okena; some would just tease him, calling him an Oleba in disguise.' Oquie told me that the group of suspicious men decided to feed him some fake information about an upcoming revolt and a plan to attack Chief Chukwuemeka-Okena, Jo's father. He said that when he saw Jo growing close to them, he knew that something was not right, so he confronted the men, asking them what they were planning on doing to Jo. The men told him to mind his own business and threatened the lives of his family if he ever warned Jo, so he decided to stay out of it.

'I had seen those men rip the skin off of corpses on the battlefield; I could not risk getting involved.' The men waited weeks in anticipation for the Okena chief to call them in for interrogation, but nothing ever happened.

Jo was tempted to tell someone in his family, but he feared the men would be hung on the spot without trial. So instead, he tried to persuade his new friends to rethink their plan. He told them what the punishment would be for such

125

a revolt and spent days researching peaceful ways to get their points across. The truth, of course, was that the men were looking for an infiltrator and had no interest in breaking the peace. Many months passed, and the men were not contacted by the royal household or brought in for questioning. It was then that they finally knew that Ojuro was an honest man.

'After that, all the old veterans trusted his intentions. It was more than just wrestling though, what he wanted.'

'What do you mean?'

'It was like he was coming up for air when he was with us and the rest of his life existed underwater.' He had a puzzled look on his face, as if he did not understand Jo's plight and was only now working it out. 'Yes, there was definitely more to that boy than what he showed us. Even though he spent almost every waking moment with us for three consecutive years, he must have held some things back – for himself, or maybe for someone else?'

Oquie went on to tell me that Jo's mother Afua started to worry that he was losing his Okena identity and tried to persuade him to spend less time with them, to no avail of course.

'Her efforts just brought him closer to us and made him resent his family more.'

Once she started to leave him alone, Oquie noticed that Jo started to spend less time with them; he would still come around or spar with them once in a while. But he started to look for other skills to learn.

'After all,' he sighed, 'he finally had all the freedom he desired. Besides, a young man has no place hanging around old men all day anyway.' He laughed, but all of a sudden I felt sad because I could only learn about him through secondhand sources.

'Why the long face?' Oquie probed. Although I was glad that he was able to tell me about Jo, I was suddenly gripped by the wish to spend some time with him myself, alone, before the betrothal ceremonies.

'I just want to spend some time with Jo alone. Find out about him for myself.'

'Do you like to fish?' What a strange question to ask a girl at her wits' end.

'No, not really, why?'

'Jo still likes to fish with us old timers sometimes. If he does come with us, it is usually on a Tuesday morning, so he should be here tomorrow. Before sunrise.' An opportunity to meet with Ojuro, without all those prying eyes. Oquie would be there, but he seemed to feel real affection and respect for Jo so that was better than nothing at all.

If we were caught, to have another person with us would be beneficial anyway. He would be our chaperone, to attest that nothing improper occurred.

'I would like to learn to fish. Thanks so much, Oquie, I appreciate this!'

I walked away from that conversation so pleased with myself. I would finally meet Jo in one of my favourite places, by the sea, and I could not wait.

All the way home I kept thinking about Jo, the paper-thin boy, only now he had so many dimensions in my mind. Like a drawing come to life. I thought about my meeting with Mama Iyeniye at the Wiri River, and I wondered if Jo possessed Yeseni, or if he knew anything of his grandmother's past and her gift. What I had learned about Jo taught me that people are neither good nor bad; they are everything. Good, bad, sweet and bitter and everything you can possibly comprehend in-between. Jo was all these things and it made him more compelling; he was complicated and troubled but still kind and caring. As the hours went by, I became more and more excited to marry such a man. I told myself that it would make life more interesting, peeling back all those the layers to reveal his true character.

What an exciting journey this will be.

~

The next day I arrived at the sea before sunrise and as I walked towards the port, I saw Oquie and Jo waiting for me at the end of the pier.

'What time do you call this?' Oquie joked. We started slowly walking towards his boat.

'Good morning, Oquie, Ojuro . . .'

'Hello, Elewa.' Jo looked up into my eyes in a coy, some-what timid way. He seemed so gentle and charming. It was hard to imagine him as a dejected and troubled person, he looked so happy and radiant.

'Thank you for coming. I just wanted to meet you before everything . . .' I paused to think of the appropriate word. '. . . starts.' As soon as I said that he looked slightly over-whelmed. Maybe his way of dealing with it was not to think about it at all.

'So Oquie said you want to learn to fish?' He quickly changed the subject.

'Just an excuse to meet you really; my little brother is the true fisherman in our family.'

'That is right; do not forget to ask him to come and see me – that boy has a true gift!' Oquie added.

'Yes, I have heard about him: the famous Komi, right?'

'That is him, but these days, because of the raids and the

white men from the sea, he is not allowed to come to the sea anymore. Neither am I really.'

'You are safe with us. One of those slavers tried to capture me once but I fought them off. I have seen them since, but they never come near me now.'

'Lucky you! Papa is so anxious about that happening to us, he would kill me if he knew I was here.' We were now at Oquie's boat. It was docked on the pier and it looked so small that I wondered how all three of us would fit in it and how Jo and I could have any kind of comfortable conversation floating around in that thing.

'Actually, Oquie,' I asked, 'do you mind if we just sit on the pier for a few minutes? I think I might give fishing a miss for today.'

'Very well. I will leave you two to talk; I will be your lookout.' And with that Oquie walked away down the pier.

'So how do you feel about the marriage?' I asked, wasting no time. I just wanted to know the truth from him.

'I do not know; I try not to think about it. I know we need peace between our tribes of course, but I do not want to be forced into a marriage.' He looked uncomfortable again.

I felt he was holding back, not telling me everything. 'It is the only way we can have peace in our land though,' I ventured.

'Yes, so they say. It feels like we are being used for a show of unity over which we have no control.' He was right about that, but if they wanted a show of unity for the sake of peace, why not give them one?

'Well could it really be that bad, marrying me?'

His face lightened again. 'Elewa, you are beautiful, one of the most beautiful girls in the village, and I have heard nothing but good things about you, but . . .'

'But what?'

'I have a light soul and . . . so do you.' He sounded so pro-found and philosophical I could not help but smile. In that moment the sun crept above the horizon, and I truly felt that Ojuro was the one for me.

'Then we are perfect for each other!' I proclaimed and he smiled back at me.

'Hey, lovebirds, the sun has risen,' called Oquie.

I stood up and regarded my future husband. 'It was nice to actually meet you, Jo. I will see you at the first ceremony.' There were still so many things I wanted to ask him that I had forgotten to ask, like if he knew about his grandma's gift and what his hopes and dreams were.

'It was nice to meet you too, Elewa; see you soon!'

'Wait, before you go, I need to ask you something . . .' I could not let him walk away without finding out this one thing about him.

'Well, what is it?' We were both walking backwards in opposite directions.

'What is your dream?'

'My dream?' He looked at me as if I was not all there.

'Yes, if one dream could come true for you in this world what would it be?'

He looked down, paused for a moment and said: 'To be free, to be completely free.' Then he turned around and walked back up the pier with Oquie.

What people had told me about Jo did not capture the true essence of his energy. He was kind, timid, romantic and trou-bled. I felt lucky to have been promised to such a deep and thoughtful young man.

~

Our parents finally arranged the dates of the meeting ceremonies when we would officially have the chance to get to know each other in person. Altogether there would be around twelve ceremonies, the first and last consisted of a party to celebrate the joining. If all the others went well, both families would agree a date for the wedding.

Mama had already commissioned outfits for all twelve ceremonies. I do not remember ever frequenting the seamstress as often as we did in the following months.

Papa would wear a deep green robe with gold trimmings for the first ceremony and Mama a bright yellow hand-woven cloth. The patterns on our outfits had innate meanings, unless of course we wore a more delicate fabric with no pattern, in which case the meaning would be revealed in the colour. Particular colours were reserved for certain events.

There were hundreds of prints to choose from and they would be repeated uniformly all over a garment. A popular print that symbolised loyalty was made up of five circles, four of which formed a square, the fifth overlapping the others in the centre. Another popular print was an opaque black box, with four white leaves shooting from each corner. This one meant good fortune and was often the print of choice for wedding guests.

It was important to know what the patterns stood for and to choose them wisely. This is because you would be judged by your choice of outfit. Mama was well-versed in this area, so we did not need to worry too much. If any of us picked something that was unsuitable, she would not hesitate to put us right.

I would wear a deep pink robe with purple heart-shaped embroidery. The pattern symbolised patience and that outfit would be for the first ceremony. It was the most beautiful dress I had ever seen, and it was fashioned in the Okena style as a mark of respect and a symbol of my transition from my tribe to theirs. Komi's outfit matched Papa's and Fumi's matched Mama's.

With all the preparation for the ceremonies and all my research into Jo, there was little time for me to think about what my Yeseni was asking me to choose. Whether I would risk it all to go and save King Yemi and our land from a great evil or stay here and be the Daughter of Peace. I tried to put it to the back of my mind, but I knew I had to make the decision sooner rather than later. Mama Iyeniye had said that I needed to act with urgency, and I could not live with this heavy decision looming over my head for much longer.

~

The night before the first ceremony and not long after sunset we were all tucked away in bed. I heard a tap at my window shutter; it woke me up, but I did not bother to move. I thought it was probably a bird pecking at the shutter, or the wind, so I drifted off back to sleep. Then again, that tap. I got up and walked over to my window, and there he was, standing right outside the house: it was Jo. He looked haunted and anxious; definitely not happy. Not happy at all. I raised my palms and shoulders towards the ceiling. He gestured for me to come outside. What could he possibly want at this hour, the day before our first ceremony; what could not wait until tomorrow? I signalled to him to go around to the back of the house, that way we would be less likely to wake anyone. I grabbed a tunic and made my way downstairs.

'I did not think we would be meeting under these circumstances,' I said with a bemused look on my face.

'You are going to have to disappear,' he said. He was

sweating, and his pupils were dilated; he was pacing up and down the yard.

'Disappear? Jo, what do you mean, what is wrong? Why are you sweating?' He stopped pacing.

'I cannot do this, Elewa, and the only way it will work is if you disappear. I will make sure you have enough money. I will make all the arrangements for you, but I cannot marry you.'

My heart sped up.

'What are you talking about? This has all been arranged!'

'I do not love you,' he blurted out.

'Of course you do not, nor do I you – our marriage was never about love; it is about peace, peace between our tribes, an important and essential part of the treaty.'

'My parents do not own me to give my hand away as if it is their own. I belong to myself, and besides, I love another.'

My mouth dried up and my heart beats pummelled as I wiped my clammy hands on my tunic. At that point he exploded; he took a blade from his pocket, pushed me against the back wall and held it to my throat.

'Disappear . . . or I will make you disappear. I will give you time. I will be too sick for the first ceremony to go ahead, but if you are not gone before it is rescheduled,' his hand was shaking and all my limbs were trembling too, 'I will see to it that you are gone!'

I was unsure if he was going to slit my throat then and there, until I looked into his eyes and saw fear, not hatred. He panicked, dropped the blade, and then ran off into the night.

'Jo!' I shouted. 'You are a coward, you know that? You keep running until you fall off the edge of the earth!' I did not know what I was saying. I was heartbroken and afraid all at the same time.

The light went on inside the house. I must have woken Mama up with my shouting. Papa could sleep through a hurricane but breathe too heavy on the other side of the house and Mama would wake up. She came out back where I was standing and still shaking like a leaf. I quickly kicked the blade away.

'Elewa, why are you shouting, are you sleepwalking? You are shaking, come inside.' She made me a warm drink, my favourite, with ginger, honey and lemon, and she gave me a long talk about how nervous she had been before her ceremony, but all I could think about was Jo.

I thought about how I might not even be here, in this time, for the rest of our marriage, or maybe I would not even make it to the wedding. If he had given me the chance, I would have told him that I might disappear. Or if he truly did love another, he could still be with them, and we would be a marriage of pretence. Like how Sessie was not really our slave. I would tell him tomorrow at the ceremony. With my warm ginger tea resting between my palms, I could hear Mama in the background offering advice that was no longer relevant.

'What if my destiny is not here, with you and Papa?' I interrupted her monologue. I was tired of lying to them.

'What do you mean? Of course it is not; it is with Ojuro and the Okenas,' she gulped.

'No, I mean, I may have to leave you and you may never know where I am, and if I ever leave you, you have to know that I am doing it for the sake of our land.'

'Elewa, I think you just need to get some sleep; you are overwhelmed. You will be fine in the morning, but not unless you get some good rest tonight.'

'You are not listening to me, Mama. You may never see me

again, and I need you to know that if that happens I am fine, and the reason I left was for the good of our land.'

'That is not how marriage works, Elewa. You still get to see your parents – look at Grandpa and Grandma. We still see them, do we not, and I am married to your father.' It was no good – no matter how hard I tried to warn her, she was not hearing me. 'And I know you are doing this for the good of our land, you are doing it for the peace of your people.'

'Yes, Mama,' I said, finally defeated.

'Now get some rest and I am sure you will be just as bright as the sun in the morning. Goodnight, my Elewa.'

I wished my mother goodnight and went back up to my room. I hoped that Jo had gotten home safely and that he had calmed down by now. I felt awful for letting him run off into the night like that, although there was really nothing I could have done.

Mama had already laid out all my clothes on the bed by the time I had woken up. When I walked downstairs her eyes were bright and she had a smile so wide it could light up the land.

'Are you ready, Elewa, for your big day?'

16

Before sunrise on the day of the meeting ceremony I set out to go to the Makutano market. It was a long-held Okena tradition that the bride's family would bring gifts of sustenance on the 'first night' or the 'first meeting ceremony' and it was customary that the bride went by herself to collect the offerings. I always loved going to the Makutano market early in the morning, while the stallholders were still setting up – that way I could have my pick of the freshest produce before everyone else arrived. I bought yams and fresh peppers and I put Ojuro's threats from the previous night to the back of my mind. I decided to carry on as normal, like nothing had happened. I told myself that maybe once he had returned home and calmed down, he would realise that our joining was more important than just the two of us and we would find a way to reconcile.

The market was a strange sight at this time of day, the stallholders were busy setting up their stands and there was something eerie about complete silence in the presence of hundreds of people, especially people whose job it was to make as much noise as they could. The only other time I could think of hundreds of people together in silence was at a burial, when a body was being lowered down into the ground, and even then, you would sometimes hear uncontrollable screams from the bereaved. In our culture we believed that during a burial, while lowering a body into the grave, complete silence should be observed. Just in that moment, because screaming, crying loudly or even talking during this time would provoke or distract the spirit from connecting with the ancestors, and if the spirit was distracted it could spend its life haunting the living. So whenever there was silence in the presence of many, it felt unnerving to me, as it reminded me of the sinister nature of death.

At the market the only noises that occurred were the occasional clinking and clanging of metals from traders tousling with their tools to set up shop as soon as possible. It was like a race amongst the traders, as whoever set up first would be the first to make money, and the first to go home. Although I enjoyed the silence of the market at this time of day, by contrast I also adored hearing the stallholder cries; they sounded poetic to me, the desperation and passion in their voices. The sheer need to sell their produce meant the cries ensured the buyers knew which product was the best in price, size, colour or freshness. They were synchronised like a seamless melody and through their efforts we knew that they had what we needed. We were just a player in their game, and they steered and ushered us throughout the market, bartering and haggling you into exhaustion if you let them. But if you went early, they were fragile and it was your game; they were busy and focused on setting up and not fully focused on you; they could not turn you away for fear of losing custom. So, this was the best time of day to come to the market, especially for those who dreaded the theatre of it.

~

On the way back home, I saw a figure in the shape of a girl, quite far away in the distance. The girl reminded me of Fumi, but she was playing Tak Tak on the boulders alone. It made me think about the days when Fumi and Komi used to follow me around begging me to take them places. They had not asked for a while now; in fact, I could not remember the last time they had asked me to take them anywhere.

As I walked the dusty path towards the water, I thought about the last few months. The young lady in the distance was effortlessly and elegantly jumping the boulders. *If Fumi could see this now*. The closer I got to the figure the clearer she became, then as the splatter of mist from her last jump settled around her, I could not believe my eyes: it was my little sister; it was Fumi.

'Elewa!' she screamed, with one hand waving in the air to catch my attention. 'Did you see that?' she boasted as she effortlessly floated between two boulders, landing gracefully on the other side. I laughed; I laughed so hard my stomach hurt. I bent over with my hand over my mouth, and tears filled my eyes; the yams and peppers fell to the floor and so, it seemed, did my heavy heart. I had just been thinking about Fumi and there she was, right there before my eyes doing exactly what I had missed us doing together. Fumi's facial expression changed from excited to concerned as she ran over to me.

'What is so funny?' she asked. 'Did you see I made it? I made the jump!' She eagerly waited for my response, as if it was just yesterday that she was tagging along with us and falling in the shallow waters.

'Yes, I saw, Tretre, I always knew you would,' I said, while wiping my eyes dry with my sleeve. I collected all the yams and peppers from the ground, dusting them off and scooping them into my tunic.

'Why were you crying? Elewa, I know that something is not right. I heard when Ojuro came to the house last night, I heard him threaten you. Why are you still marrying him after that?' I froze. She had caught me off guard.

'You should not be listening to other people's conversations. Besides, it was a joke, Ojuro did not mean it. Do not worry – everything will be just fine.' I hoped that would be enough to reassure her, at least enough so that she would tell no one else. I looked at her, waiting for her response.

'Why are you staring at me like that?' It seemed she was not going to respond directly to my reply; perhaps she sensed it was just put together to hush her. Had I underestimated Fumi? I needed to be more direct with her.

'I have just missed you, that is all. Fumi, you must keep what happened with Ojuro to yourself. I do not need you worrying anyone else, you understand?'

'Very well, Elewa,' and with a concerned look in her eyes she placed her arm around my waist and then we made our way home.

~

Mama was already fussing over all the garments when we got back, and she immediately took the yams and peppers from my tunic the moment I arrived at the front door.

'Fumi, you should be bathing – what are you doing out so early in the morning?'

'I wanted time to play before the ceremony,' she said. As if playing could ever be an adequate excuse for Mama. I could never have gotten away with a response like that, but Fumi was the youngest, the baby, so Mama and Papa overlooked a great many of her antics.

Fumi and I went upstairs to get ready; with all the anxiety

in the air a knot began to form inside my stomach. Within the next two hours the meal was ready and packed and so were the six of us. We made our way to the Okenas and the knot that had formed in my stomach hours before felt like it had all my organs in its web. I closed my eyes and tried to focus on the Wiri, a place where I had always felt calm and at ease. I pictured the water moving, the cleansing sound of it, and the soothing view of the subtle waves as the water made its way to wherever it needed to be. I thought of all the life that it carried along with it, all the different fish, the plants and all the people too. I started to feel much calmer, and when I opened my eyes the knot had unravelled, and we were nearly at Ojuro's house.

I felt Mama's hand squeeze mine tightly and we left the cart with their staff to make our way to the front door.

$\approx$

Ojuro's family met us in the lobby; they were all beaming with joy. Afua embraced me so tightly that I almost felt lightheaded once she finally released me. There were hundreds of guests and music playing. These people must have been extended family members because I had never seen any of them before in my life.

The day would consist of a short meeting with Ojuro's immediate family, followed by one with both of our parents, and then finally just Ojuro and myself. In this meeting I would eventually go upstairs alone to be received by him, so that we could begin getting to know each other. Those events would eventually be followed by a meal and a party.

Mama Iyeniye was there, in the first ritual. I smiled at her, but she looked at me with deep sorrow, just like at Mama Tiiandas's remembrance ceremony. A look of unconcealed grief. I wondered if she was upset with me because she thought that I had chosen not to travel to the future to meet her niece and instead I had decided to marry Ojuro despite all of the time and effort that she had invested in me. But she had promised me that she would be happy for me whatever choice I made, and I had not sensed any dishonesty in her. Besides, I still had not decided what I wanted to do, though I had vowed to tell Ojuro all about Yeseni, King Yemi and my conundrum. I planned on telling him once we finally had the chance to be alone.

~

The house was decorated with the most beautiful fresh flowers hanging from the ceilings, windows and doors. The scent of frankincense flowed through the walls, rooms and corridors, which gave the occasion a pure and sacred sentiment. We all wore what we had planned, and I felt as majestic as I probably would ever feel.

During the first ritual Ojuro's mother placed the ceremonial paint on the centre of my forehead, either side of my eyes and in the centre of both palms. It was an Okena tradition to symbolise the time had come to meet with my betrothed. After this, my family entered the room to see me now I had been anointed and accepted.

We laughed and drank, and our mothers reminisced about Ojuro and me as children. After this I made my way upstairs, the whole family standing at the bottom in anticipation. The further I went up, the smaller they appeared. When I finally reached the top, I looked back one last time before I turned the corner to make my way to the room where Jo would be waiting for me.

I took one deep breath, exhaled, and opened the door to the room where he was.

I had barely finished exhaling when my whole body dropped to the floor. The loudest scream that I had ever heard came from my gut, through my chest and then out of my mouth. I had never heard my voice in that tone; it felt foreign, like it was someone else's screams echoing through the walls. Ojuro was hanging from the ceiling's bare joist with a make-shift noose tied around his neck. His eyes were open, and they looked cold and fixed. Beneath him lay the stool that once supported him, in his last act of self-destruction. Under-neath his feet was a piece of paper with writing on it. It looked like a letter to me, but I was frozen on the floor and could not touch a thing.

The family came running up the stairs and a symphony of screams followed mine. His mother untied her son and cra-dled him in her arms, chanting something to herself, the two of them rocking back and forth. Papa picked me up from the ground and we all left the house. I looked for Mama Iyeniye, but she was nowhere to be seen.

17

We both sat there, Mama and I, a few days later, on Afua's couch, with cups of tea vibrating in our cradled palms from the nervous shaking of our bodies. Papa was with Ojuro's father in another room trying to offer some condolence and support, and to work out what would happen next with the treaty. Chief Babatunde had asked Papa to visit and try to ascertain some kind of plan, even though Papa thought it was too soon after the tragedy to talk about politics, especially with a man that had only just recently lost his son. He suggested that they should wait a little while longer, however Chief Babatunde insisted that he go.

Mama had planned on us all visiting the family, but she would have preferred to wait a few more days, ideally a week or so. Nevertheless we all went along with Papa. I say all of us, but Fumi and Komi stayed at home with Sessie; there was really no need for them to come along, and Sessie did not deal with death very well at all. Mama wanted to keep all of them as far away from this as possible, at least until the funeral.

In their upstairs living room Mama and I sat there as Ojuro's mother read from a piece of crumpled-up paper that she gripped tightly in her hand.

'*Dear Mother and Father.*' She paused and took a deep breath in.

'You do not have to do this, you know,' Mama offered. 'We just came to make sure that you were supported in your grief and that is all that matters right now.'

'I want to, I want to share with you how my Jojo felt.' We nodded, and she continued.

'*I had to find a way to give myself the freedom that my soul craved and deserved. There was no other way out for me – this was the only way. I thought about it long and hard and concluded that your lives would be better off without me. I was in a long, dark tunnel with no exit in sight. I could not marry Elewa, I did not love her.*'

She came and put her hand on my shoulder. I smiled politely, so she continued.

'*I loved another, and a life without my true love would have been no life at all. Please be happy now, in the knowledge that I am free. Please do not use me as an excuse to resume another war. As your beloved son, I beg you to find a way to preserve peace amongst our people. Forever in your heart, Ojuro.*

'That is it,' she concluded, 'that is all I have left of my son.' She folded the creased note neatly into a square and placed it in her pocket before burying her head into her chest and crying. She had lost everything in the world that mattered. Mama and I comforted her as best we could, but she was truly inconsolable.

There it was, an uninvited guest; I felt it coming over me like a grey cloud on a sunny day. Guilt, followed by shame. Why did I not tell someone that Ojuro came to see me the day before the ceremony and threatened me if I went through with it? If I had told someone, maybe they could have spoken to him? Or if I had tried to speak to him later that night, I could have told him my plan, which might have put him at ease – to pretend with him or to disappear and give him all the freedom that he desired.

I stood up and walked out. My legs just walked, without my brain's consent, one foot in front of the other. *Stop, sit back down, what on earth are you doing, where do you think you are going?* But my legs just told my brain to be quiet: *This is our time now*, they said.

'Elewa! Where are you going?'

I did not listen. The truth was my legs were right: I could not breathe in that house anymore. I heard Mama apologise to Afua, saying it was because of the grief. I kept walking, through the hallway, down the stairs, and out through the front door, until I found air and then I slowed down slightly. I closed my eyes and kept going until, unsurprisingly, I walked into someone. I fell to the ground and when I looked up, there she was. Mama Iyeniye.

'Did you know this was going to happen? Did you know he was going to die?'

She helped me up. 'Where were you going?' she asked, ignoring my questions. 'You looked like you were in a rush. And why are you walking around with your eyes closed?'

'I could not breathe in there. I needed to get away. So, did you know? Did you know that Ojuro was going to die?' I repeated.

'I knew that there would be a loss in the family. I felt a deep sorrow in my heart as soon as the sun rose that day.' She looked very sad, but it was a different type of sorrow, mixed with acceptance.

'So, you did not know that it would be Ojuro?' I persisted.

'I only knew it would be someone dear to me, like I said; I just got the feeling of grief but with no vision. I wept all morning for an anonymous person; it was the strangest thing. He came to see me that morning and asked me why I was crying. He wiped tears from my eyes and told me he loved me. He would always come and see me in the morning.' As she told me that story, a river of tears flowed from my eyes.

'He had a true love; he did not love or want me. I could have disappeared and then he could have been with whoever he wanted to be.'

'Even with all the powers in the world nothing is more powerful than destiny,' she said.

'What do you mean?'

'This was the plan for Ojuro, in this world at least.'

'So you mean that he could still exist in some sense?'

'Yes, in another world, but that is not just Ojuro – it is you, me, your mama and papa, and everyone you and I know. We all exist in multiple worlds.'

'You say the most extraordinary things, Mama Iyeniye,' I sighed. I just wanted to get out of there now.

'Elewa, you must know that people are not going to take this well. The Okena are going to be suspicious of this death; this is not going to be good for the peace treaty.'

'Do you mean that people will blame us? Blame me? Could this cause another war?' I thought back to the Oleba in Omolara's who were sure we could not pull it off. *They were right.*

'It could. It all depends how the news is relayed to the people – it could go either way. The message from both the Oleba and Okena will need to be unified to convince the people that this was a dreadful suicide and not an inside attack.'

Papa was already meeting with their chief, Ojuro's father, so I was sure they were working on a collaborative way to tell the people what had happened.

I thought back to the day I met Ojuro at the pier before sunrise.

'He was so romantic, I do not understand how he changed so abruptly.'

'Ojuro was romantic with you?'

'Yes, I met him one morning at the pier and he said he has a light soul and so do I; it was like he was telling me we were destined for each other.'

'Elewa, that is not what a light soul means . . .' *She was not there, how could she know what he meant.*

'What does it mean then?'

'The Okena believe that people with a light soul, whether male or female, are attracted to males, and people with a heavy soul are attracted to females.'

So Ojuro was not being romantic after all; he was telling me that we were not destined to be married to each other. I played the moment back in my head and it all made sense now. I felt so foolish.

'Can I not go back to that moment and tell him that I understand and plan on travelling to the future anyway?'

'If you went back, who is to say Ojuro would not do it again, because you would still be asking him to marry you and that is what he could not bring himself to do.'

'But at least it would save his life and allow the peace treaty to continue. What about the peace of our kingdom?'

'You should listen to your Yeseni, Elewa. That is something that you can control; you should focus on that now,' she told me before walking away.

～

The Makutano market square was packed to the brim with both Okena and Oleba. Papa said he had not seen so many in the same space since before the war. I had never seen such a thing in my life. The atmosphere was uneasy; it felt like there could be an insurrection at any moment.

'The Okena have finally gotten what they deserve!' a man at the back of the crowd screamed out; that was followed by a roar of affirmative yowls from men and women standing around him.

I could see contempt in the eyes of some, while others appeared apathetic but still nervous, unsettled and on edge.

'Be quiet and just listen to what they have to say!' a frustrated woman from the front row yelled.

'The chief had better start soon or this event will turn into a riot,' Mama whispered to Papa, as she squeezed my hand behind her back.

We all stood on the podium in the centre of the market square, in an assembly to address both Oleba and Okena citizens. It had been decided that Chief Chukwuemeka-Okena would address the crowd and Chief Babatunde and Papa would stand by his side. At the end, the chief would give a few people an opportunity to ask questions, but he could not stay for long.

It had only been a few days after the tragic death of Ojuro and both chiefs hoped that, if we put up a united front, that would quash any suspicions and stop any violence or hostility. Just as Mama Iyeniye had suggested to me when I bumped into her on the day Mama and I went to console Afua.

'We stand here today in unity, Oleba and Okena alike. We are servants of all people of Idanbule, and we want nothing more than peace between our tribes.

'We had planned the most inspirational, unprecedented marriage in the history of our land. The marriage would have symbolised our intentions of peace between our people, but as people of Idanbule know, probably more than any other people, not everything intended will turn out as planned and . . . unfortunately, this is just one of those occasions where, though our dreams and intentions were of the highest order, they have not been fulfilled as we had so earnestly hoped.

'I stand here before you, not only as the proud chief, but also as a broken-hearted father of the Son of Peace, Ojuro Chukwuemeka-Okena.

'Ojuro, my son, always loved both Okena and Oleba. He was an Okena boy that learned the Oleba language and culture; even when we scolded him and told him it was treacherous to do so, he did not care. Because where we saw an enemy and a threat, he saw opportunities to connect, learn and build lifelong friendships. My wonderful son, Ojuro Chukwuemeka-Okena, is no longer with us, and so the betrothal that we had planned between him and Elewa Olanrewaju, the beautiful Daughter of Peace, cannot be.' A wave of gasps, tuts and scathing sounds consumed the square.

Chief Chukwuemeka-Okena continued.

'This is a desolate, wretched state of affairs, but it does not have to mean the end of the intention for peace, because I know that peace between the Okena and Oleba was one of the only things that Ojuro wanted in life.

'And so, I ask you all, Okena and Oleba alike, to use this devastating loss as a reason to stick together and not grow further apart; to do what Ojuro would have wanted us to do; to band together and work out a way to live together in unity. Thank you!'

Chief Chukwuemeka-Okena took a step back and then his son Tawa hastily stepped forward.

'We can only answer a few questions, so if you have one, please raise your hand.'

'What happened to Ojuro?' an Oleba woman shouted out.

'My son was found dead at the betrothal ceremony; we believe he intentionally caused his own death,' Chief Chukwuemeka-Okena replied.

'How do we know that the Oleba did not cause him to do this? People are saying he was poisoned by the so-called Daughter of Peace when they were alone together?' an Okena man queried.

'We have no reason to believe that Elewa would do this to anyone, never mind the man that she was betrothed to marry and the man that she was falling in love with.'

I wondered if Ojuro had told him that he had a light soul. Even though he was right, and I was falling in love with him, it was all because I thought we were creating a deep connection to each other when we may as well have been speaking a different language.

'How will you prevent another war from breaking out as a result of this?' another voice yelled. I could not see a face; they must have been at the very back of the market square.

'That is why we are here today, both Oleba and Okena chiefs, to let you know that we are not suspicious or hostile towards the Oleba, we are instead hostile towards war itself. We still want peace more than anything in the world, even more so because that is what Ojuro wanted.'

Tawa thanked the crowd for their attendance and patience. Then we all stepped down from the podium in the hope that the address was enough to maintain peace until the treaty had been finalised.

'Chief, does all this talk of peace mean you will finally allow all the tribes under the Okena domain the freedom to express themselves as who they really are, under their own tribal names?' a man called.

'That will be discussed as part of the peace treaty!' Tawa responded, before dashing off to catch up to his father.

Another man jostled through the crowd towards us.

'Chief, people are saying Ojuro did this because he had a light soul and was forced to marry another with a light soul. Did you know this about your son?' The chief stopped walking and looked back at the man who had asked the question. He lowered his head despairingly and carried on walking.

A myriad of questions continued from the crowd and although we heard some of them, we kept walking in the opposite direction.

~

When we got back home, Papa said the weekly meetings were now focused on the peace treaty agreement, they were trying to rush it through before any kind of hostile action commenced. Morale was at an all-time low throughout the kingdom and peace between our people did not seem promising now that Ojuro was gone.

I wanted so badly to go back to the day that I met Ojuro on the pier, but whenever I thought about doing it, I remembered Mama Iyeniye's warnings, so I resisted even trying, although it felt almost impossible to do so.

18

After so much pain and anguish, the peaceful quiet of the Wiri River was calling me, and I needed to listen to my Yeseni, as Mama Iyeniye had told me to do. I needed to find out what exactly I would be saving my people from by going to the future if I did decide to go.

I sat down at the river's edge, just where the earth met the water. I crossed my legs, closed my eyes and asked the great forces of Yeseni to come back to me. And I waited.

My mind was full of questions. What would be the consequences of Bilal's betrayal of King Yemi? What would happen to our land and our people because of it? What catastrophe would I be trying to rectify? Was it even possible that I could physically go to another time? My family were in such agony now, could I bear to leave them and risk never returning?

I sat there waiting, but nothing happened. All I saw were blotches of static colour. I kept thinking, *Any minute now these fuzzy splodges will turn into that beautiful kaleidoscopic wheel and the adventure will begin.* But there was still no movement. I grew frustrated; I opened my eyes and screamed in sheer exasperation. A flock of birds flew out of the nearby trees. I kept screaming – it felt good just to let out all the anguish.

What I had not noticed until I looked up to the sky was the weather: it had changed. Clouds had blocked the bright yellow sun and they were heavy and grey. Before I started screaming the weather was calm, the sky was clear and the sun was bright – had I caused this? I screamed one more time to check if my Yeseni had caused the weather to change and the moment I stopped, a bolt of lightning struck a tree across the river.

I closed my eyes and asked Yeseni to come to me, once again. Then the heavens opened, and the heaviest downpour soaked me through. That was the point that I should have given in. I was wet, cold and uncomfortable. *Time to go home? Try another day? Is this what Yeseni is trying to persuade me to do?* a voice inside my head suggested.

That is what you want, another voice inside of me replied. *Well, you will be disappointed – I am not going anywhere.*

Drenched to the bone and determined as I had ever been, I asked again, and finally crystals appeared through the smudges of colour, like stars in the midnight sky. Soon the smudged canvas of my mind was replaced with a beautiful precise, sharp pattern, the colours deep and meaningful – it was finally the kaleidoscope I had been waiting for. I felt warm and peaceful, and even though I was still soaking wet, I felt dry and comfortable now. It was working. I felt my breath getting lighter and lighter and then the next thing I saw was King Yemi.

~

He was in a room like the one I had first seen him in. *He is back at home*, I thought. This was a continuation of the last vision I had, but it gave me more detail. King Yemi appeared at his wits' end. He just sat there, in his ostentatious room, looking beautifully hopeless and alone. I wondered how such a wealthy powerful man could be so disheartened.

The visions played out, and another scene began. It showed me Bilal speaking to his comrades about King Yemi in that same devious, underhanded way. They were all sitting around the same table that I had visualised in the last Yeseni. It seemed that he had brought these men together to tell them about King Yemi's immense wealth. He proclaimed that the price of gold had dropped drastically just by King Yemi's voyage through Africa to visit him in Arabia. One of the men asked how that was possible, and Bilal replied that King Yemi gave away heaps of gold to the poor and needy, so, as a consequence, by the time he reached Arabia the value of gold had dropped.

'By the movement of just one man . . . Gentlemen, we need to conquer this land and take a share in this gold. Such a man who carelessly gives away his wealth does not deserve to have it in the first place.' He spoke in a highly polished, persuasive way. The group nodded in approval. Bilal told the men it would not be difficult to take his wealth and then his country. He told them that King Yemi had imprudently agreed to buy the gold back to help bring the value back up once he returned. He called him generous and foolish, easily manipulated – '. . . the perfect combination,' he said.

Indeed, the men were interested but they insisted on taking a trip to Africa to find out more about this 'golden man' for themselves, after which, they promised, they would regroup and meet again with Bilal. Little did Bilal know that none of these men intended to deal any further with him – they were going in alone or not at all.

'Why would one do business with a man whose proposal was based on his deceitfulness?' They made fun of the way he spoke and then the English men reasoned in secret amongst themselves. It was clear the other men had the same intention, but Bilal had not the slightest idea. It seemed what he had done to King Yemi was now happening to him, and he was just as oblivious as King Yemi had been.

~

As I sat there on the banks of the river, the visions continued to come to me in all kinds of ways. They might start in the middle of a conversation or finish before the end of one. They would change completely to another scene in my mind's eye. I soon realised that once they started, I had little control over their sequence and content. I wanted to find a way to gain some control over my visions, but it was difficult to do it when I was already in one.

~

The next vision that came to me was of another group of men that were with Bilal. These were the Portuguese men; I knew where they were from because I remembered the map that Mama Iyeniye had shown me, and in the vision they pointed at Portugal on a huge map pinned to the wall, and one of them said, 'Portugal too will have its slice of the African pie,' before they all cheered and danced in excitement. After that, another vision came to me of the same men landing on the ports of what looked like my home. They stood close to the port in a V shape. Their leader was at the tip, and various soldiers formed the remainder of the shape, probably in some special hierarchical order.

They brought silk, textiles, exotic herbs, spices and various other items that they hoped to exchange for gold with the tribal leaders. They met with chiefs from every single town along the coast and made an arrangement with them. The chiefs were dazzled and impressed by their foreign goods, mostly their guns. Once one chief found out that another tribe had guns, they were forced to deal with these men, whether they wanted to or not, so they could also obtain guns and protect their tribe.

I saw these men negotiating and becoming tougher on the chiefs regarding what they would accept in exchange for the guns, simply because they knew each tribe had to have them.

I grew weaker in this state and started to feel dizzy, but I did not want to leave this connection with unanswered questions. I needed to find out if I could control my Yeseni, and direct the content of visions.

I wondered if one way of gaining more control of the visions would be to ask a question in my mind. If an answer came to me in the form of a vision then I would know that I could control my Yeseni. I had no idea if it would work, but I asked: *what was the deal, what was the deal, what was the deal.* I concentrated hard, and then in a flash I was privy to a trade negotiation between these men and one of the chiefs.

The men displayed the power of the gun to the chief by placing a piece of fruit five metres away on a tree stump; one of them aimed and fired, the fruit burst into the tiniest pieces and splattered all over the yard. The crowd gasped, and animals of the air fled their nests in the surrounding trees.

'These are the tools we have traded with your rivals in exchange for captives. They go through human flesh just like they went through that piece of fruit,' the leader explained to the chief.

'I will never sell my own people to you, no matter what fancy trinkets you bring to me,' the chief pushed back.

'No one has agreed to sell their own people, and we would not expect you to. We are talking about your enemy's people,

people from other tribes, your war captives, your repeat offenders, the citizens in debt who refuse to, or cannot pay back their debts, and your orphans.' The discussions and negotiations went on, and eventually the chief agreed to supply these men with people, in exchange for firearms. They brought other exotic goods with them that they would only exchange for gold, and since there was an abundance of gold, it seemed that if the goods were right, the men got the gold that they wanted in exchange for them.

There it is, I thought. They had made a trading arrangement with foreigners to capture people from other tribes and sell them to these foreigners as slaves. I asked another question in my mind.

Slavery already existed in our land, long before these foreign men came. Tell me why this is different; show me, please. This time I begged Yeseni. What I saw I will never forget as long as I live, no matter what world or time I was living in.

~

I was on a boat, in the lower deck. Bodies were lying in their own faeces, vomit and other bodily fluids, piled one on top of the other without an inch of space to move; stripped naked, sweating, coughing, heaving – and those were just the living. If these captives spoke, tried to escape, or even coughed at the wrong time they were brought to the top deck and beaten through their flesh to their bones. One man was brought to the deck to be punished and humiliated for humming out of turn. The slave trader pulled down his trousers and shat in the captive's mouth. He laughed and forced the slave to swallow the faeces. Once he did as he was told, he was returned to the lower deck and tied up along with the rest. I had never witnessed wild animals, never mind humans, being treated this way before.

I looked at all the bodies on the lower deck and they were covered in lashing wounds, some healing, some still bleeding and raw. They were packed forcefully and tightly, alongside numerous others, including the deceased. Some of them had passed away during the night and slavers did not always notice. They went through to check for any dead and if they found any, they threw them overboard like a piece of rotten meat. A slaver with the surname Newton kept a log of the dead in what looked like an asset logbook. I saw the book in my vision: 'Sir J. Newton Property Log' and I witnessed him writing *No. 84, slave man, died, cause: flux, disregarded, thrown overboard. No.172 died of the gravel and stoppage of urine, disregarded, thrown overboard. No.47 ...** The list went on and on. This was not at all like the slavery that already existed in our land.

After a while, below deck, I no longer saw every face, just shades of brown and limbs amongst heads, hands and feet; they were that close together that they may as well have been one giant person with hundreds of limbs. *If they thought that way maybe they could have all escaped and broke free?* The ship was either headed for the Americas or the islands of the Indies, or possibly both. I kept thinking that these were all people from Alkebulan; they could have been relatives of people that I knew and for the first time ever I cried within a vision. It was a cruel, violent, inhumane fate. I could not believe that this was what we had sold our people into, this is what the foreign man of the sea called slavery – and it looked more like torture to me.

As a tear dropped down my cheek, within the vision, a

* Paraphrased from James Walvin, *Black Ivory: Slavery in the British Empire*, p.38 (Blackwell Publishing, 1992)

woman from the lower deck looked directly at me. 'Sister, save me, please, I know you are there. I have the gift too.' She sensed me in her world – how on earth could she do that?

How can I help her!? I screamed to Yeseni.

'I am trying!' I responded to the woman, but her once hopeful eyes turned dull and her shoulders dropped. Another woman managed to break free. I do not know how but she ran to the stairs on the other side of the lower deck, even with all the other captives grabbing her ankles, arms and legs; they literally grabbed anything they could grasp on to. She scrambled up the stairs and then jumped overboard. She began swimming in the direction of the shore, but the slavers shot her before she got far.

A red pattern took the place of the woman in the blue water, as she fell to the bottom of the ocean. Moments later, the red pattern disappeared and the water was just blue again, as if nothing else had ever been there. I could not help but feel that now, at the bottom of the ocean, she was in a more peaceful place than where she would have been had she not mustered up the confidence to escape.

After this incident the men argued with each other over the loss of their 'property'. And as if my heart could not sink any deeper, it found a new depth as the man, J. Newton, noted the woman's death, time, place and cause.

The smell of rotting flesh and human excrement was putrid. The scars and open wounds from their violent captures were horrific and even though I was only there to witness, I could not wait for the nightmare to end.

The vision changed and I was no longer on board the ship. They must have finally reached the new land. A female captive was giving birth in some kind of barn. I cannot imagine how she and the child survived a full pregnancy on that horrific ship. It seemed the slavers had planned on selling her and the baby separately if they needed to.

'Two for one,' one of them whispered while the woman lay there exhausted with her newborn baby in her arms. They turned their backs to the woman, shook hands discreetly and raised their eyebrows as they smiled slyly. While they faced away, the woman firmly covered the child's nose and mouth with a rag. Her eyes were fixed and red. Tears flowed down her face but her expression was determined, unwavering yet broken-hearted. Before she could attempt her own life, the men saw that the child was now dead. Their smug expressions turned to shock and then anger when they realised the woman had *stolen* their *bonus*. One of them began lashing her with his whip but her face showed no fear or feeling whatsoever, no matter how hard he hit her. The other man pulled him back and reminded him that she still had to be sold and presented to the public. So he stopped, yet her face did not change, even when he did stop beating her.

The vision moved to the other captives – they were being displayed on a public platform in what seemed to be the centre of a foreign town. They looked different than they had on the boat: their skin was shiny, and they appeared slightly docile. Had the months on that boat taken their souls from them, I wondered. They were examined publicly, teased, mocked and then either bartered over, taken or left.

There was one man on the platform that stood out to me because he did not appear docile at all; he was struggling, openly trying to break free. The man in charge of the sale pointed at him and said something as he struggled, and then the crowd laughed in unison. Women were encouraged to let their children run up to the platform and inspect 'The Beast'. The man seemed somehow undefeated, and he just continued to struggle. When he turned around and I saw his face, I froze.

It was my father.

'Papa!' I shouted, and the vision ended abruptly.

I was back on the banks of the Wiri, still soaking wet. All I could think about now was Papa; I needed to see him right away, needed to make sure he was still here. I ran through the forest, all the way through the village. I do not know where I got the strength as the prolonged vision had depleted me, but once I arrived, I jumped over the gate and swung the door open.

'Elewa, where have you been? Why are you soaking wet?' Mama quizzed me.

'Where is Papa?' I asked, while running past my mother, through the kitchen and out through the back door. He was there, standing as peaceful as anything, sharpening some tool. I grabbed him with both arms.

'I do not know what has come over your daughter this time,' Mama said, shaking her head as she walked back into the kitchen.

'Elewa, what is wrong, girl, you are soaking wet?' He dropped his tool and sharpener as he lifted his arms up to save the rest of his shirt from my drenched blouse.

'I thought you had been taken away, by the white man. I had a scary dream,' I sobbed.

'When did you have this dream? When did you get the chance to dream?' he probed with an amused tone to his voice.

'I must have fallen asleep at the river and then I got caught in the rain on my way back.'

'I see. Go and change out of those wet clothes and meet me back downstairs. You have been through much sorrow this last week, and we need to talk.' I walked past Mama, who had one hand on her hip and her lips pursed together, holding her scolding words from pouring out. I went upstairs and changed into something dry and comfortable and as I made my way downstairs Papa was already waiting for me. He asked me to sit down and tell him all about my dream, so I told him about the vision, although I still called it a dream. I told him everything I saw on the boat, in the foreign land; after that I told him about the man at the market that I saw struggling on the platform and then I told him that that man had his exact face.

'Elewa, I have never told you exactly why I am so strict about you children going to the seashore, have I?' he asked. I shook my head, still sobbing from having to convey that awful vision to my father.

'Well, when I was younger, before I met your mother, I was looking for work with my brother in a place we did not know very well. It was far away from our home village ...'

'I did not know you had a brother?' That was the first time my father had ever mentioned him.

'I know, Elewa. His name was Itoro.' His shoulders sank and regret manifested over his face. He took a piece of folded paper out of his pocket and handed it to me. When I asked him what it was, he said it was a letter that he wrote to us children, intended for us to read when we were much older. He had planned on giving it to Sessie first. But I had had this nightmare, so he thought it apt to share the letter with me now.

He told me that he could not bring himself to explain everything that he went through in one conversation, but that everything I needed to know was in that letter. I clenched it tightly in my palm; all I wanted to do was rush upstairs to my room, shut the door and read it. But Papa was still talking to me. He was saying that he and his brother were looking for work around the time that his father's farm was in trouble due to a failed crop, and so they both decided they would find work to help the family out.

'We must have walked about eighteen miles and my feet were starting to bleed,' he recalled. He suggested that they turn back but Itoro wanted to keep going. Itoro was older and felt that he had more responsibility with regard to the family and the farm.

'He was always blaming himself; he really took it on, the weight of the family problems.' They took a short break on the beach and then carried on until they saw two men in the distance. Papa said the men were carrying a net and a machete, and when Itoro saw the men, he started to get excited.

'What would a man be doing with an empty net and a machete if it did not involve work, paid work? We are about to prove to these men that we could make their life a lot easier and perhaps even fill their net with fish and chop all the wood they need,' Itoro had said. But as they got closer to the men, there was something not quite right about them.

'Something I could not quite put my finger on,' he said. Itoro announced they were not from around there but were looking for work, selling their attributes to the men: strong, hardworking and had a great deal of experience working on a farm.

'Yes, you have come to the right place, we have been looking for an extra pair of hands,' one of the men replied. As Papa and Itoro got closer to the men one of them grabbed Itoro and put him in the net. Itoro told Papa to run but he would not leave his brother. The other man grabbed Papa and they both tried to fight them off, until the men's comrades arrived to help. The two of them were sold to the white man and after waiting in the forts for what felt like months, they made their voyage on sea.

'I do not know how I survived on that ship – there were many times I thought that I had died until I woke up and realised that I was still alive and another day in hell was about to begin. It was just as you described in your dream, Elewa, except a thousand times worse.' Papa told me that Itoro became gravely sick on the journey and one morning when he woke up Itoro was dead. Papa knew that they would throw him overboard with no regard so he—

'I do not know why I did it, but I chopped a piece of his finger off with a piece of metal that I found within the timbers of the deck and made a blade out of. If I ever got back home, I wanted to have some of my brother to bring back with me.' I imagined just how desperate he would have been to chop a piece of his sibling off as a keepsake, for peace of mind.

He told me that when he arrived in the strange land, he was given a strong jug of some form of liquor, but when the men were not looking, he spat it out. They oiled down his body and then chained him to the platform stand in the centre of a town.

'What did you do with your brother's finger?' I enquired. My question incited a look of shame and horror on Papa's face; he froze, his eyes fixed somewhere behind me. 'Surely they would have found it on you when they oiled you down?'

'I swallowed it just as we were about to leave the deck. Like you said, they would have found it and I could not let them take anything else away from me.' As strange as it was to learn that my father had swallowed a piece of his brother, the alternative was losing all of him forever. I now understood how that mother could suffocate her baby knowing that if she did not, the child would spend a life like hers, enslaved in a living nightmare. How a woman could jump overboard in the hope of swimming to freedom, because for these people, there were only two choices: freedom or death.

'You struggled, did you not, Papa?'

'Yes, I was trying to break free. I did not care whether it would work or not, I never wanted to accept that situation.' I knew what he meant.

After seeing him on the platform, helpless and struggling, I felt so guilty for all the times I did not listen to him and went to the shore. I felt guilty for all the days that I wished that I would be captured by the white man and taken on a long and exciting journey to an exotic land. *What a fool I was back then.*

Now I was filled with a raging desire to do something about it, to use my powers to change history. To make it better for the people of my land. I vowed to myself right then and there that I would travel to the future to change the past, as Mama Iyeniye had said I should. Even if it meant never seeing my parents again. They would always be in my heart and in every fibre of my body, but now might be my only chance to take away the pain from *all* my people. *Perhaps I could still be the Daughter of Peace, in some way*, I thought.

19

Relations between Papa and Chief Babatunde had been strained since the captains' visit to our house, and though Papa could easily avoid Uncle Kwame for a while, sooner or later they would have to see each other; after all we were a very close family and Uncle Kwame was often at our house for dinner or other family events. It felt like there was a gigantic mountain of tension emerging through the centre of our lives and the events of the past week had put even more pressure on all of us. But none of us could be prepared for the fiasco that was about to take place.

It was not long after the public assembly. Our house was peaceful for a change – we were all our own worlds, seemingly trying to make sense of the catastrophe that had recently occurred – when we heard a loud bang on the door. I wondered if it was the captains again, after all they did say they would be back, but this time I could not have been more wrong. Papa got up to open the door and Chief Babatunde stormed right in as if we should have been expecting him. I tried to hide the shock on my face.

'What is troubling you, Mawuli?' Chief Babatunde seldom called Papa by his first name, so it felt a bit odd, like he was distancing himself somehow.

I made to leave when Papa stopped me.

'No. Anything the chief has to say, he can say it in front of all of us.' Mama looked bewildered; she walked over and put her arm around me and we both stood there awkwardly, watching the two of them. Now that I had increasingly been allowed to take part in these complicated meetings, I felt stifled by how much I had to control every part of my body and I missed the days that I could just sit on the top of the stairs and listen in.

'Why have you been so distant these last weeks? I know you are dealing with the business of Ojuro but it seems there is something else going on. How long have I known you, Mawuli? What issue could there possibly be that you could not come to me with?' The chief swung his hands up into the air. Papa turned his back towards him and paced slowly in the opposite direction.

'The white man, he came to the house, said you and he have had a deal for years now, and since I was becoming chief, he wanted to make sure nothing was going to change.'

'And what did you tell him?' Chief Babatunde responded quickly, as if he did not understand that that was the whole point.

'What do you mean *what did I tell him*? I told him what he could do with his dirty blood contract!' Papa yelled.

'Oh, Mawuli, how do you think we have managed to live in such comfort for so many years? We do what they say and in return they do not bother us!'

'What does that mean exactly?' Papa walked towards the chief and stared right into his eyes.

'We turn a blind eye, let them capture whoever they can get. Of course, we warn and prepare our people; we tell them not to go out at night, or near the border, by the sea. We do not actively help the white man or take any of their exotic goods. We just turn a blind eye for the protection of our families.' The chief sounded like he was still convincing himself that what he had agreed was reasonable behaviour.

'Is that what you have to tell yourself so that you can sleep at night?' Papa mocked.

'Mawu . . .'

'Do you know what you are saying? Do you know how abhorrent and pathetic that is? Not dealing with the white man is the only thing . . . no, the most important thing that the Oleba stand for, yet you have been doing it behind my back all this time.'

The chief collapsed onto a chair. 'They threatened my family – they threatened *your* family.' He gestured towards Mama and me. 'And they promised us protection if we agreed to look the other way, so I thought that was a small price to pay to ensure our families were safe.

'Once you become Chief, you can do it your way, but until then we are all protected, and after the peace treaty, it is to be hoped that we will no longer need their protection.' I had not realised that Papa was still going to be Chief even though the betrothal had been cancelled.

'And you think they are just going to let us walk away? You have no clue, do you? You do not know these men like I do. You have dishonoured our tribe and now you want me to come in and clean up your mess? You think it is acceptable that they take anyone they can catch, as long as they do not touch our families? I was hoping this was all a lie, a terrible misunderstanding, but it is true and you are not the man I thought you were.' Papa marched towards the front door, opened it and stood next to it.

'Get off your high horse, Mawuli. I did this for us, for our families.'

'Get out of my house and do not ever come back. I never want to see your face again!'

Chief Babatunde stayed seated.

'What about the peace treaty, what about you becoming chief?'

'What do any of those things mean if you cannot recognise the person you see when you look into the looking glass? Leave – I will not ask you again!'

'The world is not as simple as you think it is, Mawuli. I had to find a way to buy us time so we could figure out how to get them off our land for good. I will give you some time to cool off. I can make excuses for you next week, but I expect you at the peace-treaty meetings the week after.' He shuffled forward in his seat, rested his elbows on his knees and cradled his head in his palms.

'Nobody is perfect, Mawuli; if there is a way to right the wrongs I have caused, I will do whatever it takes, but I cannot do it alone. I need you – we all need you!'

Papa bit onto his bottom lip as if it was the only thing that could keep him from flying into a rage, and the chief finally walked out. Papa slammed the door behind him so hard that Mama and I jumped, almost in unison. Even though it was uncomfortable to watch, I was glad it was finally all out in the open.

I thought about Papa having the same conversation with Uncle Kwame, and I wondered what his excuses would be. I hoped that Papa would eventually see what I saw in Chief Babatunde: a man that made a stupid, detrimental mistake, but a man who was still worthy of forgiveness.

～

With my back braced up against the bedroom door, I hastily pulled the letter that Papa had given me earlier from my pocket. My heart was racing. My first instinct was just to read it, but I wanted to be there, to see and feel everything that he had. I did not know if that was possible with Yeseni, but I wanted to try at least. I held the letter to my heart and asked Yeseni to take me to the world within the pages of the letter.

I unravelled the folds of paper and two more sheets, full of Papa's handwriting, fell to the floor. I was surprised; the letter was longer than I had expected. I bent down to pick up the additional sheets of paper, closed my eyes and repeated the request: 'Yeseni, take me to the world within these pages . . .' I held my breath as a surge of magnificent colours that took the form of letters appeared all around me. Some were grouped into words, but they spun around me so fast that my toes curled back into the soles of my feet.

They seemed to pick up speed with every second, then a cold, tingling sensation started from my fingertips and worked its way through my arms to the rest of my body. As soon as I felt it on my chest I exhaled. My muscles tensed up like before; the scariest part of accessing Yeseni was the paralysing feeling of your muscles contracting, warning you there was no going back. I could tell that it was going to be a powerful experience by the way that my body felt going into it. A prickling sensation covered my skin and I started to panic; I wished I had gone to Mama Iyeniye and asked her for help before I tried this out alone. Suddenly the spinning letters disappeared and were replaced by another scene.

～

This was the strangest thing I had ever felt. This was more than just a vision; I was sitting outside, near the sea. I was not seeing myself do it though – this time I was *in* the world, wherever this world was. I took a few seconds to gather what I believed were my thoughts.

A strange, detached thought ran through my mind: *We better get back before dark, Mama and Papa will need help on the farm.*

What was that? I thought.

I cannot wait to see the look on Mama's face when we come back with a job, maybe then she will finally stop worrying. There it was again, someone else's thoughts in my mind. They just kept flooding in; it was like another person was in my head, or maybe I was in theirs.

These other thoughts, this other sense of self, although it belonged to someone else, their temperament felt so familiar to me. I looked down at my hands, but they were not my hands. I knew those hands so well though: Papa's hands. Finally, it clicked. I realised that my consciousness was somehow in Papa's body. His feelings, memories and desires were coming through me, and I was in that moment with him. I saw the world through his eyes. I felt the cool sea breeze on his face and neck.

'What are you doing with your hands, brother – did you fall and bump your head again or something?' I stopped inspecting Papa's hands and turned to the voice on my left. It was Itoro. They looked so alike – staring into his eyes gave *me* butterflies, but it gave Papa a sense of calm and serenity. He was my beloved older brother and the uncle I had never met, a peculiar stranger and a precious, idolised sibling all at once. I instinctively knew exactly how to respond to him.

'Just giving them a stretch; those of us who actually *work* on the farm get achy joints from time to time,' I gibed back at him.

'Whatever you say, brother!' He flashed me a bright, brash smile.

I decided to try and totally quieten my inner-voice, and fully embrace Papa's mind. To get what I wanted out of that experience, I needed to let his mind, soul and spirit fully come through. But every time I tried to do it, I would hesitate. I was scared that I would either lose myself in this world or inside his thoughts somehow. The pull from Papa's consciousness was so powerful though; it felt like the heaviness of your eyelids when you are exhausted yet trying your best to stay awake. I finally realised that I could fight it no longer, so I took a deep breath in and just let go.

'Why did you jump back like that? Everything well with you?' Itoro looked back at me with a concerned expression on his face. 'Maybe we should just head back home?'

'No, I am fine, I thought I saw a crab; you know how those things pinch.' I got up and ran towards the water then dipped my feet in it to cool down. It felt so soothing that I decided to walk further in, and before I knew it, I was waist deep in the ocean.

'If you say so!' Itoro yelled as he followed me into the water. We stood there watching some mystical, invisible force push the current towards us and then pull it away again. The waves started to come in more forcefully. It was a bit too unpredictable for me; I felt uneasy.

'What a tease!' I looked up at Itoro, and chuckled nervously.

'What majesty, little brother!' he corrected me with a smile. For a few precious moments we did not think about looking for work, how bad our feet were hurting or the guilt we both felt about the failed cacao crop. Instead, we were just there, in the moment, my brother and I and the ocean.

We were strolling back to the shore, towards the rocks,

when we saw a group of men in the distance: one held a machete and another had a net.

'Heyyy! Over here!' Itoro waved to get their attention. 'This is it, brother – this is our chance to make some gold and finally help Mama and Papa!' He was so excited.

'We are not from around here – we are Oleba, and just looking for some work!' he yelled. The men got closer and Itoro jogged towards them.

'Let me do the talking, you hang back!' he warned me. Something did not seem right though; perhaps it was something in the breeze, or in their stance. Maybe it was their eyes?

'Brother, something does not seem right, just wait a minute.'

'What are you talking about? Stop worrying – just hang back, will you?'

'I will come with you. Just slow down.' I started walking faster to catch up with him. Even though Itoro was right about most things, I could not seem to shake the bad feeling I had about these men. We finally approached them. Five altogether. I could not see all their faces clearly, only that one had a thick moustache and another was heavy-set, with large droopy cheeks. They were all wearing loose white shirts that had turned different shades of beige with age and sweat.

'I thought I told you to stay back,' Itoro scolded me. I shrugged my shoulders.

'I am Itoro, this is my little brother Mawuli. We are looking for work. I am a great labourer and he can fix just about anything broken that you put in front of him. We must go back home before dark today but we can start first thing in the morning.'

'You should have listened to your little brother; you are not going anywhere!' said the one with the thick moustache. The other men cackled while Itoro frowned. He opened his mouth again to try and explain what we wanted and then the one with the droopy cheeks threw the most vicious punch at Itoro's jaw and he immediately collapsed onto the ground.

'What are you doing?' I screamed, and I crouched over Itoro, trying to get him to come back around. The men laughed and held me back while the one with the thick moustache picked Itoro up and flung him over his shoulder.

'You cannot get away with this!' I struggled as they held onto my arms and torso. They must have knocked me out as well because the next thing I knew I was waking up in what seemed like a slave fort but I could not be absolutely sure. I had an extremely sore and heavy jaw and it felt like someone was vigorously pounding on my head like a drum. I looked around the room for my brother and thankfully he was right next to me.

'Where are we?' Itoro was already awake when I came to; all the light in his eyes had dissipated. It was cold and dark in the fort and there were hundreds of men, women and even children there. My heart sank when I realised that I was probably right: we were in one of those dreadful slave dungeons along the coastline. I tried to move my arm up to stretch and realised that not only were we crammed into this dungeon, but we were also shackled at our wrists and ankles.

The rest of the people in the dungeon looked as if they had either lost hope or they were just too sick to care. We must have been part of the last group they had brought in. I tried to ask one of the men next to me how long he had been in there, but he did not speak Oleba and I did not understand his language either. Not only did the fort stink, but there were no windows or ventilation in there.

'Those strangers kidnapped us,' Itoro groaned.

174

'I knew there was something not right about those men. But you had to go running over to them!' I was heated – I felt so angry at him. *If only he had stopped and listened to me.*

'I am sorry. You are right, it was my fault, I should have been more careful. I was just so desperate to get work, you know?' Not only did I not have the energy for the effort it took to hold a grudge with Itoro, but I also hated fighting with him. I knew if we were going to get out of this dire situation, we would need each other. Besides, I knew deep down that this was not Itoro's fault.

During our time in the hellish fort, I thought about our parents, and how worried they must be about us. I am sure Itoro thought about them as well, but we never spoke about it together – for me, speaking about them would have made us weak and vulnerable in a place where we needed to be strong.

~

'I have a plan,' Itoro whispered. We knew that they would be moving us from the fort to the ships in a week or so, and that would be our last opportunity to escape. 'If we can break free when they move us, we could escape into the sea and see if we can make it to the shore of the next village along the coast.' Talking like this with my brother kept my spirits up.

'That sounds good, but how would we get out of these chains?'

'Look at that.' Itoro pointed towards a tiny silver dot in the wall, a piece of metal that was sticking out of an old door joint. 'I can make a blade out of that and saw us free.'

'That sounds good, brother.' The joint was still partially plastered over so every night after that conversation, when everyone else was asleep, we chipped away at the plaster until

175

we reached the metal joint. Once we got the joint out of the wall, we used small rocks from the dungeon floor to shape and sharpen the blade.

'We did it, Uli!' There was a look of hope on Itoro's face as the plan slowly came together. Now all we had to do was test it on a link in our chains. I tested on Itoro's chain and it was sharp enough to cut right through, but it would take a lot of sawing.

'Do you think we have enough time to get it done?' I could not see how we could saw through all these chains in just a few days and without the other captives noticing.

'Of course we will, we will need to work hard at it!'

'How can we do it without them noticing?'

'We will just have to do it like we did the wall, at night,' he assured me.

We both took turns using the blade to chip away at our chains, focusing on the links that were behind our wrists and ankles to obscure what we were doing. Itoro was right, we did get it done. Both of our chains were almost completely loose, and we left them like that until the day of our planned escape. We decided to do the last section just before we boarded the boats, then we would run to the sea, dive in and disappear.

I visualised our escape a million times. I would wake up in that putrid dungeon with a grin on my face thinking about Mama and Papa's faces once we showed up back home.

There was a heavy storm the night before the slavers planned to load us onto the ship.

'This is perfect – weather like this is distracting, trust me!' Itoro claimed. 'This last section should only take a few seconds, just make sure no one sees this!' He pointed towards the severed link in my chain. Itoro would hang onto the blade, set himself free and then either come and help or throw me the blade so I could do mine.

Once we left the giant walls of the fort, the wide-open space and the bright lights felt overwhelming. It had been weeks since we had seen the sun. When we were all chained up, standing along the shore, getting ready to board the boat, I remember seeing everyday people just going about their daily lives – not one of them made eye contact with us; it was so strange. *Maybe they think we are criminals.* Maybe that is why none of them looked in our direction. Some of the captives shouted out to them pleading for help, but that did not work.

After a few minutes Itoro gave me a look to signal that he was going to cut himself free. He did it in a few seconds then started over towards me, but the other captives screamed and grabbed his arms and legs, begging him to help them too. The chaos from the other captives' cries caught the attention of the slavers who had been preparing the ship for sea; they moved towards Itoro with a rifle before he could either get to me or throw me the blade. At that point Itoro was free to execute the plan by himself: he could have run into the sea and then swam to the next village like we had planned.

'Run, Itoro, leave me – I will find my way back home somehow! Go and take care of Mama and Papa.' I pleaded with him, but he just stood there, frozen and conflicted. One of the slavers fired a shot towards his feet and when he missed the other two guards started towards him. Another guard attempted to fire a shot, but it seemed as if the musket ball jammed in his gun. He inspected the gun and cursed at it. This was the perfect opportunity for Itoro to run free.

'Run, brother, please!' I begged him. I saw in his eyes that he could not bring himself to leave, and as the slavers closed in on him, he walked towards them with his hands up in the air. They chained him back up and loaded us all onto the boat. They beat us senseless and starved us both until I was sure we would both die, but eventually they started feeding us once again. I picked up quite quickly after some water and a few steady 'meals', but Itoro never did fully recover.

'How are you feeling now, brother?' I asked him once we had been fed a few regular 'meals'.

'Fine, I am doing fine, little brother!' I knew deep down he was not so well; his eyes told me the truth. I grew angry with Itoro once again for not escaping when he could have and giving my parents at least one son back. Then the next morning when I woke up and called over to him, he did not answer, and that was when the woman that was chained up next to him shouted out, 'Itoro, your brother, he died last night.'

I screamed so loud, I think it moved the ship's direction. When they unchained us for our weekly exercise on the top deck, I ran over to him and chopped a piece of his finger off before they could get to him. I made a hole through the nail and threaded a piece of string through it. I wore the piece of my brother around my waist and tucked in, where it could not be found. The only way it would be found was if I got into trouble or was suspected of something. If that happened, they would strip-search me, find it and then throw it overboard.

I have to keep myself out of trouble for the rest of the journey so they cannot take away the only thing I have left of my brother.

The next morning, they came down to the deck and found Itoro's body. They unchained him and threw him overboard before arguing with each other about the loss of numbers that week.

After my brother died like that, something changed deep

inside of me. At night sometimes I would fantasise about him leaving me; in my fantasy he trusted that I would survive and would find my way home. Then I would visualise him at home with Mama and Papa. I would dream that he would tell them that while we were away, I had found a job and was not able to come back for a while, just so they would not worry, because he and I would know that I would be fine and I would be home someday. Then I would wake up and realise he was gone, and it was all just a ridiculous fantasy. I would get angry and then sad. I felt every emotion possible on that journey and when I looked around at all the other faces, I could see that they had their own crosses to bear.

～

When we finally reached land, more captives on my ship died. As soon as their feet gripped solid ground, they just fell and perished. Most were sick throughout the journey, either of what they called flux or dysentery; this was probably due to the rancid conditions we were in on both the fort and the ship. On the ship we were arranged more 'like corpses than living beings', and there were only two buckets per deck to relieve yourself in and sometimes the bucket would be on the other side of the deck, which meant that people would just relieve themselves where they lay, for fear of the fights that would take place if you tried to stand up and make your way towards one of them. People were lying for weeks on end in their own faeces and other bodily fluids; I do not know how those of us that survived did so. We were packed in from what the slavers would call 'fore to aft' and 'from the nose of the ship to the rudder', we were 'arranged in tightly packed rows'. We filled the main storage decks and where the ship bulged at what they called the 'midship', we were slotted into the resulting spaces. We filled the alleyways, and we were squeezed into the gaps between the other captives. We were 'shoulder to shoulder along the length of the ship, head to toe or head to head', and chained in irons, both hands and feet. We could not turn or move without great difficulty, and we could not rise or lie down without either hurting ourselves or others close by.*

I managed to keep the promise I had made to myself of staying out of trouble so they would not search me and take my brother's finger away from me but before they sold us on, I noticed that they were changing other captives' clothes, throwing water and soap on them and scrubbing them down before oiling them up and then giving them a strong liquid substance so that they remained docile and controllable. We all stood in a line waiting for our turn to be prepared for sale and just as it was my turn, I ripped it from my waist and swallowed it whole.

It was all I cared about at that point – I would probably have killed myself or let them shoot me if they ever took it away from me. But now that I had swallowed it, there was nothing more they could take from me. Now I was ready to fight for my freedom.

~

Once I got to the front of the line, they poured that soapy liquid over me and began scrubbing my skin, then took a bucket full of water and threw it over my face. When I jolted they laughed, then they used this strange, greasy substance to oil me down. I saw captives in front of me smiling and stumbling about in an inebriated way.

* Phrases drawn from James Walvin, *Black Ivory: Slavery in the British Empire*, pp.41–2 (Blackwell Publishing, 1992)

That must have been the drink they gave them. When they came to give me the substance, I held it in my mouth then spat it into the bucket when they turned away. I saw all the captives being sold and taken off with their new 'owners' and although I had been on this dreadful journey for months on end, I still could not accept this as my destiny.

My plan was to break free once one of those people had 'bought' me, and if they wanted to, they could shoot me – at that stage I felt like I had nothing to lose.

Finally, it was my turn to be auctioned off. They tied me to the platform, and I started struggling. I think they chose to make a joke, to put the crowd at ease; it seemed to work because they all laughed, but still it seemed none were brave enough to purchase me, so they sold the rest of the captives and decided to put me back up one last time, at the end. They whispered something threatening in my ear, but I did not understand everything they said.

What felt like hours went by and no one wanted to buy me. The slavers began to get nervous and started shouting at me, like they had on the ship, when an older-looking man wearing a three-cornered hat and a white collar beneath a black coat wandered into the crowd. He looked up at me and immediately placed an offer. There was no one to barter with like there had been with the other captives because most people had already gone, so his offer was accepted right away. True to the promise I had made myself, in the cart on the way home I leapt from the back and started running, but as soon as I set out, I felt vulnerable.

Then the reality set in – where was I running to? I was now in a strange land, thousands of miles away from anyone I knew. I froze. A handcuffed brown captive running in a land ruled by white men would surely bring attention. It was not like back home – here I was the alien. I was caught almost immediately by my new master.

'What are you doing? You will get yourself killed,' he reprimanded me. There was something different about this man though; he had concern in his eyes. He placed me back into the cart without rebuke or lashings. I decided in that moment that I would wait a few days before I planned my next escape.

As the cart drove to our destination, I looked out at the lush scenery and the landscape. We drove past many farms, with hundreds of brown people that looked like me working the land, cutting the thick stalks of a tall grass that grew almost twice the height of them. The white overseers were on horses with long leather whips to hand. *Is this my fate? Is this man taking me to one of these farms?* We drove past grand estates and I began to understand that people that looked like me only existed in this world as labour and nothing else. We lived in their world, but we were just the ill-treated cogs that kept the wheels turning and oiled. I started thinking of my plan to run away and that is when the fear crept into my mind; I started questioning myself. If I ran, someone would surely catch me and return me to whoever owned me – if they did not beat me to death or hang me instead.

I could see now how truly hopeless and stuck in this world my people really were. If only I had the powers that my father said some Oleba possessed. If I did, I would vanish in less than a second. We would have disappeared that day on the shore when we realised those men were slave catchers, then we would not have known the pain, terror and heartache I now knew.

～

Once we got in the house, he reached his hand out to me. 'Reverend Sidney Burke.'

I took his hand, bent it back and tackled him to the floor—I thought he was trying to attack me. It had been over a year of captivity and no other white man had put their hand towards me unless they planned on lashing or attacking me.

'No, no, no, I am not trying to hurt you, I am merely introducing myself to you!' He stood up and smoothed his clothes off. 'Do you speak English? What is your name?'

'Yes, I do.' If I did not, I would have probably been dead by now – if you did not speak English to the slavers on the fort or the boat, you would be beaten until you did, so suffice it to say we all learned that language very fast.

'What is your name?'

'I am Mawuli.' I did not know what to expect. After everything that I had been through I thought he was biding his time, waiting to lash me for running away earlier in the day.

'Mawuliiiiii . . . ?' He hung on to the end of my name as if he was waiting for something else, like Mawuli was not enough. I had never met a white man like him before.

'Mawuli Olanrewaju.'

'Very well, Mawuli Olanrewaju, shall I show you around?'

'Err, yes,' I responded, waiting to be shown to his basement where he kept his captives.

Reverend Sidney Burke was the younger brother of Mr Thomas Burke, who owned the estate with all of that towering unruly-looking grass that they called sugar cane. His estate was called a sugar plantation and many of the slaves I had seen from the cart as we made our way there worked for him. But while Mr Thomas had hundreds of slaves, Reverend Sidney had only one, a young girl called Emily whom he said he had bought at the desperate request of her mother, right after she was born.

He showed me around his home, which was a house by

itself, with its own gardens, in a secluded corner of the estate. 'You can wander around here as much as you like but you need to be discreet and never leave my compound,' he warned. 'If you do, you will be captured and resold, or made to work on my brother's plantation – a dehumanising prospect.'

I wanted to ask him why he had chosen to save me and what he planned to do with me, but I was afraid if I did, I would wake up from this dream and be with everyone else that looked like me in this land.

I spent the next few days wandering around the gardens, helping Reverend Burke out with chores that he did around the house and teaching Emily about back home. I wanted her to know where she came from and understand that the world she lived in was by no means normal.

Later, Reverend Burke told me that, as the younger brother of a wealthy family, it was his duty to serve what he called the church. He was, he said, a man of the Christian god, and he abhorred the buying and selling of slaves.

'Though it must be admitted,' he said ruefully, 'that most of the men in this beastly "trade" still have the gall to call themselves Christians, yet they have no qualms in owning hundreds, if not thousands of slaves. Including my dear brother.'

He said that if finances allowed, he tried to achieve the repatriation of an African slave at least once a year. He had made trips to Africa on his brother's ships, to return the slaves he bought and take the word of his Christian god to the people of our land.

'My brother has a shipment of sugar leaving for England in thirty days' time. From England, there will be another ship taking goods to Africa. I will make the journey with you to ensure your safe passage. We can say that you are coming with me to help me convert your people to the Christian faith.' I cannot tell you how excited I was at the prospect of finally returning home, after all that I had been through. I felt hopeful for the first time in over a year.

~

During the time that I stayed with Reverend Burke, more than once, people referred to Emily and to me as 'N*****' or 'that N*****'. I did not understand what the word meant but it was delivered in such a loathsome way I could tell it was a repugnant term that they had chosen for us, and maybe they called all people from our land this name as well. Reverend Burke never called us N***** and he seemed to pretend not to notice or care when anyone else did. When I asked him about it, he said that if he objected, they would arrest him and have him lynched as well; he had seen it happen to others who had challenged their treatment of slaves. The best way, he said, was to remain underground in both his thoughts and actions.

Everyone knew that Reverend Burke was a respected man of his god, and so his slaves might be needed to help him in different parts of the world. They could not stop him from taking the slaves he had bought to wherever he wanted to. I felt guilty when I saw small children and women younger than me working the fields for hours on end, and when I heard the piercing shrieks of them from being whipped and beaten. I asked Reverend Burke why he could not try to set some of them free as well.

'I do what I can, Mawuli. If I make a move once they have already been bought into the system, people are more suspicious; that is why I try to buy captives from off the ships instead of from other slavers. I am but one man, though I am working hard to make others see the inhumanity of this vile trade.'

Reverend Burke modestly attributed his good works to his Christian faith, but most slave owners were of the same faith and did not act at all like Reverend Burke. He had a clarity of heart and a sensitive soul, and I knew that no matter what spirits he chose to believe in, he would still be doing a righteous service to mankind.

When I went to town and saw slaves on the podium being sold, it made me think of my brother Itoro. I knew the terror they had been through, and the terror that they had to come. I could not wait to get out of this world. I told Reverend Burke about my mother and father and their farm back home, but I could not muster up the courage to talk about Itoro, not to anyone; it was far too soon for that.

~

The day before we left the shores of that horrific land, I walked around the garden of Reverend Burke's home one last time. It was a beautiful day. The sky was blue, and the sun was bright and warm. The birds were singing in the sky, in between the shrieking of captives and lashing sounds of the leather whipping through flesh. The garden was so well manicured, and in every corner there was some beautiful exotic plant that had come into flower. When I first arrived, Reverend Burke had walked me around the whole garden and told me the names of all the plants, but I could not remember any of their names now. They were all strange names, though Emily knew every single one by heart. She skipped behind us, making a game of it, calling out the name before Reverend Burke got the chance. I walked through the house one last time, with its solid shiny timber floors and framed pictures of all the Burkes hanging from the walls, which were painted a sand-like colour. The ceilings were high and engraved with fancy cornice patterns around the edges. It was a sanctuary to me, for a moment in time, and I was sure it had been a sanctuary to many over the years. I did not want to leave the refuge that was Mr Burke's estate until I had it firmly fixed in my mind. Once I had taken it all in, I wandered back up to my quarters. I packed the few belongings that Reverend Burke had given to me and got ready to set off once again.

We left just as he had promised. I hesitated to get on the ship. I must have stood at the dock for a good five minutes, clearly haunted by memories from the last journey, but Reverend Burke insisted. 'We are not turning back now, Mawuli!' he said as he put his arm around me and gave me a friendly nudge in the right direction. Once I stepped on the ship it was like another world. We had space to walk, move and sleep with our limbs outstretched. I could walk up to any deck and watch the ocean or the sunset. *If Itoro could see me now . . .* I still wept whenever I thought of him.

After months of travelling the rough sea, a brief stay in the English port of Bristol, and another sea voyage, we finally arrived home.

As I stepped over the threshold: 'Mawuli, my son, you are safe!' Mama ran over to me and touched my face like she could not believe her eyes and only touch could convince her that I was real.

'Itoro?' Papa asked, following close behind her. I just looked back at them and shook my head. She howled and fell to her knees.

≈

After that I started feeling dizzy. I saw a wave of coloured letters spinning around my body, and then in a flash, I saw Papa standing in his mother's house consoling his parents after telling them about Itoro. For the first time in the vision, I saw Papa from a distance rather than being part of him. I looked down at my hands as those letters spun around me and they were mine now. I concentrated really hard for a thought that was not mine, but nothing came. I was alone in my mind and I felt dejected. I had quietened my mind so much that I almost forgot that I was in a vision and the lines that differentiated Papa from me had now become obscure, at least in my eyes.

I was grieving for an uncle I had never met and suffering deep wounds in my heart from a plight that I had never really been through. My palms started heating up and the warmth worked its way from the tips of my fingers, through my arms and then to my chest; my muscles relaxed, and the letters around me disappeared and there I was, back in my world, lying on my bed.

20

After being in Papa's mind through those experiences it would be an understatement to say that I now understood him. It was more than just understanding him – I was now acquainted with his demons, his fears and his grief. So, although the vision was over and I was now back in my life, my experience would not leave me.

I wished I had simply read the letter or consulted with Mama Iyeniye before doing what I did and I wondered if, in time, I would get over the pain or find a way to separate Papa's past from my present. I thought often about the barbaric slavers and slave catchers, Itoro, Reverend Burke and little Emily.

The easiest thing for me to do was to slide into melancholy; it felt like the path of least resistance. I indulged those sullen feelings and it felt scary and unnerving. I worried that I would never be able to pull myself back out of it. Mama and Papa were worried about me because I had not left my room for days.

While I isolated myself in my room and fell deeper into that gloom, they argued about whether Papa should have given me the letter in the first place. I had no idea what was happening in the kingdom or with the peace treaty; I had never felt so out of touch with current events. And then it struck me: the only way out of this sorrowful place was to start fighting the sad feelings by going against the flow.

'I will swim upstream!' I told myself. I had been letting the flow of the current take me into this miserable place, so if I wanted to be happy again, I knew I had to fight for it. I started to challenge myself to think about the good feelings that I took from being in Papa's mind. Because if I had all his wounds and damnations, I probably also had all of his gifts and good fortune as well. *Let's face it*, I told myself, *Papa had a great deal of good fortune. He managed to stay alive and healthy throughout the forts and on the slave ship and then he was purchased by a uniquely good man and sent back home.* As I thought about his luck and his blessings, the heavy feelings that had been burdening me started to lift.

I needed to get out of the house though, so I decided to go for a walk. I did not know where I wanted to go, but I did know I needed to be somewhere else. I had been in my room for days now, so I went in search of a change in scenery. I hoped the change would help me see my situation from a brighter perspective.

'Elewa, where are you going? Did you read the letter?' Papa asked. 'Now I know it is a terrible story, but you cannot let it consume you.'

When I looked at him my heart ached; all I could see was the pain of his losses and the horrific experiences he had had. If I had read the letter, I could feel sympathy for him, but because I had been there with him, all I felt was torment and agony. I broke eye contact with him; when I looked into his eyes, I felt like I was being pulled back into that world.

'Papa, I cannot talk right now.' I walked right past him and left the house. I ended up at the beach on the pier, in the same place I had met Ojuro that morning that seemed so long ago. Oquie was there taking a break after finishing his first shift out on the water.

'Elewa, what are you doing out here?' He looked surprised to see me.

'I am just thinking.'

He came and sat down beside me. 'I was sorry to hear about Jo. He was a fine young man – you would have made a wonderful couple.' He wiped the sweat off his brow with the towel he had hanging around his neck.

'Oquie, what do you know about my father?' Oquie had been around a long time; maybe his perspective on my father could help me.

He scrunched his eyebrows together. 'Your father? Well, he is next in line to the chief, is he not?'

'No, I mean do you know anything about him other than what everyone else knows?'

'Well, he used to be a lot like Jo – when he was younger, that is . . .'

'Really, how so?' I could see how that was possible, but I had never really thought about Ojuro and Papa in that way.

'Well, he was troubled, acted as if he had a point to prove, especially after his brother went missing, but he was special, highly favoured, you know?'

'Not really. Why do you think he was special?'

'Well, it is not often that a common farm boy makes their way up to be second-in-command to the chief and he just seems to be one of the lucky ones.'

'What about all the bad luck, like the difficulties he's faced?'

'Well, that is the measure of a man, is it not? How he fares after he has faced hardship. After all he's been through, your father has found a way to come out on top – if you ask me, that is special.' He had a point, and deep down I knew how special Papa was, I just needed to take a step back from the situation for a moment. I needed to find out what I already knew, but I had to hear it from someone else, someone outside my mind.

'Yes, it is; thank you, Oquie.' He ruffled my hair, got up and started to prepare his boat to go out on his second shift.

Oquie was right, Papa had come out on top despite all his scarring experiences and if Papa had it in him, then I had it in me as well. I was fortunate and gifted just like Papa, and he and I would both experience adversity, but we would overcome it, because there were more important things in the world than our pain.

~

After my talk with Oquie I decided to go and visit Mama Iyeniye. I wanted to tell her that I had finally made my mind up and was ready to go to the future. I went back home and started to pack a bag. *What do you pack when you are visiting the future?*

Then Mama came to join me.

'Elewa, is everything well with you? You have spent the last week in your room and now you are packing a bag, what is going on?' she probed.

'All is well, Mama, it was just sad reading about Papa's experiences, that is all.' I did not have time for a heart-to-heart. I had waited long enough to make this journey and now that I knew exactly what I needed to do, I just wanted to get on and do it.

'I knew he should not have given you that letter yet!'

'Mama, I am glad I know now. I asked Papa about his past and he told me what he could and then gave me the letter to fill in the blanks. I am glad I read the letter. I have got to go now though, I am visiting Omolara.' I had to lie; if I said I was visiting Mama Iyeniye I think she would have worried even more, but with Omolara, she knew I would be safe.

I continued to pack my belongings as a great many thoughts and questions spun around in my head.

I sat on my bed, feeling butterflies. I heard Mama in the kitchen, I think she was making breakfast. Papa had already left for the day. The past week while I was isolating in my room I heard Mama persuading Papa to forgive Chief Babatunde and he did. I think he would have forgiven him without the pressure from Mama, but even so, I was glad that they had sorted out their differences.

I had heard nothing about Uncle Kwame in weeks, but I assumed that since Papa had forgiven the chief, he would more than likely forgive Uncle Kwame as well. Fumi and Komi were already in the backyard playing a game that seemed to involve water; I heard splashing and spraying sounds, then Fumi's distinct high-pitched laughter followed by Komi's shrieks.

'You got me wet!' he cried. It seemed he had underestimated Fumi once again.

Sessie was in the kitchen talking to Mama about her plans for becoming a junior tribal envoy.

I tucked a note into the pocket of Papa's favourite robe, the one he always put on in the evening. I folded it along with the letter that he gave me. I knew that Papa would not put on that robe for at least another seven hours, so this would, hopefully, give me enough time to get away undetected.

The note I left explained everything I planned on doing, and once he and Mama had read it, I guessed they would probably think I was out of my mind and come to look for me. I hated to do that to my family. But I knew that I had some control over my Yeseni now, at least a great deal more than when I first discovered it, so I was hopeful that once I arrived in the future, I could get a message to them in some way. A message that would give them peace of mind about my safety.

I picked up my bag, took a deep breath in, ran downstairs, and headed through the front door. I did it! Now I was finally free, out on the road, awaiting my new adventure in the future. *Do not look back*, a voice in my mind said, so I kept my head firmly forward, keen to learn what the future would bring.

～

As I walked the well-trodden path to Mama Iyeniye's house, I began think about how important perspective is, and that even a hug in reverse could be described as someone taking their embrace away from you: the same action but just viewed in a different way. I visualised the white men of the sea coming to our shores and taking back their guns then giving the gold back to the chiefs; I visualised them unchaining all the slaves they had caught and letting them out of the dungeons on the coast.

I hoped I would be doing the same sort of thing now, but instead of just imagining it in reverse, if I was successful, I would be changing it altogether.

When I finally arrived at Mama Iyeniye's house, she was already standing at the door.

'I am ready to go now,' I said, as I approached her quarters. I was slightly out of breath; I had to cut through an uphill path to get to that side of the estate. The only other choice was to go through the main entrance, and if I did that,

I would have to face Ojuro's parents. If I was still hurt over Jo, I could hardly imagine how they felt.

Mama Iyeniye smiled. 'Brave young woman!' she responded without an ounce of worry in her voice or doubt in her eyes.

'Well, we had better not waste any time. I only have a few hours to spare – after that I think Mama and Papa will start worrying about me.' I was anxious to get going; I did not want to risk anyone finding my note before Papa got home.

Mama Iyeniye quickly grabbed a bag that looked like it was full to the brim of strange contraptions, snatched her crocheted shawl from the back of her old wooden chair and then scanned the room for something. After a few seconds her eyes fixed on a brown wide brimmed hat, which she grasped, plonked on her head, and then hurried out the door.

◈

We were finally at the banks of the river. I looked out over our land and in the distance, I could see the ocean. I wondered if there were any lost ancient worlds underneath its waves, like I had heard of in stories from the elders.

What if something goes wrong and I travel too far in the future or past? Could I end up underwater in a lost world too? I had to gather my thoughts; it helped me to put things into perspective. *A few hundred years, in the grand scheme of things, is not very long at all,* I thought.

'What is on your mind?' Mama Iyeniye asked.

'Rivers and oceans, time and distance,' I replied.

'Child, if you no longer wish to do this, there is no obligation. It is your decision.'

There it was, my way out, my opportunity to say 'forget about the past, forget about the future' and just stay in my present. But I had already made up my mind: I could not take the easy way out. The time I had spent in Papa's mind would stay with me forever; I had experienced what being a slave was like, first-hand. 'It was not me, it was Papa!' I mumbled.

'Well? What do you say, child?'

'I have made up my mind, I am going!' I replied, in as firm a voice as I could muster.

'There is something we need to talk about before you make your final decision.' She looked across at me with immense intensity. *Perhaps my tone did not fool her.* I fretted.

'I have not been entirely honest with you, Elewa.' My breath grew rapid and shallow as those words left her mouth for my ears.

'What do you mean?' *Has she deceived me – was this all a lie? The possibility of me being able to physically travel to another time?*

'Do you remember when I told you that Mama Tiiandas and I got stuck in this time and that we might have been able to make it back if we tried to come back individually?'

'Yes, you said you just did not want to risk trying to go back alone in case one of you made it, but the other got stuck in the past.'

'Indeed. Well, there was more to that story. As the years went on, Mama Tiiandas and I discovered that we probably would have been able to come back together had we not stayed in the past so long.'

'How did you find that out?'

'By copious trial and error,' she chuckled ruefully, then went on to tell me that Mama Tiiandas was so doggedly determined to find out what went wrong that she decided they would jump back and forth through time until they worked out the exact laws governing their time travel.

'We learned that we could not stay in one period of time for too long without getting stuck.'

'So how long is too long?'

'The longest we were ever able to stay without getting stuck was forty-eight hours, any time – even a second after that amount of time meant we always got stuck.'

'So you are saying I only have two days?'

'No, no, no, no, you have to listen to me now, Elewa – you do not have two days, you have forty-eight hours. They are quite different . . .'

'How so?'

'Two days does not always equal forty-eight hours, and this could be the difference between you being able to see your family again or not. You must pay attention. If you arrive at night, forty-eight hours could cover three days. My point is that you must make sure you keep your eye on the time. My four-times great niece Scyra will have a device that you can use to count the hours, but you need to count the time from when you first arrive to when she meets you, and after that you need to keep a close eye on the time through-out your stay.'

I remembered when Papa had first taught me to measure time the Idanbule way, by facing the sun and counting the number of fingers it took to reach the sun from the horizon.

'Every finger counts for about an hour, so half a finger is . . .'

'Thirty minutes.' I had caught on quickly.

'You have it!' Papa had declared. I could not have been much older than five at the time.

'Very well. I had hoped I would have a little longer than forty-eight hours, but I still want to go. What do I need to do?' I asked Mama Iyeniye.

'It is like going into a vision, only this time you must make a jump, in your mind. You need to tell Yeseni exactly what you want to do, clearly, over and over again, and then when you feel like something is happening, that is when you must jump, without any apprehension.' It sounded too simple. And what about that bag full of contraptions that she had brought with her?

'Very well, but what about all the things you brought with you? In that bag, I mean. Do I need to use any of those?' I said in disbelief.

She laid all the items that she had brought with her on the ground in front of her. One was a large golden stone that looked like it had a butterfly, or a moth, captured inside of it; she said it was made from the sap of an ancient tree and that it would bring me a sense of calm when I found it hard to find it within myself. Another was a piece of hand-woven cloth in the Oleba colours. It was embroidered and in the centre was the symbol for bravery and fortitude. The rest of the items were for Mama Iyeniye's four-times great niece, Scyra. There was a letter, a spear, and a bow and arrow that our warriors fight with. There was also a drawing of Mama Iyeniye, which was striking and eerily convincing; it looked like she had found a magical way to capture her face and fix it to the piece of paper. And lastly there was a map of our land, with points of interest marked out in a key column to the left-hand side. At first, I had assumed that one of those objects would be helping me to make the journey but after going through them one by one, I realised that, as fascinating as they all were, they were just gifts – this momentous undertaking would be entirely up to me and my Yeseni.

'Thank you, Mama Iyeniye ...' I thought it graceful to thank her for the gifts that she had given me, but I was still concerned about how or if I was going to be able to actually make the journey. '. . . but what if I . . .'

'The time for doubt has long passed.' Her voice had deepened, as if she was channelling a greater force. 'Come, hold my hand, child.' Her eyes were closed as she reached her fingers in my direction. I quickly gathered all the items and placed them back into the bag. I wrapped the bag around my torso and hurried over to her. As soon as I joined hands with her, I felt a power more immense than I had ever felt before. I looked at her and her eyes were still shut so I closed mine too.

'Yeseni imcuba, Yeseni imcuba, Yeseni imcuba,' she chanted. With each repetition the power and connection grew stronger, as it flowed through my veins.

I joined in. 'Yeseni imcuba, Yeseni imcuba.' I continued to repeat it while Mama Iyeniye spoke directly to Yeseni.

'Yeseni we are grateful for your gift of knowledge. Now Elewa wishes to use your gift to make right a most heinous wrong. She will need to travel to the future to gain more knowledge so that she can change the past for the good of humanity. We humbly ask that you allow her safe passage through time so that she can undertake this task and then her safe return.' She repeated the same sentence, almost five times over, and as the kaleidoscope started to form within my mind, it felt right to cease chanting.

I started to focus on what I wanted Yeseni to do for me, in the plainest words that I could find. *Take me to Scyra, take me to her time.* I asked, over and over again, and at the point where I would normally get a vision there was just a pure white path. At that point, I visualised taking a huge leap, a jump way beyond my potential, like the one that Fumi had finally made when I caught her playing Tak Tak alone that day. I kept repeating the same sentence until everything that was white turned to black, like when you first close your eyes to go to sleep. I opened my eyes and there I was, in a gigantic grey maze.

I had finally made it. I was in the future.

21

I gasped desperately for air, standing there confounded in that mystifying world. There were metal machines that moved at speeds I had never witnessed in my life; they carried people and travelled three, maybe four times faster than any cheetah I had ever seen.

That world was mostly grey in colour: the ground, the walls, the buildings were all grey, or different shades of it. I could see a few sectioned-off green areas with perfectly manicured crisp blades of grass, uniform trees and elegant flower beds.

There were gigantic shiny buildings, of varying shapes and sizes – some square, some pointed, some circular – and they penetrated the sky and reflected the clouds around them. What did it take to construct such objects?

There were people, hundreds of them, coming in and out of those strange buildings, talking to small boxes that they pressed up against their faces. Had they all gone mad? The people were wearing the strangest garb I had ever seen. They seemed very serious but when they looked at me, they frowned as if I was an obscure object.

In this land there were people of all colours, heights and sizes, seemingly living and working together. Were they all one tribe?

I looked up to the sky and suddenly felt a beautiful sense

of calm and freedom from this grey maze. The sky, the clouds, they were the same, the same as they were back home. For a moment I had peace until I brought my head back down and then it hit me, from the bottom of my stomach to the top of my neck and finally through my mouth, everything that I had eaten the night before. I fell to my knees, panting, hands palm down on the floor, and then I remembered.

'The time, the sun . . .' I groaned, lifting my head back up and trying to rise and face it like Papa had shown me all those years ago but now, for some reason, I just could not seem to find my balance. I pitifully collapsed back to my knees, then reached my left hand out in front of me while on all fours and raised my head again to find the horizon. All around me, the buildings rose so high that I could not find it. Panic rose in me as I remained on all fours looking frantically for a gap between those grey towers. How could I measure the time if there was no horizon? Dropping my arm and head back towards the ground, I was grateful to take the weight off the rest of my limbs, when in front of me I noticed the light had, all of a sudden, dimmed. Two legs covered in a grey cloth appeared before my eyes.

'Elewa?' I lifted my head up and saw a lady that looked like she came from the Okena tribe, but she was dressed like the rest of this tribe, in that strange cloth. She had bent down and was staring at me, half smiling while shaking her head.

'Yes.' I sat up and wiped my mouth with my sleeve. 'Are you Scyra?' I rolled my sleeve up, embarrassed by my vulnerable state.

'Indeed, I am she,' her tone was perky, 'come on.' She leaned down and took my hand to lift me up from the ground. 'Let's get you cleaned up.'

'I am sorry, I do not know what came over me. I do not

normally get sick like this.' I tried to explain my condition, but the truth was, I did not understand it myself. What I mean to say is, I understood myself, but I did not understand myself in this context, within this world, and neither, it seemed, did my body.

I had one arm wrapped around Scyra's shoulder as she helped support me while she guided me to where we were going. I still felt so weak and sick, but I also felt ashamed of the impression I was giving to Scyra. 'I mean to say I have only ever vomited once before and that was when Fumi . . .' I was going to tell her the story about the only other time I had ever vomited, when Fumi picked unripe berries and served it to me as a surprise—

'Elewa, this is normal,' she asserted. 'You have just travelled hundreds of years into the future. I keep telling them that it is better to meet travellers from the past in more rural settings the first time, but they never listen to me.' *Wait, what?*

'So you mean there have been others? And what do you mean, you keep telling "them" – who are "they"?'

'There have been a few, well, that I know of anyway. But you must be hungry – let's get you fed, and then I promise I will catch you up on everything.'

The journey to Scyra's home was confusing and unnerving to me; the sounds alone made me feel physically unsteady. One sound in particular made me jolt whenever it came, and it came often, in rhythmic blasts. In my time, a sound like this would indicate war, but in this world, it was like people did not even hear it. I think it came from the moving machines, but I could not work out how they made the sound or what it meant.

Then there were the lights, though they did not come from the sun, or through fire. These people had found a way to create light and they used it everywhere. Some of it came through large square or rectangular boards that were placed at very great heights. These boards exhibited intense, captivating pictures with multi-coloured lights instead of paint.

There were lights on the moving machines that carried people. There were lights penetrating through the windows of all the buildings; lights came from the little flat boxes that people carried around and pressed against their cheeks. Lights seemed to come from everywhere.

And the smell: this world smelt like animal fat that had been burning for days. Yet it was not the smell that astonished me; it was more the lack of smells. The earth, the soil, the ground – that smell had vanished. The grass, the trees, the plants – that smell was also non-existent. And the air, it felt thick and heavy; the longer I spent there the more trapped I felt.

At every junction I had a million questions. I felt like a child again, wanting to know what the coloured lines on the road meant, what the words on the moving machines were, how many tribes were in this land and who was the chief. I decided to keep quiet until we got to Scyra's house. I did not want to open my mouth again in case I threw up. If I did, this time it would be all over Scyra, so I was sure to keep my mouth firmly shut.

'We're nearly there, Elewa,' she assured me. I smiled and nodded back at her. If we did not get there soon, I was sure to pass out, so I tried to distract myself by thinking about other things.

∽

After walking for what felt like an age, we finally arrived at Scyra's house. As we approached her huge building, I wondered why one person would need such an enormous house, then other people started seeping in and out of the building through what appeared to be a revolving door. *How odd*, I thought. *Either all these people work for Scyra, or she does not live here alone.* I was so exhausted by the time we reached her quarters that all I wanted to do was sleep.

'Would you like something to eat?'

'I think I am more tired than hungry actually, Scyra.'

'Are you sure? I tried to get something that's similar to the fish stew you have back home. I cannot promise you that it's as good, but I like it.' I could not possibly risk eating their food just now and vomiting in her beautiful home. I pushed the embarrassing thought out of my mind.

'The time!' I remembered Mama Iyeniye's warning. 'How long have I been here? I only have forty-eight hours, or I could get stuck here.' I rushed towards the window in her living room.

'Elewa, slow down, it's okay.'

I had a clear view of the sun through Scyra's sparkly windows, they were like walls of glass. The sun was now fairly low in the sky so I knelt down and lifted my arm towards the window, turned my palm inwards, then lined up my smallest finger with the horizon. 'I think it has already been perhaps two hours!'

Scyra followed close behind me then dashed over to help me back up to my feet.

'Don't worry.' She flipped out a small black portable machine that had a long blue string attached to both ends.

'What is that?'

'It's a digital timer . . .' She pressed a red circular button on the face of the device then all of a sudden, numbers started racing upwards on its small rectangular screen.

'It's counting the time passing. Now that we know around two hours have already passed, we'll make sure you're ready to go back way before it reaches forty-six hours.' I felt a small sense of relief, knowing that this device would now be monitoring the time for me, so I started to relax a bit and take in my surroundings.

Scyra's home was pleasant and immensely comfortable, from the soft padded piles of thick woven floor coverings to the panoramic views from the glistening glass walls.

'Come, I'll show you your room,' she said, gently guiding me to another room within her quarters. She set the machine down on a cabinet then sat next to the bed. 'We'll leave it running here. That way we'll always know how long you have left.'

'That is one less thing to worry about, thank you!'

'This will be your bed.' I climbed on to the bed and revelled in how soft it was. *This is something they have definitely got right, in this time.*

'I bought some clothes that you can wear while you're here, I've put them in the cabinet. If you don't like any of them, don't worry, I can just return them.' *How do you buy someone clothes without taking their measurements?* I was curious to see what she had picked out for me.

As soon as she said her goodnights and disappeared, I turned the digital timer around on its face then melted into a fabric case on the bed that was stuffed with soft materials. Then I drifted asleep almost instantly. Everything on my mind would be tomorrow's issue; all would be dealt with in the morning.

∼

When I woke up my eyes were drawn to the one thing that was moving in the room. It was some type of toy animal; its paw kept moving, back and forth. Scyra came in to offer me some tea.

'What is that?' I asked.

'Oh, this?' She turned towards the ornament, and I nodded. 'It's a maneki-neko, or a lucky cat.' I stared at her blankly. 'It's supposed to bring you good fortune – it's Japanese.' I knew that word, 'Japanese'. Japan was one of the places that Mama Iyeniye had shown me on her map.

'Japan, that is next to Korea in . . .' I paused for a moment: *It began with an A*. Finally, I thought I had it. '. . . Asia, is it not?' None of this had anything to do with what I was there for, but I think I just needed to test my brain. Make sure that time travel had not messed with my memory and comprehension in any way.

'Yes, that's right!' she responded reassuringly.

'So how do you get its paw to keep moving like that?' I asked, unsure why I had become so fascinated with this little toy.

'It's solar powered, powered by the sun,' she replied, as if it was an everyday method that everyone knew.

'Interesting . . .' *What strange trinkets.*

Scyra advised me that her quarters were typically called a flat. Hers was a small space in a large glass building, but you could get them as large spaces in small brick buildings or medium spaces in small glass buildings or a whole host of variations. As you walked inside there was a lobby and then we took some kind of hoisting machine called a lift, which elevated us to Scyra's floor. Once you got to Scyra's floor there seemed to be hundreds of doors with different numbers on them and each living space was numbered and belonged to a different person. Scyra's was number 54.

'Elewa, there are going to be a lot of things that are strange and obscure to you, and it's okay. All I ask is that you keep an open mind and ask as many questions as you like. I'm here for you, okay? Like a sister slash best friend.' She sat on the bed and draped her arm around my shoulder.

'You remind me of Mama Iyeniye,' I smiled.

'Let's get you some breakfast.' She stood and beckoned me towards the kitchen, like the little Japanese toy.

I had had the best night's sleep in a long time in Scyra's house. She told me that the bed I slept on was made of a material called memory foam; I could have lain on it all day, in fact I found myself looking forward to the night, when I would get to curl up on that beautiful invention once again.

For breakfast I tried some of the fish stew that she had prepared for me the night before. It was not bad, but it was not the same as back home.

Scyra was the same height as me and had the same eyes and nose as Mama Iyeniye; she told me that she was related to Mama Iyeniye on her mother's side of the family. Then she told me how she had come to connect with Mama Iyeniye as a teenager.

It all started with her finding an old picture in her parents' attic. The picture was of two young girls; later she would find out that the girls were Mama Iyeniye and Mama Tiiandas. She said she did not know why, but whenever she saw the picture, it was like they were crying out to her, screaming almost. At first, she was frightened of them because of how they made her feel every time she was around them, but her fear turned into fascination as she got older, and she became more curious, until one day she picked the picture up. When she held them in her palms and focused on them, the cries became more coherent; she found out that those young girls, Mama Iyeniye and Mama Tiiandas, were stuck in the past.

She heard their long conversations that revolved around their tireless attempts to try and return to their correct time together.

'It was like listening to clips from a film with a frozen visual,' she recalled. She asked her parents who the girls in the picture were, and her mother said that her grandfather used to tell her a story about two young girls on his mother's side that went out to play and never came back. Although Scyra's mother did not know for sure, she thought that the picture could be of those girls. After that, Scyra kept the picture close to her pillow, and that was when Mama Iyeniye would visit her, in her sleep at first. She built a relationship with her that way and told her exactly what happened that day when she and Mama Tiiandas went missing. She confirmed that she and Mama Tiiandas were the girls in the picture, and she told her all about her gift, Yeseni; she explained to her how to use and grow her powers. After that, Scyra was able to connect with Mama Iyeniye any time that she summoned her, and she said that more recently, Mama Iyeniye had started to tell her about me, and my mission.

After breakfast I told Scyra all about Mama and Papa, Sessie, Fumi and Komi and all about my life back home. I handed her the items that Mama Iyeniye had sent for her, and I had never seen a smile so bright over a simple spear, but Scyra told me that items like these, in such good condition, were priceless in her time, because there were not many left. She wrapped them in a silk cloth and stored it away in a cupboard.

Finally, I told her more about my mission, my terrifying visions on the slave ship and how I had managed to find out what may have started it, or at least prompted the white man's interest in our land which ended up with the trading of human beings, our people.

'If we could just get a message to King Yemi and warn him about making the journey to the foreign land.'

'Wait, who is King Yemi?'

'Sorry, King Yemi was the man in the first visions I received; I think he was responsible for drawing the wrong attention to our land.'

'What makes you think that?'

'Well in my vision he travelled to foreign lands flaunting his riches. Not only did that signal to foreigners that our land was rich, it encouraged them to visit us and trade their goods with us for gold and other precious items, and once they were already trading with us, that is when they saw an opportunity to trade not only gold, but human lives as well.'

'Right so you think that if you warn King Yemi about this it will stop the transatlantic slave trade from taking place?' She seemed unconvinced. 'I mean surely if it wasn't King Yemi it would be some other monarch that followed him?'

I must not have done a very good job of explaining my visions to her. I had not mentioned my experience with Papa's vision yet.

'Well, I was thinking we could warn him off and encourage him to put laws in place to prohibit the trade of people in Africa. What do you think?'

She gave me a sceptical look and then walked over to the contraption she used to boil water for tea; a kettle, I think.

'I don't know, Elewa, let me think about it okay?' She fiddled with a sparkly ring on her finger while dolefully gazing down at it. I grew frustrated with her; it felt as if she did not realise the magnitude of the situation. I was surprised that Mama Iyeniye put me in touch with someone who would be so on the fence.

'I could give him the visions that I had, those on the slave ship and in the new land. Maybe they could come to him in a dream or something,' I suggested, hoping that if she knew I had put some thought into it she would be more likely to agree.

'Your idea could change the past or the future as we know it entirely.'

'This world could be a true paradise if this dreadful atrocity had never taken place.'

'But there were hundreds, if not thousands of crimes against humanity well before the Maangamizi, or the transatlantic slave trade as you call it, and there have been many since.'

'Maangamizi, what is that? Look, Scyra, we must start somewhere. Why not start with something you have the power to change?'

'It's a Swahili word, meaning a kind of holocaust. It's what people call the transatlantic slave trade now. The Maangamizi means the intentional and immoral crimes of genocide and ecocide in the continuum of chattel, colonial and neo-colonial forms of enslavement. The word *trade* is no longer acceptable to use because there was no "trade". It was a genocide amongst other things.'

'I see,' I said, though I did not quite understand all the words she used. My mouth dried up and my palms were wet and clammy. I rubbed them against my clothes; how could I have used such a word that clearly did not match what actually happened? The word 'trade' implies a benign exchange between two agreeable parties, and this was certainly not the case with the mass kidnapping and unspeakable cruelty taking place now in my time.

'Of course, you are right,' I continued. 'Maangamizi? It seems entirely more appropriate than *slave trade*. But no matter what we call it, we can still change it, perhaps stop it from ever happening.'

'But that could mean that no one that either of us knows and loves now would exist. Or that my mother never met my father, they never got married and so maybe I wouldn't exist either!' she exclaimed. I could not understand what she thought my visit would be about if not to change an event in time, which would obviously involve all the risks she mentioned.

'Scyra, I have jeopardised the peace of my kingdom and risked never seeing my family again to make this change in history. I understand if you cannot help me do it, but if you will not help, I will have to do it myself.' I wondered why Mama Iyeniye had not explained to Scyra what my intentions were.

'I'm not saying I will not help, Elewa, I just need some time to figure out what our options are, that's all.'

'I do not understand – did Mama Iyeniye not explain to you what I intended to do?'

'She said that you needed to find out what life was like for the descendants of the people from the 1640 Maangamizi and that you may need some help with your Yeseni.'

'Oh, well that explains everything then!' I could not help my irritation and confusion coming out in my tone of voice.

'What do you mean? You know, Elewa, I don't think it will be a bad thing to find out what life is like for the descendants of the survivors of the 1640 Maangamizi – it might change your mind about changing the past.'

'Why? Do they live in some kind of paradise now?'

'Not quite, but there's been so much ingenuity from the great people that came about through the struggle. Like Olaudah Equiano, Frederick Douglass, Sojourner Truth and Harriet Tubman, just to name a few.'

'Who are all those people?' I asked. I had never heard those names.

'They are all people who were kidnapped from Africa and who suffered and fought for the abolition of slavery, for the humanity and equality of our people. They were heroic men and women,' she replied, as though I ought to know.

'But, Scyra, if they had not had to fight that atrocity, they might have been even greater and more heroic. Who knows what they might have achieved in their own lands for their own people?'

'I hear you, Elewa, but like you said, you've had time to think about it, now all I'm asking of you is that I have the same courtesy.'

'Fine, take your time!' I worried about exactly how much time she would need to take. I had less than forty-eight hours and I did not want to get stuck in their time. If she did not come around soon, I would have to think seriously about taking it into my own hands; after all, my Yeseni was probably stronger than Mama Iyeniye knew. I took a deep breath in and tried to be patient with Scyra.

'Scyra, you know I have less than forty-eight hours. I do not think I will have the time that you need.'

'Why don't you let me take you around so you can see for yourself? You can meet the descendants of the 1640 Maangamizi before you decide to wipe them out completely!'

'Scyra, I do not want to wipe anybody out, I just want to right a terrible wrong from the past.'

'I know, Elewa, but you're here in the future, in *my* present now, okay?'

I nodded reluctantly.

'Very well, but only if you agree to one thing. I need you to view the visions that I have had.' I wanted her to witness

213

everything that I had seen so that she would see the pain, the brutality and the fear that I had experienced. And so that she could fully understand my motivation in possibly risking everything as we knew it, to erase this event from history.

'Deal!' she proclaimed as she shook my hand. 'But you're in my world now. First we do it my way, then I'll view your visions, okay?'

That was what I had in mind anyway. The visions or experiences I wanted to show her were not easy to view and not even I was ready to view them again in that moment.

'Indeed, that sounds like a plan!' *Finally, we agree on something!*

22

Scyra told me that the city she lived in was called London. We stood on a platform with a fence around it that she called a balcony, looking down on a long, murky body of water called the River Thames.

'At half tide, when the water speeds up, if you lean out onto the railings it feels like you're on a cruise ship.' Scyra stretched both arms out and proudly pushed her chest forward, then meditatively closed her eyes. Her features softened and she radiated pure joy as the rays from the sun bounced off her gleaming cheeks. I suddenly felt an aggressive yank in the bottom of my stomach so I wrapped my arms around the area, squeezing firmly, in the hope that the pressure would lessen the pain. The knot gradually unravelled, and the pain finally started to subside, but watching her in that meditative state made me realise that no matter what was happening in her world on the outside, she had created an inner peace, a deep and blessed, almost sacred place within.

When she opened her eyes and noticed I was in pain she rushed up to tend to me. 'What's wrong, Elewa?'

'I think it is just a mild stomach pain, it is going now.' I unwrapped my arms from around my waist so that she would not panic, then she sat back down with her elbow on the table, propped up by her chin in palm. She stared back at me as if I was the most obscure spectacle she had ever seen, so I felt compelled to say something, anything, on my mind. The truth was, seeing her so contented made me feel even more guilty for what I planned to do, but I could not say that.

'I think I was just a little . . . taken aback by your ritual; it is just so beautiful, that is all!'

She flashed me a smile then switched her gaze across the water. 'What, me pretending to be on a fancy cruise ship on my balcony?'

I hesitatingly nodded. Though I knew what a *ship* was, I wondered what a *fancy cruise* meant.

'Why is it so muddy though?' I stared back out at the river.

'I dunno, they say it's from the silt that runs off it. Apparently around ninety per cent of London's drinking water comes from this river.' I subtly pushed away the fresh cup of tea she had made me and thought about the shiny pebbles at the wetland of the Wiri. Would I ever see them again?

She walked towards the corner edge of the railings, then with her back towards me, she discreetly extended her left arm out in front of her. I wondered what she was peering down at, so I tacitly got up and crept over to find her gazing down at that shiny ring on her finger again.

'Careful or it will fall in!' She jumped.

'Christ, you gave me a fright!' she squealed.

'Did someone special give that to you?' I wondered why she was being so secretive about it.

'What?' She quickly moved her hand towards her hip, but I grabbed it just before it got there and lifted it back up to inspect the ring. It was a very sparkly ring. I had never seen anything like it; it was silver and had around a dozen shiny stones set into the band.

'Oh this, well yeah. It's an engagement ring.'

'You are betrothed then?'

'Well yeah, sort of, but we just say "engaged".'

'How did your parents find him?' She looked back at me blankly. 'Your intended?'

'Well, they didn't; these days it's mostly up to the individual to find his or her own partner, although some cultures do still observe arranged marriages.'

'That must be difficult. Where would you start? How would you know if his family were honourable or if he could even afford a wife?'

She laughed and shook her head as if what I was saying was completely out of this world.

'Well, I met Henry at a party . . .'

I could see that she was deeply excited, in love and looking forward to a lifetime with this man.

'So, when is your marriage ceremony?'

I got that tight feeling in my stomach again but this time I tried to ignore it.

'It's this summer!' I dropped my head to the ground and looked back up at her with stoic eyes.

'I am sorry, Scyra, I . . .'

I now understood why she was hiding the ring from me: once she told me about it, the reality would set in that she may never marry Henry.

'No, it's okay . . . I understand.' She exhaled deeply. I grabbed both of her hands and brought them into my chest.

'This thing, it is bigger than you and me. It is for the greater good of the world. You understand, do you not?' I released her hands, and she stepped back and nervously smiled.

'All I ask is that you give me the time I need to come around.' Though I hoped with all my heart that she would come around, whether she did or did not, I knew that I had a promise to deliver to the world, but the longer I spent in the future the harder it was to imagine risking the lives of every single one of the people I met.

Energy does not die, it just changes form, a voice inside my head assured me.

'An agreement is an agreement, but time is running out!' I warned.

∼

Scyra worked at what was called an office as a Geographical Information Systems Analyst.

'I develop systems to address environmental, exploration and land mining issues,' she explained.

'So, what is it that you actually do then?'

'I make maps. Well at the moment that's the majority of my workload, but I also do spatial analysis, data collection and asset management consulting.' Scyra showed me maps of my village back home. I felt as though I was being interrogated; she asked me hundreds of very specific questions about the location of landmarks, mountains streams and rivers, all for what she described as her 'passion project'.

Scyra took me to one of their 'supermarkets', which stocked endless supplies of produce, meats and grains amongst a multitude of supplementary peculiar commodities.

'What have you not thought of in this time?' I exclaimed. You could grab anything you liked as long as you had a little rectangular card, which you had to tap on a strange machine before you left the store. Any item you collected in your 'trolley' was yours.

I could see why this shop was referred to as a super market: everything was so sleek and enticing, from the gigantic glass doors to the polished floors. A part of me was thrilled and excited to be there but another part wanted to curl up into a ball on the floor until all the madness disappeared.

'So do you think you might stay then?' Scyra enquired.

I neither responded nor made eye contact with her. The truth was, I was starting to enjoy life in her time, and once I admitted that to myself, a sickening feeling emerged at the back of my throat.

'*Qui tacet consentire videtur*,' she said.

'Is that English?'

'No, it's Latin. It means "silence equals consent or he who is silent seems to consent".'

'Oh, well no, I just wonder is it really all as good as it seems here?'

She shrugged her shoulders and linked her arm through mine.

~

'It won't stop if you stare at it!' Scyra teased me as I stared at the time counter. 'Elewa, I have to run an errand for my mum. I wouldn't want to drag you along. You can rest here for a while, and I promise I'll be back in a few minutes, okay?'

'If that is what you want,' I answered nervously.

She put two thumbs up towards the ceiling, grabbed her bag and coat and headed out the door. 'Do not leave the flat!' she called.

I wandered frivolously around her quarters for a while. I knelt down in front of the flat black box that stood upright on a low table, and ran my fingers along the edges looking for a way to open it. There was nothing obvious or protruding but when I got to the underside of it, I finally felt a button, so I pushed it in and then the most alarming thing happened.

A man that looked like he came from my tribe, addressed me through the box, right there in Scyra's room.

'At 0800 hours station time the Romulan Empire formally declared war against the Dominion.'* I jumped backwards towards the sofa and my heart sank; I could not believe I had come this far, only to end up back at the cusp of another war. I tried to open my mouth and say something, but nothing came out.

'They have already struck fifteen bases along the Cardassian border.' *So this must be the chief*, I thought. Finally, I mustered up the confidence to respond.

'What can I do to help? I can throw a spear at least twenty feet.' Perhaps he did not hear me; he kept talking over me, or maybe he just did not reply to unsolicited comments.

'So this is a huge victory. This may even be the turning point of the entire war.'

I ran to find the spear that Mama Iyeniye had sent for Scyra. 'I will be right back, wait there!' I shouted. I could not see it anywhere and when I got back, he was still talking.

'A guilty conscience is a small price to pay for the safety of the alpha quadrant . . .' Scyra came rushing through the door.

'Oh, you figured out how to turn the TV on, good for you; but you shouldn't sit so close, your eyes will go square.'

'What are you talking about? We must get ready! Your chief has spoken; war has started, Scyra. Where did you put the spear Mama Iyeniye sent for you?'

Scyra looked confused. She took one look at me, then another back at the box. She took a deep breath in, bit her

* Captain Sisko, 'In the Pale Moonlight', Episode 9, Season 6; *Star Trek: Deep Space Nine,* 1998

bottom lip, then covered her mouth with her hands. What on earth could she find amusing at a time like this?

'What is wrong?' I asked desperately.

She choked back a sound then exploded into laughter.

'Elewa, this isn't real, it's make-believe, just for entertainment.' My jaw dropped.

'A declaration of war for entertainment?'

She fell to her knees and laughed so hard that tears streamed down her face. *Even war is entertainment for these people.* I felt relieved, then embarrassed and finally angry.

'This could only be entertaining for people who have never experienced war.' I ran into my quarters, slammed the door shut as tears splashed down my face. Scyra followed me, sat beside me, and stroked my hair.

'It's okay, Elewa, I should have shown you how everything worked; I'm sorry, will you come back out?' I nodded reluctantly and followed her back into the living room.

'You should have seen your face!' She looked as if she was holding back another fit of laughter, but I flashed her a scowl, then looked back at the chief who appeared to have frozen in the middle of his speech.

'What is it called anyway?' I gestured towards the television screen.

'*Star Trek: Deep Space Nine*. It's my favourite show.'

~

After she had stopped laughing, Scyra showed me how the TV box could be changed to see many different things happening in different places and times. She showed me a gathering that was called *Question Time*, where people of many colours and tribes sat with a group of their leaders and asked them questions about what the leaders would do to make their lives better. There were many questions about what these people were paid for their work, and how difficult it was for some to afford a place to live. I had thought everyone here could go to the super market, but it seemed that many could not.

A woman who could have been an Oleba asked the leaders what they thought about a statue of a famous slave owner which had been torn down and thrown into a river.

'Isn't it time to apologise for the transatlantic slave trade?' she asked.

'Oh, that's all in the past!' a white woman on the stage replied. 'I think people are suffering here and now with fuel poverty, unemployment, low wages, insecure jobs. Slavery was awful but it was hundreds of years ago; we need to deal with the here and now.'

A brown woman with long dark hair turned angrily to her from another seat on the stage. 'I'm sorry, but W. E. B. Du Bois was right when he said the enslavement of 12.5 million Africans was "the sum of all villainies, the cause of all sorrow and the root of all prejudice."'

A man sitting next to her, white and spindly but with a reddening face, intervened:

'Look, slavery was obviously atrocious, but we can't keep looking back – at some point we have to look forward and stop living in the past.'

People in the audience tutted loudly and were clearly annoyed by his comment.

'I'm sorry,' he continued, undeterred, 'but nobody here ever knew anyone that was a slave , so how could this terrible event in the past, that happened hundreds of years ago, affect anyone here personally?'

A growl of discontent consumed the room and people

rolled their eyes in frustration, looking fed up and frankly exasperated.

'You really believe that nonsense?' the lady with the long dark hair chimed in.

'You really think two hundred years of free labour from over fifteen million people kidnapped from Africa would have no impact on their ancestors today?'

The spindly white man was getting more agitated. 'Fine, you may have been impacted, but why should my children have to pay the price for their ancestors' wrongs? My children are innocent, and I'm bringing them up to love all people no matter what colour they are. Is it really fair to punish them?'

'It's not about punishing your children, or anyone else's children.' A black man on the stage raised his voice over the rumbling displeasure of the audience. 'It's about seeking justice, reparations. Do you know that British taxpayers only just, in 2016, finished paying off the debt which the British government borrowed to compensate slave owners due to the abolition of slavery? And not a penny was paid to those enslaved!'

The audience erupted into a mixture of cheers and jeers.

'So, you can tell that the Maangamizi is still a very heated topic, Elewa,' said Scyra, turning to look at me. I was still staring at the box even after she had turned it off.

'At times it seems like this world is some kind of utopia, and then I hear a conversation like this.' I shook my head in confusion.

23

The television had made me restless. I wanted to get outside and walk and think about all I had heard.

'Not at this time of night, Elewa,' Scyra said firmly. 'It's not a good idea for women to go out in the dark.'

I wondered why she thought it was dark with so many lights everywhere in the windows and the streets.

'This world, it's not as safe and luxurious as it looks.' She paced up and down the room. 'My life is sort of privileged. Not everyone enjoys the freedom and safety I do – I have worked my butt off for where I am today. I certainly didn't grow up like this, but there is a lot of crime and struggle out there.'

'What do you mean?'

'I mean you could be hurt if you go out at night.'

I wondered why Scyra was so afraid of the world that afforded her such a comfortable lifestyle. Then I thought about the people who had low-paid jobs and had to live in bad homes.

'Of course, I am sorry. That was not very thoughtful of me! I did not know so many people were living in fuel poverty and in houses threatened by floodwater and with insecure jobs . . .'

'Wow, you really did take all that in from *Question Time*, didn't you? Well, yes, our time is not everything it seems. When you look closer, you start to see all the inequality.'

'Well, it has now been thirty hours. My time is running out, Scyra!'

I knew that I would have struggled to decide what to do if I came to the future and witnessed a kind of utopia, and when I first landed here, from the outside it did indeed look like one. People of all colours and beliefs were living together in one land with the absence of war. Yet when you scratched the surface, you found inequalities, injustices and discrimination. And most of it seemed to stem from the Maangamizi. It had not gone away, I realised; they had just gotten better at hiding it.

~

All those painful knots in the bottom of my stomach haunted me whenever I felt guilt about changing their world. 'A guilty conscience is a small price to pay for the safety of the Alpha Quadrant . . .' I kept hearing those words from the chief on Scyra's television box.

'He's the captain, actually. His name is Benjamin Sisko,' Scyra corrected me, after I asked her to replay that scene where *the chief* spoke about war.

He was right: my guilt at possibly disrupting Scyra's world was a small price to pay to save the lives of over 12 million people.

But it was hard because I could not bear to erase the hope and excitement that I saw in Scyra's eyes when she spoke about marrying Henry. Living in Scyra's world sometimes made you believe that everything was better now, and everyone had been fairly compensated, but I realised that was not true at all.

I thought about back home and I pictured the slave boats that we saw on the shore every day; we played Tak Tak while they loaded the ships. We heard the captives crying from the forts, but we kept our family safe and did not worry about the others. When I thought about it, I felt nauseous and my old friend guilt started to consume me once again. I tried to shake off the feeling, to stay hopeful and focus on my task. I felt that if we could get the message to King Yemi and he took the right actions, millions of lives could be saved.

Although it had been a fascinating experience, nothing I had seen on my journey convinced me that this future was worth the suffering of the past.

As the seconds and minutes went by, I started to feel more anxious and I realised I was ready to contact King Yemi.

'Scyra, it is time. I think I have honoured my part of our agreement. Now it is your turn.' She flung down her keys on the coffee table and sighed deeply.

'Fine, a deal's a deal!' She removed her bag from her torso, hung her coat up on the hooks behind the door then began removing the cushions from the sofa. I brought the dim lamp in from the bedroom, and waited for her in the middle of the circle. She took my hands and asked Yeseni to show her what I had seen. It was strange, different from when I experienced the visions alone. This felt like someone was sucking all the energy out of me. It felt like days, but after we had finished, just thirty minutes or so had passed. I felt faint, but I could see in her eyes something had changed. The blank spaces in her comprehension were coloured in and she knew what we had to do. We sat there and wept together.

I suggested that we attempt to reach King Yemi within the next hour. We needed to have all the evidence in place so that he would not simply disregard our contact as a bad dream. We started to get everything ready for our communication with him. Now we would finally see if history could be changed once and for all.

24

We sat there in the middle of the floor. We were ready to contact King Yemi, but now I had some doubts about the effectiveness of just simply sending him the visions.

I thought I should try and do what I did with Papa – visit their time through Ola's mind, King Yemi's servant. Ola was already apprehensive about King Yemi bringing his gold and wealth along, so he could be the perfect person to join forces with. I suggested it to Scyra, and she agreed, although she was not sure that she could do it.

'I'll give it my best,' she promised.

'We do not have long,' I worried.

My experience with Papa was different from the experience I wanted to attempt with Ola and King Yemi. I needed Ola to somehow allow me to act through him, whereas with Papa I experienced his world through his actions. We would need to do it in two stages. First, we would need to connect with Ola, and through him persuade King Yemi to do the right thing, and then we would need to send them both all the significant visions.

I explained all this to Scyra. 'Maybe Ola could give King Yemi the visions while you're joined with him,' she suggested.

'Yes, if persuading him alone does not cut it, that is an option.'

'Right, so shall we do it then?'

'Are you scared?' I asked. What I really wanted to say was: *I am scared!*

'I was, but now I have a strong feeling that we'll be fine!' I hoped that she was right. So much was at stake. If King Yemi listened and then the Maangamizi never happened, what would become of all the revolutionaries throughout time and what would become of us and our families?

'The only way we will find out what will happen is by taking action!'

I thought about the Oleba and Okena back home. I knew that what we were doing could also change the reality of life there. It could cause another war or, just as likely, mean that there was never any war in the first place. I went back to my vision of people going backwards, undoing the damage they had caused. I visualised the white men returning to their boats after taking back their guns and giving the gold and captives back to the chief. I smiled.

'Scyra, I want to thank you for joining me in this quest for peace, for sacrificing everything you know and love for this!'

'You don't have to thank me: this is the right thing to do!' She fiddled with her sparkling ring and her eyes filled up with tears. I held the back of her left hand in my palm and she held the back of my right hand in hers.

'I will lead, but I need you to follow. Focus on the vision you see and try to keep me connected,' I said.

Without Scyra there, reaching Ola would take a lot more effort; now that Scyra had seen both King Yemi and Ola from when I had shared all my visions with her, it would be easier for her to help me connect to him.

'If you can make a connection with anyone around King Yemi it would help, but do not worry if you cannot.'

Scyra told me that she had never attempted anything like this before, but she promised to try. If she could not come through, then she would just support me in the vison and help me keep the connection by staying focused in the circle.

'Yeseni, bring us to Ola and the wealthy man.' I used 'the wealthy man' term and not King Yemi because I wanted to reach King Yemi before his trip to the foreign land, and before I knew his full name. After I said it once, Scyra joined in with me and we both said it together, focusing intently on Ola's image.

Colourful particles suddenly started to float in the air, so real that it seemed like you could reach out and grab one. They reacted to my touch, as if they were actual living, sensory objects that cared about touch and attention. It was the first time I had physically seen the forces behind Yeseni behave in such a sentient kind of way. The kaleidoscope that I usually saw when I closed my eyes came to life, and it revolved all around us, twirling as we progressed deeper into the spell. My fingertips started changing temperature, but this time instead of cold, they were freezing. Such an extreme difference startled me and made me even more anxious about the part I hated the most: *If the temperature is worse, what will the muscle contractions feel like?* and before I could even indulge the fear, my body flipped backwards. I could not believe how extreme this experience felt. It was worse than any of the other times. I looked over at Scyra as she pulled herself back up and grabbed onto my hands again. The particles raced around so fast that we could no longer see the room, and when they disappeared, there I was, standing in front of King Yemi. I noticed that I had a silver plate in my hands; I brought it up towards *my* face and Ola's face stared back at me.

'What are you doing, Ola?' King Yemi said, bewildered by my behaviour.

'I am just making sure that they are doing their jobs right and that there are no scratches or smudges on the silverware, Your Highness.'

Something does not feel right, Ola thought.

All is well, Ola. My name is Elewa. I am from the future. I need you to help me get a message to King Yemi.

'Did you hear that, Your Highness?'

'Hear what? What are you talking about, Ola?'

He will not hear me, Ola. Only you can hear me.

'Ola, perhaps you should go and take the weight off your feet for a moment? You look a little tired,' the king suggested.

See, I told you – he cannot hear me. I know this must be alarming but the sooner you cooperate with me, the sooner I will be out of your mind. You are going to feel a heavy pull, like a desire to fall asleep. When it comes, you must go with it. Do not fight it. I am going to take over for a while and then, once I have got my message to the king, I will leave you alone in peace.

'Are you crazy? Who are you?'

A man walking past Ola gave him a strange look and whispered to his colleague.

Ola, it is best if you just think your answers to me; if you talk out loud, people will think something is wrong with you.

Who are you? Why are you doing this to me?

I am not going to hurt you, Ola. As I said, my name is Elewa. I feel we already know each other. You came to me in a vision about a year ago – it was before I even knew that I had this gift: the Yeseni. After that vision, I found out that I had to warn the king of a terrible thing that will happen. And then it hit me: everything had come full circle and I was now back in the first vision I had ever received, but this time I was not a powerless onlooker. I was now an active participant and someone who had the power to effect change.

What is this 'terrible thing' you talk about?

Ola, I know you are concerned about the king travelling with all his gold, and you are right to be concerned. If the king does this, it is going to bring the wrong attention to our continent before we know how to control it. Ultimately over twelve million people will be captured and brought to the new world, where they will be dehumanised in slavery. They will be made to work for centuries, they will lose their language and their culture, and even after the dreadful slavery system is abolished, they will still suffer.

I hoped that was enough, but I suspected I would need to give him my visions so that he could fully understand.

That sounds awful, but you are talking about hundreds of years in the future. The king is concerned about next week.

I could not expect him not to push back at all; it was understandable that he was confused.

The king will also be affected two weeks from now. The man he is going to visit, Bilal, will betray him. Stay calm and seated – I am going to show you what happens.

Very well, if you say so. Thankfully Ola had started to calm down.

Another one of King Yemi's servants came and sat next to him.

'Elewa?' It was Scyra. She was in an older woman's body; she could have been a kitchen maid. I was glad she had made it through; she could help me deliver the visions to Ola.

'Yeah, it's me – you need to help me get these visions to Ola. Is there somewhere private we can go?'

'Let us go down to the kitchen, there is no one there at this time of day.' Scyra led the way; we had to walk down two flights of stairs to get there. As we walked down each step, the temperature got cooler and cooler. When we finally arrived in the kitchen, we stood next to the stove, and wasted no time in attempting to give Ola the vision. But as we approached Ola, a girl burst through the door.

'You asked to see me, ma'am?' The young girl was talking to Scyra.

'Amara, yes, I did want to see you – please can you collect the produce from the market? I've left you a list.' The girl scrunched her eyebrows at Ola, presumably wondering why he was in the kitchen.

'Of course, ma'am!' she replied and scurried off. Once she had gone, Scyra and I approached Ola again.

She is going to find it strange that I was down here.

All is well, Ola! It has been a strange day. You will make something up.

We held hands again. I thought intensely about the first time I got the vision of Ola and King Yemi. How strange it must be to receive a vision of yourself from the future. I asked Ola to close his eyes and relax. The visions came through quickly because Scyra was there to help. We sent that vision of him and King Yemi, and the vision of Bilal after Ola and King Yemi left him. Of those men coming to our land and selling our people into slavery in the new world. Of Papa and Itoro on the slave ship, in the forts and in the new world.

Ola ripped his hands out of Scyra's palms.

It is safe, Ola. I know how shocking it all is – just take a breath. I tried to reassure him.

Just tell me what I need to do, and I will do it.

Thank you, Ola, I promise I will bring you back in one

piece. When you start to feel tired, all you need to do is fall asleep. Then I am going to warn the king about this meeting. Do you understand? We hung around the kitchen for a few moments, waiting for Ola to feel the pull.

What is the lady's name? I asked. *The one that my friend is with.*

Oh, her name is Melody; she is the palace's best cook. She will need to be back in one piece once all of this is over as well, he warned me.

'What's happening? Is Ola on board now?' Scyra inquired.

'Yes, we are just waiting for him to allow me to fully take over.'

There it is, I feel it now, Ola alerted me and then I felt his psyche gradually fade away into the background. I approached Melody.

'It is done. I am going upstairs now to the king. Stand by just in case I need you, Scyra.'

'I got you!' she confirmed, and I made my way back to King Yemi.

'Ahh, Ola. Are you feeling better now?'

'Yes, Your Highness, I think it was just a dizzy spell.' It was exactly like the first vision I had had with Mama Tiiandas but this time, just like with Papa, I was in the world. King Yemi was in the drawing room surrounded by gold, plenty of exotic foods, and servants. He looked just like he did in that first vision: dark brown skin with a reddish undertone, his outfit displaying the most stunning colours and patterns.

'Excellency, are you certain you will be travelling with all of this?' I gestured towards the packed luggage filled with luxury items.

'Do you question my judgement, Ola? I have travelled to many lands, as you very well know.' King Yemi casually

233

strolled around the room, just like he had in the first vision, and wherever he went, it seemed, the light followed him; it reflected on and off him, from all the precious metals he was wearing. And there it was: that thick gold bracelet that had a serpent's head on one end and the tail on the other end. The serpent's mouth was open, and the cleft tongue was the lock that fixed the bracelet securely to his wrist. It was still the most beautiful craftsmanship I had ever seen.

'This is the way you gain your associates' respect; we need their respect if we want to trade and create affiliations with them.'

'No, you do not!'

'I beg your pardon, Ola.' He looked shocked to the core, as if no one had ever spoken to him like that.

'You do not need all that gold, Your Highness; I have been here before and it does not end well.' King Yemi grabbed Ola's arm and as he marched him out of the room; all the other servants looked at Ola as if he was out of his mind.

'If you had not served under me for the last twenty years, I would have had you kicked out immediately. What is going on, Ola? I demand you tell me now.' Melody followed us into the other room and shut the door behind her.

'You are right, I have served you for over twenty years and my father served your father for thirty or more, I think, so I need you to listen to me and trust me, just for a moment. Have I ever let you down or questioned your authority, Your Highness, in the last twenty years?' I hoped to heavens Ola had a record of faithful service. I needed my point to follow through.

'No, you have not . . .' The king looked as though the wind had been knocked out of him just by Ola going against the grain. I wondered how he would deal with what he was about to tell him.

'Look, I have a gift. I receive visions and I have seen you and this trip we are going to make. It is not going to end well; the man we are meeting is going to betray us, and if we bring all this gold with us, we will attract the wrong type of attention.'

'What are you talking about? What is Melody doing here?' Melody stood next to me.

'Melody has seen the visions too, Your Highness, and we can show you them now. If you see them and you still want to go, then I will help you pack, and we can just forget all about this.'

'And how do you plan on showing me these visions of yours?'

'Give us your hands and close your eyes.'

It was a good thing the king trusted Ola so much, otherwise we would not have stood a chance. We held on to his hands and shared five visions with him. The first showing him getting ready to leave, the second an extract of Bilal's sinister betrayal, when he tried to persuade men from other lands to raid King Yemi's kingdom. The third was those men arriving in King Yemi's empire, revealing his tribal leaders trading *their own people* for guns. The fourth exposed everyday life on the dreadful slave ships, and the last one showed the captives' life in the new world: being sold in a foreign land and their treatment and work on the plantations.

After we shared the last vision, King Yemi opened his eyes and stood there speechless.

'Your Highness, we cannot take a trip to that land; Bilal is nothing but trouble. We must put laws in place to prohibit the sale of human beings to anyone, but especially to the white men. In the future there is also a scramble for Alkebulan, where men from lands all over the world come and claim ours as their own. We need to prevent this from taking place because it will have a terrible and detrimental effect. We need to take action now, Your Highness.'

Luckily there was a bench behind where the king was standing because he fell back onto it and just looked right through Melody and me.

I think our work is done here. I hoped we had done enough.

~

Once Scyra and I were out of Ola and Melody's minds, there was a little bit of an anti-climax. I felt exhausted. I would have been happy to just lock myself away in a dark room for a whole year to make sense of everything that had happened. I worried about what the after-effects of me joining with Ola would be, because I was still trying to recover from my joining with Papa. Luckily though, Ola did not seem to have suffered much in life. He was the highest servant to a great King of Alkebulan. He had grown up in a respected family with kind parents, and nothing out of the ordinary, or especially distressing, had happened to him during his childhood, apart from one incident. It was the first time he had tried to swim. He had thought he was drowning, but the water only came up to his chest. All his friends had teased him for weeks on end and that experience made him a little defensive and scared to try new things in front of people.

I was able to feel empathy for him but not take on the defensive and shameful feelings he had as my own. I somehow separated his feelings from mine; maybe it was because I was so apprehensive going into that experience that I made sure the line between Ola and me was crystal clear; or because Ola and I had nowhere near as strong a bond as

Papa and I did. Ola did stay with me, though; I thought about him often and I cared what became of him. You cannot share someone's consciousness and forget about them; that was one of the prices you paid for using Yeseni in that way. I was glad Ola had no demons.

'Is Melody playing on your mind?' I wondered how Scyra was getting on.

'No, she's fine, a pretty straightforward cook. I have become obsessed with lemon chicken, though; it was her favourite dish!' We laughed.

'It is uncanny how they stay with you, is it not?'

'Yup, that's why that type of experience isn't recommended at all. Probably because you never know what feelings people keep bottled up inside of them,' Scyra said wryly.

'So do you think King Yemi listened to us and made any changes?'

'Well, we're still here, so that's something. If he did listen to us and take us seriously, we'll find out sooner or later.'

She was right. I was still here and that meant that Mama and Papa still existed too. I rushed over to the mirror that hung above the simulated fireplace and stared at my reflection; I was relieved when I saw that I looked the same. I patted my cheeks with my fingers to check if it was real.

'I really hope he did. I hope with all my heart he did.' I pulled the curtains back and peered out the window. Their world still seemed the same to me. It still looked like an amalgamation of people from all over the world living together in one tribal utopia, no different than it had on the first day that I arrived. Scyra laughed at me as I frantically checked everything.

'*Wait*, does this mean that nothing happened and that it did not work?' My heart sped up.

'Don't stress. Like I said, we'll find out sooner or later . . .'

'Well, I suppose I have done what I came here to do now.' I slumped down into Scyra's couch, thinking that I would miss some of the luxuries they had in this world. Like the couch and their mattresses.

'You know the reality that you go back home to might not be the same one that you left,' she warned me.

'How do you mean?'

'Well, just be prepared for anything, Elewa, whatever happens – okay?'

'Thank you, Scyra, I cannot thank you enough!' I reached over to her hand and squeezed it tight.

'So, is this goodbye, then?'

I tried to form words, but nothing came out, so I just nodded back at her.

Scyra gave me a great deal of information to bring back home with me, and dozens of maps detailing where to mine for precious metals, what crops would flourish in my time and many useful particulars, in case I was lost or stuck, as she fretted I might be. Perhaps she had had a vision of my future that she had not shared with me and maybe all this information would help me overcome whatever it was that I was about to face. I did not care what past I was going back to, as long as it was one that did not involve the trade of human beings, and I hoped and prayed all our hard work had paid off.

We needed to go back to the spot where she first found me, but it was a busy area. We waited until the early hours of the morning to ensure that people would not suspect anything odd happening. When we arrived, there were still a few people around, but we could not make the jump from any other place. I felt a slight resistance as we got ready to request my return to Yeseni, and Mama Iyeniye's reassuring voice echoed in my mind. '*The time for doubt has long passed,*' she said, and the energy began to flow from her to me. Scyra reached out and held my hand.

'Are you okay?' she enquired.

'A little anxious, but that is normal,' I replied, then I remembered I still had the letter from Mama Iyeniye. I reached into my back pocket and pulled it out.

'Yes, you'll be fine, you'll be an expert at this time-travel stuff soon.' She nudged me playfully. I raised my eyebrows and tilted my head in a cautionary way.

'Never again,' I assured her.

'Scyra, this is a letter that Mama Iyeniye wanted you to have. I am sorry I did not give it to you sooner. I was curious, but I did not read it.' I honestly had no idea why I had taken it.

'It's okay, Elewa.' She looked slightly confused and disappointed for a moment, before smiling at me forgivingly. 'If ever you want to know something in the future, just ask, okay? Or should I say in the past?' I felt so foolish. She chuckled at the paradox of tenses and seemed different somehow, highly focused and captivated. Her pupils had dilated.

'Let's begin,' she said, in a tone of voice I'd never heard from her before: it was deep, and it seemed to reverberate on all the surfaces around us.

'Okay,' I replied. I was not nervous this time, though; I knew I was in safe hands with Scyra.

'Yeseni, we humbly ask that you take your blessed daughter Elewa back to her true time. She has diligently done your work, based on the visions you had blessed her with. Now she needs to return to her family and to her natural time.'

I felt the energy from Scyra cross over into me. She repeated the sentences a few times and then we both chanted.

'Yeseni imcuba, Yeseni imcuba, Yeseni imcuba.' We had not discussed what we were going to chant or the order in which we would do this – it all happened in beautiful synchronicity.

I started to see dots of colours forming into the kaleidoscope that I had expected. Gradually the colours created a fully formed pattern. After this I asked Yeseni to grant me passage back home. The kaleidoscope in my mind began to collapse and in its place was just plain white. *This is the point that I jumped last time.* With all my might and will, I imagined the highest and furthest jump that I could. I could feel the veins in my neck swelling with pressure and I no longer felt Scyra's hand in mine. Everything around me seemed to bend and ripple and then, when I opened my eyes, sure enough Scyra had gone, and I was standing there at the Wiri alone.

I sat at the river for a moment, feeling anxious about the life that I would find back at home.

~

I looked up at the sky above the Wiri and tried to find the courage to head home. Could I even travel through the Okena forest or were we still at war with them in this reality?

I stood up, strapped my bag diagonally across my torso then started the journey. A million thoughts ran through my mind: did I still live in the same house, where were my parents, how much time had passed, had time paused or just continued on without me? My head started to throb as I contemplated all the possibilities.

All I cared about was getting back here in one piece. As I reached the end of the forest, I saw a man in the distance. He looked familiar to me, but he was just far enough away that I could not quite make him out yet.

'There you are! What has taken you so long?' he asked me anxiously. I could not believe my eyes: it was Ojuro; he was alive. I ran towards him and held him tightly.

'You are here . . .' I said, trying to hold back the tears from my eyes.

He tilted his head. 'Yes, of course I am here – what has come over you? You told me to meet you at sunset, here at the end of the forest. What are you wearing?'

'I did? I mean, I did! Thank you,' I replied.

I thought it was best to keep as quiet as possible and just observe my new reality for a few days. That way I would find my feet without coming across as too peculiar or unusual.

'Well, that is what friends are for. So where did you get those clothes from?' he asked. I'd forgotten to change before I left. I was still wearing the clothes that Scyra had given me.

'It is just something different that Kemi is trying out. I promised her I would wear them to see what people thought.'

'I doubt they will catch on,' he sniggered.

Since my trip through the forest went by peacefully and Ojuro and I were *apparently* friends, I could safely assume that our tribes were no longer at war. That is, if we had ever been at war, in this reality. I could not get over the shock of his existence, never mind our friendship. It was not long ago that I found him hanging from the ceiling, yet now he was standing in front of me, full of life and vigorous as ever.

'Jo, I need to go and see my parents.' I had to see them; I missed them so much.

'Elewa, you see them every day. You *live* with them.' He frowned. 'I think we need to get you home so that you can rest. All that overtime on the farm must be getting to you.'

My jaw opened and my mouth sort of just hung there. I quickly covered it with my hand, having to physically hold the words back from spilling out. *We are farmers now?* That was an honourable and respectful profession. That would be good enough for me. I smiled and nodded my head. Jo looked back at me in a puzzled way, while I was smiling and nodding to myself. I could tell that he was trying to find a tactful way to say something.

'Are you sure you are well? You are unusually quiet and you are acting strangely,' he said, trying to read my face.

'Like you said, I probably just need to get some rest,' I replied. *You try travelling more than three hundred years into the future and see how strange you seem!*

Throughout the journey home I could not help but notice every little aspect of my surroundings, and compare them to the old land that I had left behind. Most things seemed to be the same, really, although I hoped there were no slave forts or ships at the shore. *That is a way I can find out if our attempt worked: I will check to see if the forts are still there at the coast.*

I remembered Grandma's stories about her life on the farm that Papa grew up on, and it did not seem like they had much time for anything other than work.

When we arrived home Mama and Papa were sitting in the front yard; they were in the middle of what looked like a very intense discussion. Apart from the familiarity of their faces, it was like walking into another world.

'Mama, Papa!' I shouted as I ran over to embrace them. They looked at me and then over at Jo, bemused. The house was a small two-room shack. Yet there were five of us that lived there – *Where do we all sleep?* I wondered – and where were Grandma and Grandpa and Sessie?

'I do not know what has gotten into her. But I think she just needs some rest,' Jo said as he walked past our home and into one of the houses across the way. *We are neighbours,* I thought.

'*She* is fine. Do not worry about me,' I mockingly yelled out to Jo.

'Bye, Elewa,' he turned around and flashed me a coy grin.

'Elewa, as soon as you wake from your rest, I need to talk to you about the forthcoming tribal gathering with Queen Sessie,' Papa called, and I gasped.

There was a lot for me to learn about. But for now, I walked into the house, found the first room with an empty bed to lie down on and hoped it was mine.

～

As soon as I woke up, I went to look up Mama Iyeniye. I needed to get some perspective on this new world and Mama Iyeniye was the only way I knew how. I found her selling produce at the local market. I could have spotted her a mile off, but she spotted me first.

'Elewa!' she shouted from the distance, her palms towards the sky. 'What kind of life do you have me living, girl?' she asked rhetorically and sarcastically, with a huge smile plastered across her face. Everyone turned around to look at her and then at me. Then when I did not shout back, they continued what they were doing before.

'Mama Iyeniye, you remember me?' I replied, when I got closer to her. I was so relieved that someone recognised the real me. She cradled my face with her palms the way she always used to.

'A face that the world should see – how could I forget? Come, child.' She gestured me to a tent attached to the back of her stall where she, apparently, told fortunes. There was a small wooden table with two on chairs either side. It was definitely a more modest setting than I was used to seeing around Mama Iyeniye. There were no elaborate carvings or exotic fabrics; instead, she had a simple map stuck on the wall of the tent and some dried flowers in a jar.

'Take a seat, let us catch up.' She did not seem to be doing much better than our family was, selling produce on a small market stall and reading fortunes on the side. I did not know exactly how much she knew about the whole situation or what she remembered of the past, so I thought I would try to find out.

'What do you know of me, Mama Iyeniye?' I queried. I did not want to interfere if she did not fully remember the life that we had before. If that were the case, I would leave things as they were.

'Do not worry, child, I remember everything; I helped you make the trip to the future at the Wiri. I taught you all about your gift, Yeseni. Our families were wealthy and comfortable one moment and then one day, after you left, I woke up and this was my lot.' She gestured around her small tent and stall. 'That morning, when I woke up to this, was when I knew that you had arrived in the future safely. Well done, child!' She put her palm on my shoulder and shook it in an encouraging manner.

'Thank you, Mama Iyeniye, I really appreciate all the help and guidance that you gave me along the way, and I am so relieved to see you. But now what? I mean, we are farmers and really struggling to make ends meet. Mama and Papa work from sunrise to sunset – that cannot be good for them at their age. I do not need us to be wealthy, just comfortable, that is all, and of course I want that for you as well.'

'My dear, you have the tools to create any kind of life that you desire. Scyra must have left you with a comprehensive list of opportunities. She had an inkling that this would happen, that you would feel this way. But as for me, I am happy and content with this life. It is simple, I admit that. But

I can feed and take care of myself, and I do not have to put up with all the airs and graces of that ridiculous high society. This is a much richer life for me. I get to speak to a variety of people every day. I really get to connect with them, Elewa. I do not know what could be more valuable than that.'

She was right – perhaps I had become ungrateful. I broke eye contact with her and looked down at the floor. I was not comfortable in my new life, and I did not know how to get to a place where I felt content.

'Elewa, there is nothing wrong with wanting something different, but if I found myself in a life that I did not like, I would not feel bad about wanting to change it. I know you do not want to line your garden in gold – you just want to be a little bit more comfortable, so your parents do not have to work so hard and so there is enough for all your family . . .'

'Why do you not want more as well?'

'Child, my days on this earth are numbered – what would I do with more than I have now? You know they used to lock me away in my quarters? The only person that would visit me was Ojuro, and whenever I came out into town, I was *the crazy old lady*, thanks to our friend Ade.' She rolled her eyes. 'Queen Sessie has seen to him, though. She helped him see the error of his ways and now he works for her as a servant. She has done so much to bring the tribes together into a new peace accord. It was her idea that the wealth should be shared, and each family should have land to farm. There is a gathering soon where every member of the Okena and Oleba will attend and have their say on matters of all kinds. You know they are calling Queen Sessie the Daughter of Peace?'

For a moment, I felt a terrible sense of loss. I had risked everything, and no one in this new reality would ever know, except for Mama Iyeniye.

'Child, I know how much you risked, but look at what you have gained. Ojuro is restored to us, and you know in your heart that you are the one who changed this world. You might not have recognition, but you have the chance to make a better life.'

'So, you are truly happy with your life now?' I double-checked. I wanted to make sure. Mama Iyeniye was important and dear to me.

'I could not be happier. If I was not happy, I would have changed it by now. I have all the same intelligence that you do, child.'

It was true: she taught both me and Scyra everything we knew. If she wanted to start up a gold-mine tomorrow, she knew exactly where to dig. Or if she wanted to build a trading company, she knew exactly what would sell and how to find the merchandise at the best price. But what she wanted more than anything did not involve material wealth. 'Without her sister, what she really desired was human connection, and now she had that in abundance. What more could she want? What more could I want?

'I understand, but where do I go from here?' I knew I wanted more for my family. Whether we used Komi's gift or Scyra's intelligence, I just wanted to take away the struggle somehow.

'Have you thanked Yeseni yet?' She fixed her gaze at me.

'Not yet,' I replied. I knew this made me seem unappreciative, but I had only just returned yesterday.

'Then if you are grateful, which I believe you are, I would start there. Once you have done that, come back to me and we will etch out a plan. In the meantime, have a think about what you really want out of life, and we will find a way to make it happen, child. Do not fret.'

Mama Iyeniye could make anything seem obtainable; even the most complicated things in the world were neatly ordered into perspective around her.

I realised what I wanted most was to go to the shore and see for myself if the forts had gone. I thanked Mama Iyeniye and strode out on the road to the sea.

All will be well, a voice in my mind persuaded me. *It already is*, the other one replied.

Acknowledgements

In loving memory of my dear grandad, George Burke, who wholeheartedly supported this novel; my dear uncle, Paul Burke; my god-sister, Rahana Davis; family friend, Brother Berenji; Uncle Frank King; and Leroy Reid.

Thank you, Katy Guest, for always believing in and championing this novel.

The amazing editors at Unbound who have helped shape this book with me: Aliya Gulamani, Faiza Khan, Rachael Kerr, Imogen Denny, Kate Quarry, Kwaku Osei-Afrifa and Hayley Shepherd. Thank you Cassie Waters for all your support in those early days and John Mitchinson for your encouraging words.

The family that pledged: Grandmother Lydia Burke, my brother Mark Sterling, my neice Leoni Sterling, Uncle Leroy Burke, Soloman Smith, Natalie Burke, Sophia Burrell, Horace Burrell, Jacqueline Rhoden-Trader, Doreen O'Connor, Charma Rhoden, Aunt Linnette Rhoden.

Thank you to, my siblings Monique Burrell, Aziza Hewitt-Burrell and Merrick Sterling for being engaged with the project and to Terry Ann, Dotting, Shamira Watson and Salama Kefentse-Fransiz for reading the first draft and showing genuine interest and spurring me on throughout the life-cycle of the project. Thank you to my nephew Laquan

Burrell for his verbal encouragement and entrepreneurial ideas on how to promote the book. Thanks to all my nieces and nephews for being inspirational: Lashaya Sterling, Joseph Sterling, Taijuan Iwhetta-Burrell, Tiana Sterling, Shannae Sterling, Navae-Renaé Iwhetta-Burrell, Nuri Maliha Kamara and Chloe Beckles. Thank you Emily, Carl's work friend!

My godparents and mum's friends: Valarie Davis, Elaine King, Pauline McCarthy, Donna Hacket, Paulette and Constantine Blake, Verna Milligan, Delita McCarthy and Carmen Gayle.

My closest friends that pledged; Celina Taylor, Chantelle Pierre, Natalie Higgins and Simone Fearon. Carl's friends Wayne and Colin Lord. Old school friend Jessica Thomas, old St Catharines friend Laura Pollard. Old HR friends Tolulope Popoola and Helena Mithras.

Thank you to all of my in-laws for being excited and positive about the book whenever we meet.

Thanks to the Ontario Arts Council for their support through the Literary Creation Projects (Works for Publication) Grant awarded in September 2021, and Diaspora Dialogues Charitable Society and Dundurn Press Ltd. through the Recommender Grants for Writers, awarded in 2021–22.

Special thank you to James Walvin's book, *Black Ivory: Slavery in the British Empire* (Blackwell Publishing, 1992) and I'd like to acknowledge source material from John Newton's *Thoughts Upon the African Slave Trade* (London, 1788) and his journal: *Journal of a Slave Trader*, B. Martin and M. Spurrell (eds) (1788).

Unbound is the world's first crowdfunding publisher, established in 2011.

We believe that wonderful things can happen when you clear a path for people who share a passion. That's why we've built a platform that brings together readers and authors to crowdfund books they believe in – and give fresh ideas that don't fit the traditional mould the chance they deserve.

This book is in your hands because readers made it possible. Everyone who pledged their support is listed below. Join them by visiting unbound.com and supporting a book today.

Roxanne Gordon
LUSH Oshawa
Joseph K. Abankwah
Martha Adam-Bushell
Claire Adams
Viccy Adams
Keith Adsley
Tony Aitman
Neil Alexander
Sally Allen

Rhona Allin
Lulu Allison
Shelley Anderson
Kirk Annett
Sidra Ansari
Emma Antonova
Donna Arnett
James Aylett
Suzanne Azzopardi
Rachel Baker

Nicola Bannock
Vikki Bayman
Helen Bennett
Elizabeth Bentley
Senay Bereket
Jitna Bhagani
Mel Bischer
Maud Blair
Paulette Blake
Piero Bohoslawec
Laura Bold
Emily Bolton-Hale
Fran Bongard
Kate Boulton
Susie Boyt
Sarah Brazier
Catherine Breslin
Stephanie Bretherton
Carolyn Brina
Garry James Britton
Brian Browne
Marti Burgess
Leroy Burke
Lydia Burke
Natalie Burke
Paul Burke
Grassarah Burrell
Horace Burrell
Sophia Burrell
Ana Calbey
Jennifer Campney
Grace Carter

Holly Cartlidge
Rosemary Chamberlin
Bruce Clark
Rocane Clarke
Peaches Clarke-Hurst
Mathew Clayton
Sarah Clement
Lara Clements
Anastasia Colman
Jude Cook
Nick Cooper
Richard Cooper
Elizabeth Coulter
Deborah Crawford
John Crawford
Emoke Czako
Peter Dalling
Ben Dare
Rishi Dastidar
Nick Davey
Eileen Davidson
Laura Davis
Valerie Davis
Stephen Dixon
Ashley Elsdon
Emily & Tabitha
Ayla Chandni Estreich
Mary Jane Fahy
Simone Fearon
Patric ffrench Devitt
Paul Fulcher
Caroline Gale

Carmen Gayle
El Gee
Claire Genevieve
Catherine Gent
Eva Georgiou
Terry Georgiou
Rina Gill
Richard Gillin
Carl Gordon
Paul David Gould
Robert and Cynthia Graham
Jo Gray
Emma Green
Joanne Greenway
Katy Guest
Aliya Gulamani
Dawn Hackett
Daniel Hahn
Cris Hale
Eleni Hamawi
Sharon Hammond
Sophie Hanscombe
Chloe Hardy
Becca Harper-Day
Clay Harris
Elspeth Head
David Hebblethwaite
Paula Hedley
Samuel Hedley
Anna Hepworth
Jerome Hering
Sean Hickman

Jan Hicks
Natalie Higgins
Robin Hill
Tony Histed
Emily Hodder
Damian Hornett
Katy Hoskyn
Vicky Howard
Helen Hubert
Joe Huggins
Chris Hulbert
Barbara Hungin
Iqbal Hussain
Cassara Jackson
Estelle Jacobs
Mike James
Amanda Jenkins
Jill Johnson
Alice Jolly
Margaret Jones
Pippa Jones
Sheila Jones
Nikki Jones – The Bookish Mindset
Adrian Justins
Diana Kahn
Steven Keevil
Kathryn Kerr
Dan Kieran
David King
Vanessa Kisuule
Emily Kyne

George Kyriakos
Pierre L'Allier
Jane Lamacraft
Elizabeth Larkin
Capucine Lebreton
Lena Lee
Ruth Leonard
Anastasia Lewis
Jennifer Lewis
Johanna Linsler
LJ
Colin Lord
Wayne Lord
Jose Miguel Vicente Luna
Jen Lunn
Sabrina Mahfouz
Rachel Malik
Mary Mcauliffe
Melanie McBlain
Deleta McCarthy
Pauline McCarthy
Megan McCormick
Marie McGinley
Isabelle McNeill
Joe Melia
Radojka Miljevic
Verna Milligan
Helena Mithras
Ken Monaghan
Alastair W Monk
Daniel Monk
Paul Monteith

Martin Morrison
Janet Morson
Jo Murphy
Jamie Nash
Antony Nelson
John New
Emma Newell
Chris Newsom and Jasmine
Milton
Iain Newton
Sue Norris
Doreen O'Connor
Jenny O'Gorman
Mark O'Neill
Karen O'Sullivan
Ros O'Sullivan
Melody Odusanya
Wayne Olson
Jo Ouest
Camilla Marie Pallesen
Ryan Patrick
Alex Pearl
Jenny Pichierri
Jennifer Pierce
Chantelle Pierre
Yvonne Plummer
Justin Pollard
Laura Pollard
Patricia Pollock
Steve Pont
Tolulope Popoola
Janet Pretty

Tina Price-Johnson
Joanna Quinn
Daniel Rafferty
Amanda Ramsay
Angela Rayson
El Redman
Leroy Reid
Emma Rhind-Tutt
Charma Rhoden
Linnette Rhoden
Jacqueline Rhoden-
TraderJane Richardson
Pamela Ritchie
Jane Roberts
Bernadette Rodbourn
Bryony Rogerson
Melissa Rung-Blue
Janet Rutter
Caroline Sanderson
Emily Sandovski
Sarah
Lucy Shaw
Mom-Veronica Shaw
Isobel Sheene
John Simmons
Balmeet Singh
Andrew Smith
Solomon Smith
Valarie Davis
Pauline McCarthy
Deleta McCarthy
Valarie Smith

Kerriann Speers
Josh Spero
Ruth Stanier
Hannah Stark
Cathryn Steele
Gabriela Steinke
Leoni Sterling
Mark Sterling
Ruth Stevens
Susanne Stohr
Pamela Strachman
Ander Suarez
Pauline Subran
Kirsty Syder
Katie T
Celina Taylor
Jane Teather
Andy Telemacque
The Development Team
Unbound
Jessica Thomas
Kate Tilbury
Sabine Tötemeyer
Susan Turner
Zach Van Stanley
Alaina van Thiel
Mark Vent
Steve Walsh
Chee Lup Wan
Anjunette Washington
Cassie Waters
Carole Watters